The Stone Lantern

A Hawaiian Mystery

Samantha Stevens

Samantha Lei Stevens
The Stone Lantern
A Hawaiian Mystery

Print ISBN: 978-1-54390-762-9
eBook ISBN: 978-1-54390-763-6

1. Fiction, 2. Mystery, 3. Romance, 4. Hawaii, 5. Cowboys

To my late mother,
Mabel Gouveia Horner,
who inspired me

Acknowledgments

I would like to thank the following people for their kind and valuable assistance in helping me write this book: Herbert Horner, former Hawaii police officer; Lei Ann Werner, Marin County, California realtor; Big Island rancher, Annarie Shallenberger; Rebecca Keliehoomalu, Big Island realtor; Hilo resident, Jimmy Vita; my late grandparents, John and Gussie Gouveia, who owned and lived on the ranch which is the backdrop for this novel and where I spent most of my small kid time; and above all my husband, John Sollo, for his patience, endless editing, support, and unconditional love.

Prologue

It was still dark that early morning at South Point on the Big Island of Hawaii when two men carrying battery-operated lanterns started their descent down the cliff, careful not to slide on the loose rocks of the narrow, steep trail. Half way down they found a slit in the rock wall and shined the lights into it. Beyond was another bigger opening shielded by a large, free-standing boulder. The men slipped through the narrow space and found a smooth, flat rock at the foot of the boulder and stood on it, lifting the lamps, trying to see what was on the other side. As they had hoped, there was an entrance to a cave. They stepped inside and gasped. Ahead of them at the far end, sitting on four large lava rocks, was an outrigger canoe. Surrounding the canoe were wooden bowls, tools, and stone lamps among other ancient implements. Petroglyphs adorned the walls. They moved closer to the ancient vessel and peered inside. Lying on a cape made of faded crimson and yellow feathers was the head of a human skeleton. Other bones were arranged as if to simulate a whole skeleton, but the long arm and leg bones were missing.

The men held their breaths, unable to speak. Turning to look back at the cave's entrance they saw two *kahilis* – long-handled wooden staffs topped with cylinders of crimson and yellow feathers – leaning against the wall like sentries guarding a tomb. They lifted the lanterns to shine more light on the cave's interior. In the shadowy darkness to their left, near the entrance from which they had come, something caught their eyes. Slowly inching over they found another astonishing sight. Lying there wearing knee high leather riding boots and a leather belt with a tarnished silver buckle was another skeleton, this one not so ancient. The skull was bashed in.

I

As soon as she saw the belt buckle Jessie Bradford knew it was her father's. Looking down at the skeleton with the crushed skull she felt that she was going to be sick. Less than an hour earlier she had been in the warm kitchen at the ranch house talking and laughing with her housekeeper and ranch manager. She wished she were still back there.

It started out like every other morning since Jessie returned to Hawaii's Big Island to claim the inheritance left by her uncle, Rod Bradford. She and ranch manager Billy Gonsalves were seated at the kitchen table planning the weekly chores and going over her uncle's papers and ledgers which were spread out before them.

Housekeeper and cook Mary Chin was clearing the remnants of the noon meal when her cell phone vibrated in her apron pocket. She stepped out to the porch to answer. After a few minutes she returned to the kitchen, her face ashen. Mary stood inside the screen door and looked at Jessie, the phone still clutched in her hand.

Jessie glanced up. "What's wrong, Mary?" She stood and put her arm around Mary's shoulders, staring worriedly at the stricken face. She thought of Mary's husband, Harry, who suffered a heart attack several months ago. "Is it Harry?" asked Jessie. "Is he sick?"

Shaking her head, her voice soft and shaken, Mary said, "Jessie, my friend called, the one who is married to the policeman. She told me her husband is at South Point Cliffs with Reverend Joe Kanekoa and Detective John McIntire. She said Reverend Joe and someone from the University of Hawaii found a cave, a burial cave."

Before Mary could continue, Billy jumped up, nearly knocking over his chair. "So, they finally found something," he said, slapping his thigh. "They've been scratchin' around for years."

A few years ago Joseph Kanekoa, pastor of the Hawaiian Congregational Church of Waikea Village, told Billy that he and a friend from the university were searching for an ancient Hawaiian burial site at South Point. "That's like looking for the pot of gold at the end of the rainbow," Billy said. "Pah, waste time," he'd told Joe. Now he looked at Mary expectantly. "So? What'd they find?"

Mary scowled at him. "Hush, Billy," she admonished and turned to face Jessie. "Well, they don't know yet. They did find some ancient remains, a skeleton in a canoe and some other relics, but there was something else. Jessie, they think they found your father."

Pulling away from Mary, a look of incredulity on her face, Jessie said, "What? I don't understand. My father drowned years ago and his body was washed out to sea. That's what we were told. Everyone knows that. What do you mean? How could they have found him in a cave?"

"There's a skeleton in there that isn't so ancient and they think it's your father," said Mary shrugging her shoulders. "That's what my friend told me. She said there are a lot of police down at the cliffs, newspaper and TV reporters, university people..." Her voice trailed off.

Jessie picked up the keys to the Land Rover parked in the back yard and grabbed her purse that was hanging by its strap from the back of a chair. "I'm going down there," she said and strode out to the porch. She sat on the steps and pulled on her boots. "John McIntire should have called me," she muttered.

Billy joined her and reached for his own boots. "I'll go with you," he said.

"No, no. Thanks, Billy. I need to do this myself." She climbed into the old Land Rover with its mud splattered doors and tires and drove off.

Jessie spent most of the last evening going through her uncle's books and files. She'd been at the ranch house since Rod died suddenly several weeks ago. Rod Bradford had willed his ranch and his belongings to her and she was trying to sort out his affairs, especially his finances.

Billy was waiting for her at the Kona Airport when she arrived from San Francisco. They drove straight to the Bradford Ranch half way down South Point Road in the Ka'u District of Hawaii Island, commonly known as the Big Island. She hadn't left the ranch since, spending most of the last couple of weeks trying to make sense of Rod's bookkeeping. Luckily, the ranch and holdings were left in a trust, so there was no probate, no haggling with lawyers. Jessie was the only heir. It seemed fairly straightforward – get the books in order, settle the debts, and sell the place. She planned to spend a few weeks working things out and then return to her home in San Francisco.

Driving down the red dirt ranch road, dust clouding up behind her, she tried to digest what Mary said. They'd found her father? But he drowned nearly 40 years ago. It was common knowledge. He'd been fishing at Green Sand Beach. Some fishermen found his fishing gear on the rocks, but no trace of him. His station wagon, the keys still in the ignition, was parked nearby. The search lasted for weeks, but his body was never found. The police theorized that he'd slipped on the rocks, fell into the pounding waves, and drowned, his body carried out to sea. The case was designated an accidental death and closed.

Jessie turned onto South Point Road and headed toward the cliffs. She finally stopped where the pavement ended and the pot-holed, gravel road began. A lighthouse once stood near the cliff just ahead of her, but now only the foundation remained, the original building having burned down years ago. "NO TRESPASSING," "KEEP OUT," and "KAPU" signs marred by graffiti and pockmarked with bullet holes hung on the barbed wire fences that surrounded weather-beaten pastureland near the beach.

It was a clear, sunny, windy day and the ocean was dark blue with millions of tiny white caps that looked like miniature sailboats being tossed about. The waves washing against the rocks were foamy like slightly beaten egg whites.

Police cars were parked haphazardly along the road and a couple of uniformed officers milled about. Yellow police tape cordoned off the area around the lighthouse foundation and more tape was placed along the cliff's edge that overlooked the waves crashing against the rocky coastline. A policeman guarded the gate leading into the pasture. A small crowd was gathered outside the barriers, a mix of reporters and onlookers. Several news helicopters hovered overhead.

Jessie parked the truck, slipped through the yellow tape, and started toward the gate where a young police officer stood guard. He stopped her. "Police or university?" he asked. "Neither," she said. "Is Detective John McIntire here?" "Detective," the policeman called out, looking past her, "this woman is asking for you." Jessie turned and looked up into the face of Detective Lieutenant John McIntire. "Mac," she said.

"What are you doing here, Jessie?" He pushed his tan Stetson back from his forehead and reached out and hugged her. It was the kind of hug you get from an old friend you hadn't seen in a while, affectionate and warm. "I heard you were back and was going to stop by the ranch after I finished here this afternoon," he said. "How'd you find out we were down here?"

After explaining about the phone call Mary Chin received, she asked, "What's going on? Is it true about my father's remains being found in a cave? Why didn't you call me?"

Mac was tall and lanky with that tan, dusky complexion that some people of mixed Caucasian and Hawaiian heritage tend to have and he still had the handsome, square-jawed face she remembered from their younger days. He was wearing a denim jacket with a fleece collar, faded jeans, and cowboy boots. He took off his reflective sunglasses, revealing clear blue eyes.

"A crime scene is no place for you, Jessie," he said. "We're checking it out and we're pretty sure it's your father, but not a hundred percent. The investigation will take a while. I don't have any answers for you right now."

"I want to see," said Jessie. "I want to see for myself. Can you take me there?" The wind whipped her shoulder-length light brown hair across her face. She regretted not putting it in a pony tail before leaving the ranch and felt in her jeans pocket for a scrunchy, but didn't find one. Looking at the crowd that stood on the other side of the police tape, she noticed that some of the people were huddled together to keep warm. She'd forgotten how cold and windy it was at South Point, touted as the southernmost part of the United States. Her blue denim shirt and jeans gave no protection. Mac offered his jacket, but she refused.

"Are you sure you want to go down there?" he asked. He looked at her face and saw the stubborn glare, the thrust out chin, defying him to say she shouldn't. He knew it was useless to try to talk her out of it. "Okay, let's go, but it's a rough trail down to the cave. Think you're up to it?" She nodded.

"C'mon, my truck's over there," he said.

His white Ford Expedition was parked in a pasture that was owned by Jessie's neighbor, Reverend Joseph Kanekoa. When they reached the truck Mac pulled a gray hooded sweatshirt out of the back seat. "Here, put this on," he said, handing it to her.

Cattle and horses grazed nearby, oblivious of the commotion. There was no road only the dry, grassy plain, but already there were tire tracks marking a path where vehicles had driven through since early that morning. It was a bumpy ride. As he drove, Mac spoke into his phone. Jessie heard him order all police personnel to vacate the cave for a short time. He stopped the truck near several other vehicles that were parked in the makeshift parking lot.

More police tape cordoned off the area that led to the edge of the cliff. Officers stood guard. A small group of people was gathered holding iPads and other electronic devices and taking photographs with cameras and phones. The faces were a blur to Jessie as Mac led her toward the cliff. She looked down at the rocky, zigzagged path and took a deep breath.

"Still sure you want to do this?" he asked.

"Yes, I'm sure," she said. "Let's go before I lose my nerve."

"Okay. Watch your footing and don't look over the edge," he warned. It was steep and Jessie felt rocks slipping beneath her feet. The wind howled in her ears. Mac let go of her hand to make it easier for them to trod single file down the steep incline. She steadied herself with her left hand against the cliff wall.

Most everyone who'd been around for a while knew the story of Jessie's missing father, Allen Bradford. He was an avid fisherman and often fished off the rocks at the base of the South Point Cliffs. He sometimes went alone in the early morning before going to work and one day he didn't return home.

He was the manager of Kahana Sugar Company, a plantation owned by one of Hawaii's major corporations that was in existence since the late 1800s when sugar cane was king in the Islands. A number of companies were founded by early missionaries or transients who'd either married someone of Hawaiian ancestry or acquired land through bartering or business transactions with native Hawaiians. Most of those companies owned and operated sugar plantations.

Bradford was tall, more than six feet, handsome, brash, arrogant, and known for his knee-high riding boots and the silver buckle he wore on a custom-made leather belt. His initials, AWB for Allen William Bradford, were etched on the buckle.

Mac and Jessie came to the boulder blocking the opening to the cave, slipped through, and within seconds they were inside. It wasn't what she expected. She'd imagined that it would be dank and damp. Instead, it was dry and cool and quiet. Portable lights were set up to illuminate the interior. Mac nodded toward the corner on their right.

The skeletal remains lying just inside the entrance wore leather boots that were cracked and discolored, but were relatively intact. The clothes were unrecognizable and what was left of them was in shreds, but the belt buckle, though tarnished, was without a doubt Allen Bradford's, the initials clearly visible.

Jessie saw that the bright lights were not just to indicate the location of her father's remains. Beyond where she stood, toward the back of the cave, was a stunning sight. Looking past the skeleton near the entrance she saw what appeared to be a collection of ancient Hawaiian artifacts, but it was the huge outrigger canoe sitting on its catafalque of lava boulders that was most imposing. Standing near the entrance, she couldn't see what was in the canoe, so she walked over and peered inside. Seeing the bones lying on the bottom of the outrigger convinced her that it was time to leave. "Okay, Mac, I've seen enough. Let's get out of here."

As Mac led her back outside he told her that the people gathered near the cliffs were from the University of Hawaii, local museums, and other agencies with an interest in such an ancient find. They were all eager to get in the cave, but they'd have to wait until the police investigation was complete. A couple of police officers went back in after Jessie and Mac started the climb up the cliff.

When they reached the top Jessie recognized a tall, muscular Hawaiian standing beside a slightly built, white-haired older man. "Ey, Jessie!" called the Hawaiian.

Reverend Joseph Kanekoa walked over and put his arms around her. "Long time no see," he said. "I'm sorry about your Uncle Rod and now this.

I know it's a shock. If there's anything I can do let me know. I'll stop by the ranch or you can come to the church, whatever you want. We can talk."

"What are you doing here, Joe?" she asked, forgetting for a moment that it was his pasture land on which they were standing.

"I found this cave," he said. "Well, actually, Michael Campbell and I. We found it yesterday, but it was late and we didn't have the lanterns, so we came back early this morning."

He introduced the man standing next to him. "Michael is a professor of archaeology at U of H on Oahu. He and I have been scouting around here for a coupla years now and sheesh, we never expected to find anyting li' dis!" Even though Joseph graduated from the University of Hawaii with a doctorate in theology, he sometimes slipped into the familiar patois of the Islands – Pidgin English.

The professor shook Jessie's hand. "I'm sorry for your loss, Miss Bradford," he said.

Mac took her arm and suggested that they be on their way. The wind was blowing cold and Jessie rubbed her hands together trying to warm them up. Joe asked when he could come by the ranch to see her.

"I'll stop by the church one of these days, Joe. I'm sure I'll need some spiritual guidance before this is over. I'll see you soon." She nodded at the professor.

With his arm around Jessie's shoulders, Mac steered her toward his SUV. They climbed in and headed back toward the gate. The officer on guard lifted the yellow tape and waved them through. When they were outside the tape and got out of Mac's truck, he pushed through the crowd to get Jessie to the Land Rover. Onlookers, mostly press, locals, tourists, and a few hippie types who usually camped and hiked at South Point, grumbled as they were pushed aside.

Mac asked, "Are you okay to drive, Jess? I can have someone take you home."

"Thanks, Mac, but I'm all right, just a little cold and still in shock," she said. "I'd like to talk about this when you have time, though. Come by the ranch soon, will you?" She reached in her purse. "Here's my card with my cell number. You can reach me anytime."

"Think you'll be up to it tomorrow afternoon?" he asked. "I can be at your place around two o'clock. I'm staying at Mauna Loa Ranch up *mauka* from you for the next few days until I wrap up things here instead of driving to and from Hilo every day."

"How long do you think it'll take to finish the investigation?" she asked.

"A couple of days here at the site," he said. "It could take months, even years, for us to find out what happened and there's a chance we may never solve this mystery because it's such a cold case. Campbell and the other archaeologists want the police out of here as soon as possible so they can begin doing whatever they need to do. This is a big find for them and they're itching to get in there. Unfortunately, because it's also a crime scene we can't turn it over to them yet. I'll let you know when we're finished here, though."

"Okay, two o'clock tomorrow is fine," said Jessie, taking off the sweatshirt and handing it to him. "See you then. Thanks, Mac." She backed the truck away from the crowd, pulled onto South Point Road, waved, and beeped the horn a couple of times.

Mac tipped the brim of his hat, then turned to face the throng of reporters from the local and Honolulu papers and television stations. This was the biggest thing that ever happened on his watch and he wasn't sure what to tell them – skeletal remains from maybe 40 years ago and skeletal remains from hundreds, perhaps thousands of years ago, in the same burial tomb. That's all he knew. Since he was the senior officer at the scene he needed to make a statement. He'd be relieved when the reporters with their cameras and microphones went to Hilo where the police chief and the mayor could deal with them.

2

As Jessie drove home she crossed the desolate South Point landscape. The place hadn't changed much since her brother Danny and she spent summers on Bradford Ranch when they were kids. Rod Bradford and his wife, Maile, were childless and welcomed the spirited visits from the children of Rod's older brother, Allen, and his wife, Anne. Rod took them with him when he made his veterinary rounds to neighboring ranches. Back then he drove an old Ford woody station wagon and Jessie always sat in the back while Danny, three years older, rode shotgun up front.

Today she was in the driver's seat passing the dry, barren lands of the small ranches scattered throughout the area – the barbed wire fences; grazing cattle and horses; the nondescript weather-beaten ranch houses much like the one she inherited. She felt the bump as she drove over a cattle guard that spanned the narrow, two-lane asphalt road.

The biggest change, she noted, was the windmills. The Hawaiian Electric Company finally decided a number of years ago, in spite of much protesting by environmental and conservation groups, to take advantage of the windiest spot on the island. The windmills were thought to be eyesores by some and saviors by many. Electricity was expensive in Hawaii and anything that reduced the high cost of living was worth giving up the view of some of the island's cherished scenery. The towering windmills had a sort of surreal appeal, turning furiously and silently against the bright blue cloudless sky.

South Point is not what visitors to the Hawaiian Islands expect. There is nothing tropical about the place. It is so arid it could be West Texas or the Mojave Desert. Trees bent by the wind dot the pastures where rolls of barbed wire are scattered like tumbleweed on a Kansas prairie. Most of the vegetation is *panini,* the prickly pear cactus that grows everywhere on the island, and the scraggly, thorny lantana that chokes back any grass that tries to grow.

When Jessie was a few miles away from the Bradford property, the landscape turned from arid to lush. It doesn't look tropical, but it is as grassy and green as Montana ranchland. Eucalyptus and ironwood trees grow straight and leafy. She drove up to the entrance of her newly acquired ranch, got out and swung open the gate. Ranch hand Tarzan was in the corral mending the wooden fencing. He saluted as he walked over to close the gate. She waved back and continued up the red dirt road to the green and white ranch house at the top of the hill where a jacaranda tree was in full bloom, its blossoms a profusion of purple.

A feeling of comfort washed over her as the house came into view. She'd spent so much of her childhood here that whenever she thought of Hawaii it wasn't Kahana Plantation that made her feel homesick nor the white sandy beaches and palm trees that draw thousands of tourists each year. It was this ranch where she and Danny ran barefoot and learned to ride horses by the time they were three or four that she longed for. She fondly recalled that when they'd come in disheveled and out of breath after playing all day, Maile would scold them good naturedly, "Go wash your hands and faces before you come to the table, for heaven's sake, you wild Indians."

It was no surprise that Jessie was her Uncle Rod's sole heir. She was his only living kin. Maile died more than three years ago and Danny was killed in the Gulf War Desert Storm in 1990. Rod and his older brother, Allen, were the only children of William and Violet Bradford, descendants of a group of Mormons that settled in Hawaii and established a mission in the 1850s. Jessie's daughter, Catherine, lives in Marin County, California and is not interested in far off Hawaii. Born and bred in the San Francisco Bay Area, Catherine is an urban woman and proud to be a native Californian. She seldom visited Hawaii. That left Jessie as the last surviving member of the family tree with ties to Hawaii.

She sat on the back stoop to remove her dust-covered boots and called, "Yoo, hoo!" as she entered the house and was answered by a high-pitched "Hooey!" She followed the aroma of brewing coffee and freshly-baked bread into the kitchen where Mary waited eagerly for the latest news.

"I talked with Reverend Joe's wife, Ipo, a little while ago," said Mary as she stooped to pull a pan of mango bread out of the old Wedgewood oven. Placing the pan on the stove top and smoothing back a stray gray hair that escaped the knot on top of her head, she turned and said, "Ipo called after you left. She said Reverend Joe saw you with Detective McIntire climbing down to the cave. She told me what Joe found in there. Hard to believe, yeh?"

Nothing is kept secret in this place, Jessie thought. Maile called the rumor mill The South Point Gazette. Before there were telephones and televisions in this remote corner of the island, news still got around and now even with satellite dishes and cell towers, the main carrier of news is still word-of-mouth by way of the imaginary South Point Gazette. It's local news, mostly gossip, and, as Maile used to say, it traveled faster through the small ranches and homesteads than a runner in the Iron Man Triathlon.

Jessie poured herself a cup of the powerful Hawaiian coffee the Bradford family favored. They grew it themselves, dried, cured, and ground the beans. Sitting down at the long, koa wood kitchen table, she sliced a piece of warm mango bread and took a bite. "I'm not sure how I'm going to cope with this," she told Mary as she washed down the bread with a sip of the potent black coffee, her hands encircling the cup. The warmth of the cup felt good after the chill at the cliffs. "Did Ipo Kanekoa tell you what else was in the cave?" she asked between gulps.

Mary sat across from Jessie at the table and nodded. "Yeh, Ipo said there were two sets of remains in there. One looked ancient and the other might be your father. I'm sorry, Jessie. This must be so hard for you." She sighed and poured more coffee for each of them, stirred some sugar and cream into hers, and took a long swallow.

Billy came into the kitchen with Rod's Border collie, Jack, at his heels just in time to hear Jessie relate what John McIntire told her.

"Apparently," she said, "Joe Kanekoa's friend, the archaeologist Michael Campbell, was searching the South Point area for years. He was looking for Hawaiian artifacts and hoping to find something big and important for the university. Campbell and Joe stumbled upon the cave and found what appears to be an ancient royal burial site. They sure weren't expecting to find a modern-day crime scene."

"What exactly did they find?" asked Billy, getting a cup from the cabinet and draining the last drop of coffee from the pot. "Did you see anything? Were you allowed in the cave?" He pulled out a chair, turned it around, and straddled it.

"I went inside with Mac," said Jessie. "There's a lot of stuff – those koa wood bowls they call calabashes, stone tools, poi pounders, things we've all seen at museums. And there was a huge canoe sitting on four boulders. I looked inside and saw a human skull and other bones lying on a red and yellow feathered cape that lined the bottom of the canoe. Then, of course, there was the skeleton near the entrance. I'm sure it's my father. I recognized his boots and his belt buckle. Remember the silver buckle with his initials that he always wore?"

Billy and Mary both nodded. Everyone knew that buckle. It was Allen Bradford's trademark.

Jessie continued. "According to Joe, the discovery of the old canoe with all the other artifacts in the cave will probably bring archaeologists, anthropologists, and curators from around the world as well as native Hawaiian conservationists. It might be a royal tomb or at least a burial site of a high chief, judging by the way parts of the skeleton were arranged with some of the bones missing. Joe said that people of high status were buried that way in ancient times. Isn't this something?" Jessie said. "Nothing ever happens at South Point. It's not much of a tourist attraction and even the locals don't go there very often except to fish, but today it's a hub."

"What about, um, your father's remains?" asked Billy. "Will they turn them over to you for a proper burial?"

"I didn't ask," she said. "It's up to the police. I'm sure they'll let me know."

Mac told her they'd investigate to determine if Allen Bradford entered the cave by himself and if the skull fracture was caused by an accident such as a fall. He said an accident didn't seem likely. He didn't tell her what he really thought, that it looked like her father was murdered.

Jessie couldn't get the image of the crushed skull out of her mind. "I just wanted to get out of there," she said. "I felt like I was going to be sick."

Billy and Mary listened silently as Jessie spoke. Mary brewed more coffee, poured some all around, and blew lightly on hers before drinking. "I don't understand," she said between sips. "My husband, Harry, and I have known Reverend Joe and Ipo for a long time. Joe baptized our kids. He and Harry used to play softball on the Cowpunchers team. We've been very close friends all these years and not once did Joe ever mention that he was helping that professor look for anything at South Point. Funny, yeh?"

"Well, he told me about it a couple of years ago," said Billy. "Said he put off the professor for a while, but finally gave in. Where exactly is the cave, Jessie? I mean, they've been looking for a long time. I wonder why they didn't find it sooner?"

Jessie said the cave was several miles along the cliffs which bordered the Kanekoa land and unless someone knew exactly where to look, it would be difficult to find if not impossible.

"The cliff looks pretty smooth with a big, oblong rock hiding the opening. I imagine from a distance, even from a boat heading straight toward it, no one would ever guess a cave was there because it blends in so well. I'm not surprised it took such a long time to find it," she said, "but someone found it years ago, that's for sure. I wonder if we'll ever know what really happened?"

3

THE NEXT AFTERNOON JESSIE SADDLED THE GELDING ROD gave her as a birthday gift several years ago when she visited him shortly after Maile died. The horse was compliant as she reached under his belly for the cinch and began tightening it around his middle. Rod named him Koa. "He's reddish brown like koa wood," her uncle said when presenting the then two-year-old to her. That was the last time she saw Rod Bradford.

He and Jessie had scattered Maile's ashes at her favorite spot on the ranch. It was a small grassy mound surrounded by wild ginger and eucalyptus and guava trees where Maile often took her niece and nephew for picnics. After making sure her uncle was all right, Jessie hugged him goodbye and flew back to San Francisco. They kept in touch by phone several times a month.

She wasn't worried about him because she knew that Mary Chin, the housekeeper and caregiver he hired during Maile's long bout with cancer, was taking care of him. Rod was plagued with heart problems for years, so although Mary was alarmed she was not surprised when she found him sprawled on the floor at the foot of his bed one morning, his dog, Jack, standing guard next to the body.

Jessie scattered his ashes at the same spot as Maile's as Rod's will specified. She, Mary and Harry Chin, Billy Gonsalves, and Tarzan said their final goodbyes on the mound beneath the eucalyptus trees. They laid two fresh plumeria leis on the spot and removed a faded orchid lei, a remnant of Jessie's last visit.

After meeting with the lawyers and settling the trust that Rod set up, Jessie wondered whether she should sell the old place. Billy told her to expect offers from neighboring ranchers wanting to buy or lease Rod's 500 acres. He was willing to continue as manager if she didn't sell. Tarzan said he'd stay, too, and Mary promised to help out until she wasn't needed anymore. At first, Jessie didn't plan to be on the island for more than two or three weeks, but with the discovery of her father's remains she figured she'd have to stay at least until the preliminary investigation was over, maybe a month at the most.

It was nearing two o'clock and after Jessie saddled Koa she fed him an apple as she waited for Mac to arrive. Tarzan saddled Rod's favorite horse for Mac. Rod named the mare *Hoku* for the white star on her forehead. She was his favorite horse. He used to say she was "half Arabian, half horse."

A few minutes later, John McIntire drove into the yard. He got out of the Ford Expedition emblazoned with the logo "Hawaii County Police Department" on the doors. He tipped the brim of his baseball cap with the initials HPD in the front to Jessie and shook hands with Tarzan, who gave him the reins for the mare. "Well, it looks like we're going riding," he said. "I never thought I'd live to see the day that I'd be astride Rod Bradford's famous Arabian mare. I'm honored."

"She needs the exercise and I hope you won't be disappointed to learn that she's really only part Arabian, and a very small part at that," laughed Jessie. "Uncle Rod used to say she had plenty of ordinary working horse in her to be tough and a drop of Arabian to be fast."

They mounted the horses and Jessie leaned over and patted Koa's mane. "I thought you'd enjoy a ride. Billy and I were planning to take these guys out, but we've been busy trying to settle the accounts and we haven't had time. Besides, it clears my head to ride out there," she said, pointing toward the horizon and the sweeping view of the cattle ranch she'd known all her life.

She hadn't visited very often during the last 10 years or so, but it always felt like home no matter how long she was away. It was never a problem adjusting from her San Francisco life to the simple country living of the ranch. Her uncle and aunt always made her feel welcome, as if it were her home, too. "It's like the little house on the prairie," she told her San Francisco friends, "only with indoor plumbing."

Jessie nudged her horse and said, "Come on, Mac. I'll race you."

Tarzan opened the gate to the paddock and closed it after them. They gave the horses their lead as they broke into a fast canter. Jessie was wearing Maile's western-style straw hat, her hair streaming behind her. Mac kept up, though the mare seemed to be holding back to keep pace with the gelding.

They arrived at an old lava flow that nearly reached the rugged cliffs of South Point about two hundred years ago. It separated Bradford Ranch from Joe Kanekoa's property, a sort of natural boundary line. The smell of sulfur emanated from beneath the hardened lava. The odor was strong, as if the flow was fresh and had recently passed through. Rounding the tip of the craggy rock field, they came to a clearing surrounded by guava and pandanus trees and stopped, dropped to the ground, and left the horses to graze. The scent of wild yellow ginger blossoms permeated the air. Although wild ginger was a scourge to ranchers, so invasive that it threatened the grass that was vital to cattle and horses, Jessie loved the sweet scent of the delicate flowers.

This spot was where Jessie and Danny used to come with the brown bag lunches Maile made for them when they were young. Jessie could almost taste the freshly baked bread slathered with peanut butter and Maile's homemade guava jam. "Danny and I came here often during small kid time," she said. "We'd sit near the mound and eat lunch. Sometimes my aunt came with us."

"I know," said Mac. "I came with you a couple of times, remember?" reminding her of their longtime friendship. He pulled a blade of grass and placed it between his teeth, chewing on its sweetness. He wished they could reminisce about old times, but he was there to discuss the grisly find in the cave.

"How are you doing, Jess?" he asked. "I'm sorry you have to deal with all of this, especially so soon after Rod's death. I was shocked when you showed up yesterday. I planned to call you when I was on my way up to Mauna Loa Ranch to tell you what we found. I hoped to protect you from the gruesome side of it."

"Thanks," she said, "but I wanted to see for myself. I'm sorry I was such a bitch."

Although they hadn't seen each other in years, there was no awkwardness between them. They went to high school in Honolulu – Jessie at a prestigious boarding school, Mac at the Kamehameha Schools for students of Hawaiian ancestry where he was required to prove he was at least part Hawaiian in order to be accepted. He provided birth certificates of his mother and grandmother whose lineage is traced back to early Hawaiian royalty.

They'd dated in their senior year, but didn't make plans for a future together, although many hoped they'd marry. In fact, both their families counted on it, especially her mother. The thought of her daughter marrying one of the wealthy McIntire brothers was like catnip to Anne Bradford. Jessie attended the University of California at Berkeley and Mac went to Brigham Young University on the island of Oahu. The relationship lasted through their first summer and holiday vacations, but the phone calls and letters gradually stopped. When Jessie married her college sweetheart soon after graduation, it crushed any hopes their parents held for uniting the two families.

Mac gave up his plans for law school, became a police officer, and married a girl he met in college. His wife tried, but couldn't cope with being married to a police officer. After an angry teenage boy Mac had arrested on drug and robbery charges made bail and started making threatening phone calls to their home, she decided she'd had enough. Her husband's long hours and missed opportunities to spend time with his family were already putting a strain on their marriage, but now she and her children were being threatened because of his job. She filed for divorce. They shared custody of their three boys. That was more than 15 years ago.

She remarried and she and Mac had a civil, even friendly, relationship for the boys' sakes. He dated occasionally, but nothing serious ever came of those one-time dinner-and-a-movie outings. He'd never admit it even to himself, but he was still in love with Jessie.

Jessie, on the other hand, divorced her husband, an executive with an engineering firm, after learning of his affair with a younger woman. It was the usual story – he met the perfect trophy wife – tall, blonde, thin, and half his age.

At first she was besieged with matchmaking attempts by friends and dated a few of the men they introduced her to, but she never met anyone with whom she'd even consider having a long term relationship. She went back to the university at Berkeley, earned a master's degree in American history, then a doctorate, and was now a tenured professor at San Francisco State University. Summer break was just beginning when she learned the news about her uncle's death.

Here they were again, she and Mac, only without her brother and Maile's peanut butter and jam sandwiches. She gazed at the man who'd been her high school sweetheart. His earnest expression and clear, blue eyes were still endearing. He seemed to be the same gentle guy from her youth and still handsome, she couldn't help noticing. He took off his hat and laid it on the grass beside him. A few strands of gray ran through his wavy, dark brown hair. Jessie patted her hair, thinking of her own gray strands hidden by blonde highlights. She didn't remove her hat. They were both 50 now, no longer children, and she was depending on him to solve the mystery of her father's death.

She was a teenager when her father disappeared. They weren't close and he was gone so long that she felt more curious than sad. "I suppose you can't know too much in such a short time," she said, "Why don't you start by telling me the how and the why if you can. We already know the where."

"We don't have much yet," said Mac. "After almost 40 years most forensic evidence is gone. We'll try to test for DNA and we'll need you for that. I'm hoping there'll be some DNA that we can compare to yours. I'll send someone to the ranch to do a swab or you can go to the lab in Hilo."

"It's been exactly 36 years, by the way," said Jessie. "I did the math when I was driving home yesterday. I was 14 at the time. Anyway, just let me know where the lab is in Hilo and when you want me to go."

Mac said dental records were the quickest way for identification. "We'll look at those first if we can get them. Do you remember the name of his dentist? I hope he's still around and kept the records. I'm certain it's your father, though. Everything fits – size, clothes, boots, especially the belt buckle. Everyone knew that buckle. You seemed pretty sure yourself yesterday when you saw it."

"I knew it was my father," said Jessie. "I just felt it. Of course, the buckle helped. Our dentist was Dr. Kwon in Hilo, by the way, but I doubt if he's still alive. He seemed old even back then."

"If the dental records don't work out," said Mac, "DNA will be the only option to confirm identity. Our lab in Honolulu is not equipped for the testing that'll be required. There are some private laboratories in Honolulu that do DNA testing, but they're expensive and I'd need to go through channels to get it approved. We could send it to Washington, D.C. to the Feds, but that could take months, years, even. We're a little behind in the Islands. This isn't San Francisco or New York City where they have the latest technology. Everything takes longer here. I'll work on finding Dr. Kwon. We may still need your swab just in case. I'll let you know."

"I'll do whatever I have to," Jessie said. "I'm curious about what happened and I want this to be over so I can go home."

"We'll do our best," he said. "Right now, we're guessing he was fishing alone that morning. Maybe he was accosted by someone, transients, perhaps. Do you remember what he usually wore when he went fishing? I can't figure out why he was wearing expensive riding boots on those slippery rocks and in salt water at that. Most people wear rubber boots with treads on the soles or flip flops, even waders, not smooth leather-soled boots. Did he usually go alone or with someone? If he wasn't there to fish, why was he there?"

"They found his fishing gear, didn't they? Doesn't that prove why he was there?"

"We have a lot of questions," said Mac. "That's one of them. We'll try to figure it out. What do you remember about him? Did he have any enemies? Anyone who held a grudge? From what I hear, he wasn't the easiest person to get along with, a my-way-or-the-highway kind of a guy. Any information you have will be helpful. What was he like at home?"

"He was kind of rigid, I guess, maybe even a bit standoffish, a little gruff at times, not the warm, cuddly type. He didn't get too involved with Danny and me and we usually stayed out of his way. I never sat on his lap like little girls do with their daddies and I can't remember him wearing anything but those riding breeches and boots. He always dressed conservatively, not like Uncle Rod who was pretty casual in his t-shirts and jeans." She looked at her own scuffed, dusty boots. They were lying in the grass next to her, the socks tucked inside. She wiggled her red-tipped toes, the bright polish glistened in the sun.

"I never saw my father's bare feet," she said. "That must sound strange, but he and Mother were pretty formal. You knew my mother. Not a hair out of place, impeccably dressed at all times, wearing silk stockings and high heels just to go across the street from our house to the post office. Father wore his polished brown leather boots everywhere, even in the house, much to my mother's dismay. I guess the only time he took them off was when he went to bed." She laughed and shrugged her shoulders. "And I'm not even sure about that."

Mac looked down at his boots. He wore them most of the time, but at home he was usually barefoot. No one would describe him as being formal. He was beyond casual.

"You know how most of us are island-style when it comes to taking off our shoes before entering the house," Jessie said. "We'd all remove our shoes at home, even my mother, but my father didn't. The maids had fits because they had to polish the wood floors all the time to remove the scuff marks. Anyway, I wouldn't be surprised if he wore his boots to go fishing. He probably figured that he could always buy another pair if they got ruined. My parents were careless with money. When my mother died there wasn't much left. After she paid for Danny's and my educations, she spent whatever she wanted on designer clothes, jewelry, trips, anything. Her life insurance policy paid for her funeral. That saved me from dipping into my savings. They were both irresponsible."

"What about the goings on at your house during that time? Did you notice any problems between your parents, arguments, anything like that?" Mac asked.

"I can't think of anything unusual," she said. "They did argue sometimes. I didn't pay much attention."

It was August and she and Anne were packing for boarding school. Her mother wanted to buy Jessie a new wardrobe in Honolulu before classes began so that her only daughter would wear the latest in teenage fashion. "But I was just a tomboy who ran wild and barefoot on the ranch and the plantation," said Jessie. "I was such a little hick and dressing me up was not going to change that. It sure didn't help me to fit in with those uppity Honolulu girls. I wasn't very girly."

"You were girly enough for me," he said. "I always thought you were the cutest one of all. It was the sprinkling of freckles across your nose and the gold flecks in your green eyes that reeled me in. Why do you think I asked you to go steady? You wore my ring all senior year, remember? It was a sad day when you mailed it back to me." He peered closely at her. "I see you still have the freckles."

She smiled. "Yes, they're still there and I do remember wearing your ring. That was a sweet time, wasn't it? But we're getting off topic, Detective."

Tilting her head slightly and closing her eyes, she recalled that her parents were having friends to dinner that night. In the morning her mother went over the menu, making sure the cook was prepared for the dinner party when Tom Johnson, the plantation office manager, came to the house looking for Allen. Allen and Anne slept in separate bedrooms, so her mother didn't always know whether or not he came home at night. "Mother sent one of the maids to check his bedroom, but he wasn't there. None of us knew where he was," said Jessie.

She'd never forget that awful day. Tom Johnson told Anne that a couple of fishermen found her husband's station wagon parked at the beach with the keys in the ignition and his fishing gear lying on the rocks. There was no sign of Allen. The fishermen rushed to the lighthouse which was still operating at the time, and called the police. Anne was distraught, sobbing uncontrollably and was comforted by a parade of people who provided emotional support.

"People were in and out all day," said Jessie. "Police, the Mormon elders, Aunt Maile and Uncle Rod, my mother's sister, Sarah, who came from Hilo, various friends, and the plantation doctor who plied her with mind-numbing sedatives."

Anne asked the housekeeper to cancel the dinner party, but that was the only rational thing she seemed capable of doing during the ordeal. After everyone left she went to bed with a cold, wet towel on her forehead and stayed there for several days. Jessie and Danny were told to be quiet and were left to themselves most of the time. Eventually, their Aunt Sarah took them to Honolulu and enrolled them in school. Jessie was a freshman and it was Danny's senior year. When they returned to the Big Island for Christmas vacation, their mother was living in Hilo with her sister. "As far as I know, she never went back to Kahana Plantation, not even to visit friends," said Jessie.

No one questioned why Allen went to South Point that morning. They all assumed that he went to fish. The police interviewed nearly all the plantation employees, including Tom Johnson and Hideo Miyamoto who both worked in the office. "Mr. Miyamoto died years ago," said Jessie. "His daughter, Sachi, is married to Billy Gonsalves, my ranch manager. Billy told me that Mrs. Miyamoto, Sachi's mother, is in a nursing home in Hilo."

Sachi Gonsalves was a professor of economics at the Hilo campus of the University of Hawaii. It was time for finals and she was still busy at school. They spoke briefly on the phone when Jessie first arrived and planned to get together when the semester was over.

"Maybe do some shopping, you know, girly stuff," Sachi said. "We have Macy's now," she teased in a sing song voice. They both laughed, remembering when the biggest store in Hilo, the largest city on the island, was the five and dime store, Kress.

"What about the Miyamoto sons?" Mac asked. "Weren't there three or four of them? I wonder if they're still around? They might know something."

"There were four," said Jessie. "I remember the oldest one, Tak, died years ago in an accident at the plantation mill. The youngest boy, Albert, was killed in Viet Nam. One of them became a doctor. He's on the Mainland, Seattle, I think. I don't know about the fourth son."

"This is not going to be an easy case," said Mac. "As I said, the years have taken their toll on the evidence. I'll try to find out who is still living in this area from that time. I hope I can jog someone's memory. They'll be elderly and might not remember much, but that may be all we have. With

Sachi's mother being in a nursing home, I doubt that she'll be helpful. I'll go see her anyway, though. She's what? About 90 years old?"

"In her 80s or early 90s, I guess," said Jessie. "I've been thinking that it might have been a robbery. I wouldn't be surprised. You know the kind of people who hang out at South Point – gun-toting campers who shoot up the signs, hippies, homeless people, and who knows who is living in those dilapidated, old buildings. Even years ago when my father disappeared, there were misfits living in the Seabee Quonset huts from World War II. The reason they were torn down was to keep people from squatting in them."

"Yeah, we've considered a robbery gone bad," said Mac, "but he was still wearing his expensive Bulova watch and gold wedding ring when we found him, and hell, the silver belt buckle. There's money in his wallet, exactly $54.00, and some change in his pocket. Then, there's the station wagon with the keys in the ignition. If it was a robbery they'd have taken the money, the valuables, and probably the car. We're trying to cover all the bases, Jess. Not only is the cave difficult to get to, but it's sacred to native Hawaiians and now it's an archaeological site. This is no ordinary crime scene and it doesn't help that the remains are so deteriorated."

"If it wasn't a robbery, then why was he killed? I don't get it," said Jessie.

"That's what we'll work on," said Mac.

He was expecting a call from the police chief. "I thought my boss would have called by now," he said, looking at his watch. "He was trying to fend off the media when we last spoke, so I don't know when he'll get back to me. He's made this investigation a top priority. It's getting a lot of press and he doesn't want us to screw it up. If it weren't such a delicate situation – you know, the historical implications and all, it might be just another cold case. But this one's complicated. As it is, the only witness I have right now is the other occupant of the cave and he's not talking."

"Yes, I know," said Jessie, "your silent witness."

"Yeah. Well, we'll try to track down the dentist," said Mac. He was scribbling in his notebook as he talked. "He's probably retired now or passed away. If so, maybe someone took over his practice. Let's hope records from that long ago are still around. Maybe they are. You never know."

Mac told her that they were already having problems with certain groups who didn't want the site disturbed by the investigation. "They've been hunting for King Kamehameha's tomb ever since he died in 1819 and if it's him, it's a really big deal since he was Hawaii's first king. In any case," he continued, "eventually the site will be turned over to the university and the museums, but they're not getting in there until our investigation is complete. It's a crime scene, for Christ's sake. That's more important than an archaeological dig, just sayin'."

"I came here expecting to settle Uncle Rod's estate," said Jessie. "I never dreamed I'd be in the middle of a criminal investigation." She was glad to spend time with Mac, but wished it was for reasons other than a murder mystery, especially one involving her father. She glanced at her watch. They'd been gone too long. Mary was watching from a window as they rode off and Jessie didn't want to be the next news item for the South Point Gazette. "The wind is revving up, we'd better go. Mary's waiting for us." As she put on her socks and boots she said, "If you have time, why don't you stay a while? I'm sure Mary won't mind cooking an early dinner."

"I'd like that," said Mac. "I'll see what the chief says. If he doesn't need me tonight, it's a date."

They mounted the horses and started at a slow trot, then went into a gallop, racing each other to the paddock gate. Mac got there first and opened the gate. As they rode into the yard heading for the hitching post, they saw Mary waving frantically from the front porch. Jessie hurried over to her as Mac and Tarzan began unsaddling the horses.

"There was a call for Detective McIntire," Mary said, "from Chief Lindsey in Hilo." Jessie waved Mac over and Mary repeated the message.

"Shoot! I should have known I was out of cell range," groused Mac. "Good thing I left a message for the Chief giving him your ranch number." He turned away from Jessie and Mary, pulled out his phone, and was soon talking with his boss. He spoke briefly and clicked off. "I'm sorry, Jessie. I can't stay. I have to get back to Hilo tonight. Rain check?"

"Sure, another time," she said.

He bent and kissed her on the cheek, tipped his cap to Mary, waved to Tarzan, got in the Expedition, and headed back to the main road, his phone at his ear.

For dinner that night, Mary served fried mahi mahi cooked in Jessie's favorite style – dipped in soy sauce and egg, dredged in flour and fried until flaky. There was macaroni salad, rice, and green beans and tomatoes from the kitchen garden. It was a typical island meal, loaded with carbs and calories.

As Jessie was taking the last bite, she said, "That was delicious. Too bad Mac missed it, but maybe next time just a salad? These jeans won't fit me if I eat like this every night. I'll end up weighing 200 pounds by the time I go back to San Francisco," she said, laughing. She helped Mary clean up, and urged her to take the leftovers home.

After Mary left, Billy stopped in to say he was leaving for the day and a few minutes later Tarzan drove out of the yard. Probably headed for Moon's Beachhead Inn in Waikea Village, Jessie thought. Waikea is about 40 miles from the ranch and nowhere near a beach, and Moon's is a bar, hardly an inn, but it is popular with the locals, especially the *paniolo,* the cowboys from the nearby ranches.

Tarzan lived at the ranch in a small cottage behind the main house. He'd worked for Rod Bradford since his teens and his father before him. Half Hawaiian, half Portuguese, or *hapa,* island lingo for half or mixed, he's stocky and fair-skinned with sandy hair and blue eyes.

He acquired the moniker Tarzan when he was in high school. On his way home from a football game in which he scored the winning touchdown, he saved the day when a car skidded into a ditch. Before the tow truck arrived, Tarzan helped the stunned driver to safety and pulled the car out of the ditch. Within minutes, the car was upright and back on the road. There was applause from onlookers and some of them shouted out the names of Superman and other super heroes. The one that stuck was Tarzan. "It's just a Honda Civic," he said modestly. From that moment, Kawena Ernest Lorenzo became known as Tarzan.

After everyone left, Jessie sat down at the kitchen table and spent another evening going through her uncle's papers. Knowing what was left after she paid the debts would determine whether she'd have to sell the ranch. All she really wanted to do was go back to San Francisco. Selling seemed the best option no matter what the finances were.

As she pored over the papers and typed the info onto a spreadsheet on her computer, she suddenly remembered that Moon's Beachhead Inn was a popular watering hole when her father disappeared. Moon, a burly Lithuanian, whose real name was Stanley Toli, opened the bar about five years after the end of World War II. It was just off the highway and was still a favorite spot for anyone hankering for a cold beer or a shot of cheap whiskey. Jessie was sure Stanley Toli was an avid participant in the South Point rumor mill and that he probably saw and heard everything and knew everyone who traveled that road. She wondered if he still ran the bar. Maybe he remembered something about that day.

Her parents often argued about her father stopping at Moon's. Anne Bradford was a teetotaler and a practicing member of the Church of Latter Day Saints. As a Mormon, she disapproved of Allen's drinking, especially at a place like Moon's. Although Allen Bradford and his younger brother, Rod, were the sons of devout Mormons, they never practiced Mormonism or any other religion once they left for college and never limited their vices. They smoked cigarettes, drank liquor, and copious amounts of the strong Hawaiian coffee that Rod grew on the ranch. While Rod did everything in moderation, Allen did not. He loved his vices and enjoyed the intensity of excess.

Jessie clicked on her phone to the notes app and typed the heading To Do. She began her list: Call Sachi, visit Sachi's mother, talk to Moon Toli, see Joe Kanekoa, DNA test, plan burial, find out when remains will be released.

She planned to bury her father at the Mormon cemetery in Hilo alongside her mother. Danny was interred at Hilo's veterans' cemetery. She made a mental note to visit his grave. Should I write an obituary for my father, she wondered, and then reasoned that it probably wouldn't be appropriate under the circumstances. The newspapers and newscasts were covering the story, so every detail was out there for all to see, anyway. It was even on CNN.

Since there was so much media coverage about the "gruesome and amazing discovery on the Big Island," she didn't even turn on the TV or check the news online anymore. The only concession she made was to watch an uncomfortable Mac on the local six o'clock news the day she left him at the South Point Cliffs. He was surrounded by reporters shoving microphones at him and he was trying to answer questions without being too specific. It was painful to see.

Her daughter, Catherine, saw the news on CNN and left a voice mail asking if Jessie was all right. "Should I come to be with you?"

Jessie returned the call and left a message. "Don't come yet, maybe later. Don't worry."

She looked up the Beachhead Inn online and called the number. A man with a gravelly voice answered, "Moon's." There was the usual bar noise in the background – clinking glasses, the click of a cue ball, laughter, and loud music. Jessie asked for Moon Toli. "This is Moon," said the man.

She identified herself and asked if she could meet with him to ask a few questions. "Is this about the Bradford murder?" asked Moon. She hesitated before saying yes, agreed to be at the bar around 11 o'clock the next morning, and clicked off.

Murder? Why would anyone murder my father?

4

HIDEO MIYAMOTO WAS 28 YEARS OLD IN 1935 WHEN HE IMMI-grated to Hawaii to work as a laborer in the sugar cane fields of Kahana Plantation. He was poor and couldn't make a living on his small farm in Wakaya-ken, a province in southern Japan. When the call came that workers were needed in the Hawaiian Islands, he was eager to go. His wife and infant son had died in childbirth and he was alone. He planned to make a fortune in Hawaii and return to Japan to find a bride and start a new life.

On the Kahana Plantation he worked hoe *hana,* the back-breaking work of weeding the cane fields with a hoe, hana being the Hawaiian word for work. Later, he was promoted to slashing and cutting the cane with a machete. While living in the free Japanese bachelors' quarters, he saved nearly every penny of his meager salary. It took 10 years to save enough money to return to Japan and find a wife.

In 1946 at the age of 39, Hideo traveled to Japan by ship to meet the bride found through the matchmaking custom, *nakodo.* He had been writing letters and sending money to a matchmaker for several years. When a suitable and willing bride was located, Hideo eagerly made the trip to Ehime prefecture, a coastal village in southern Japan, to claim the beautiful 16-year-old Sumiko Nakashima. Hideo fell instantly in love. Sumiko's glossy black hair fell nearly to her waist, thick lashes fringed wide, almond-shaped eyes. Her porcelain skin gave the appearance of the dolls Hideo saw in the shops in Hawaii and reminded him of the actresses in the Japanese movies that played at the plantation theatre one night a week. He couldn't believe his good fortune.

Sumiko on the other hand, was inwardly disappointed in the work-worn older man her family chose for her. Hideo was able to pay the price they asked and they couldn't afford to keep her on the farm where they struggled to feed and clothe their large family. Sumiko, the eldest daughter, was the sacrifice her parents made.

The solemn marriage ceremony was brief. The wedding night was spent with Sumiko crying and Hideo gently trying to comfort her in a small room in her parent's house. A few days later they were on a ship sailing to Hawaii where Hideo decided to take his bride instead of staying in Japan. The sea voyage was no discomfort for him, but Sumiko was constantly in the throes of dysentery and nausea in the cramped quarters of the ocean liner. It was a great relief to finally land in Honolulu where they spent the night at a hotel in Japantown. The next day they flew to Hilo. Hideo hired a taxi to drive them the 75 miles to Kahana Plantation where he was granted a married man's house in the Japanese camp.

When they arrived at the house, neighbors met them with banners of welcome printed in Japanese characters. Sumiko was pleased to meet her new friends and to see the neat and tidy wood frame building that was to be her home. Hideo, with the help of the wives of his Japanese com-patriots, furnished the house with futons and tatami pillows of the best quality he could afford. He bought a black lacquer kimono chest and filled it with several new kimonos and the tiny kitchen contained all the utensils a Japanese wife would ever need. He even built a *furo*, a precursor of the modern hot tub, so Sumiko could take the hot baths that were the Japanese custom. She began to feel less disappointed in her new husband.

Although he was older, he was gentle and only wanted to please her. Unlike most of the other wives, she was not going to work as a hoe hana woman in the cane fields. Hideo wanted her to stay at home, keep house, and have babies.

His wish was fulfilled when nearly a year later, Sumi, as he came to call her, presented him with a son, Takeshi, who soon had the nickname, Tak. Another boy, Isaburo, was born two years later, followed by a third boy, Nobu, and a fourth, Albert. By 1952, Hideo and Sumi were the parents of four boys, all healthy and robust. Even though she experienced the ordeal of childbirth four times, Sumi was still a beauty. Her life as a stay-at-home wife and mother allowed her to maintain her good looks. That was not the case with most of the other wives who worked in the fields and also managed household chores and child-bearing. Their skin became wrinkled from the hot tropical sun no matter how hard they tried to protect their faces and hands. Their bodies were prematurely bent and worn from the hard work of cutting the cane with machetes and digging weeds with hoes.

Sumi rarely left the camp, but she was active in the Japanese community, teaching Japanese language to children at the Buddhist temple school and learning to speak English. Though the war with Japan ended years ago, most Islanders could not forget Pearl Harbor. There was still anti-Japanese sentiment among the local people. Even those Japanese who were born in the Islands and were American citizens weren't spared the abuse. They kept to themselves and stayed in their segregated plantation camps as much as possible.

World War II brought hardship and upheaval to the thousands of Japanese who had immigrated to the Hawaiian Islands since the late 19th century. Much the same as their counterparts in other areas of the United States, they were ostracized and in some cases sent to detention camps on the U.S. Mainland. The plantation workers, though, were safe in the camps and their lives didn't change much except for an occasional slur called from a passing car or when they shopped at the company store in town. They were very familiar with the derogatory term Jap.

Allen Bradford treated his workers fairly, leaving them to their respective ethnic customs, including the Japanese. While some plantation managers restricted their Japanese employees' activities outside of work after the war ended, Bradford allowed his workers to live as if Pearl Harbor hadn't happened and nothing was changed. Kahana was one of the most successful sugar plantations on the island and he wanted to keep it that way. His was a well-run, profitable operation. He did not tolerate racism and grievances about the war.

He frequently visited the Japanese camp to make sure all was well and to let them know they were safe. One evening Bradford was invited to speak at a meeting at the camp community hall. It was then that he saw Sumi Miyamoto for the first time. He had spoken there several times before, so this was not unusual, but that night he saw the beautiful woman in the audience. Sumi usually attended the meetings only when Japanese leaders spoke, but Hideo urged her to go to this one because he held Allen Bradford in high esteem and wanted his wife to hear his boss speak.

"Come on, Sumi. I want you to go. He is such a good speaker and a wonderful man. You'll like him, you'll see." Finally, she agreed and sat in the front row along with the other wives.

Bradford couldn't keep his eyes off her as he sat on the stage. He was mesmerized by her beautiful face with its porcelain-white skin. When he stood at the podium during his speech he seemed to speak directly to her. Sumi possessed an air of confidence and poise as she sat in a metal folding chair, straight and prim, unlike most of the other Japanese women who displayed subservience in the way they hunched their shoulders, heads bent forward, and eyes downcast. She stared steadily at the man on the stage, never looking away, giving no semblance of subservience. She doubted that the plantation manager was speaking directly to her, but noticed that his eyes rarely shifted away from hers.

At his office the next day, Bradford asked his secretary for a list of all the Japanese workers on the plantation including their wives and children. After going over the list, he crossed off the names of the men and women who worked in the fields. He knew most of them and those women were work-worn unlike the beauty he saw at the meeting hall. The list of married women who didn't work was brief and one name stood out – Sumiko Miyamoto. Under her name was listed the names of her sons and one of them was Tak, who he knew was Hideo's son.

Bradford remembered that Hideo Miyamoto married a young mail order bride from Japan and was sure she was the beauty at the meeting hall. He worked closely with Hideo on a number of occasions and found him to be intelligent, well-spoken, and industrious. He thought at one time to promote Hideo to a supervisory position because he spoke English well and was a leader in the Japanese community, but hadn't acted on it after the bombing of Pearl Harbor.

A few weeks after he spoke at the community hall, Bradford paid a visit to Hideo's home. Although Hideo invited him in, the plantation manager didn't want to remove his boots. He knew the Japanese custom of removing one's shoes before entering a house. That custom was evident at the back door of the Miyamoto home by the rows of shoes and *gita* – Japanese wooden clogs – lined up outside the door. "Too hard to take off my boots," Bradford said, laughing as he asked Hideo to step outside so they could talk. He noticed the fishing poles and nets leaning against the wall near the door, so he asked where Hideo fished. Hideo was stunned to have a visit from the head *luna* – the boss. He hid his surprise and told Bradford that he fished at the black sand beach near the plantation sugar mill and sometimes Green Sand Beach at South Point.

Bradford made small talk for a while hoping to get a glimpse of Mrs. Miyamoto when suddenly the door opened and the beautiful woman from the meeting hall looked out.

"Oh, *gomen'nasai*, I'm sorry. Hideo, I didn't know you have company. Good Evening, Mr. Bradford." Her voice was soft with a sing-song lilt that sounded melodic to Bradford. Sumi bowed and quickly closed the door.

Bradford apologized for intruding and asked Hideo to come to his office first thing the next morning.

Later that night during dinner he asked his wife, Anne, if she knew a Mrs. Miyamoto. Anne was the perfect manager's wife, often visiting the homes of the other managers as well as calling on the wives who lived in the various camps. She put them on committees, met with them at PTA meetings, held fund raisers for the families in the camps, and played bridge with the top managers' wives.

"You mean Sumi Miyamoto? Yes, I know her. Why?"

"I'm thinking of promoting her husband, Hideo, to a supervisory position and I wondered if she met the qualifications of a supervisor's wife. She would have to interact with you and the other supervisors' and managers' wives and she'd be visible outside the Japanese community. What do you think?"

"I can't say enough good things about Sumi," said Anne. "She speaks English well, her boys are well-behaved, and she's a role model for the other camp wives. Yes, she'd be the perfect supervisor's wife. She's delightful."

The next morning Bradford offered Hideo the job. Hideo was jubilant when he went home from work that night with the good news. "We'll have a bigger house, a supervisor's house, Sumi, and you will spend time with the other luna's wives. What do you think of that?" He laughed as he drank the *sake* Sumi poured for him. She was proud of her husband and opened a celebratory bottle of rice wine to toast their good luck.

The boys were thrilled. Although Tak at 15 had quit school by then and was a laborer at the mill, he still lived at home. His brothers were smart and American in every way. They belonged to Scouts, participated in school sports, and attended Japanese language class. They were elated at their father's success and joined in the celebration – happy that Hideo would be a luna and that they'd live in a bigger house.

It was not long after Hideo began his new job that Bradford began to invite him to go fishing. Sometimes his brother Rod joined them. They'd fish for mullet at the pond at Punalu'u black sand beach and sometimes for flounder and red snapper at South Point.

They became friends, often meeting to go fishing in the morning before work while it was still dark. Sometimes Bradford had Hideo drive the station wagon on the way home so he could sleep. Several times a week, they met in the evenings for beers at Moon's Beachhead Inn. Neither Anne nor Sumi liked that idea. While Anne often chided Allen about it Sumi, always the dutiful wife, never said a word against it to Hideo.

With more responsibility and authority, Hideo began to work longer hours at his new job. He was a supervisor under office manager, Tom Johnson. Johnson was friendly and easy-going and got along well with his staff. He and Hideo became good work mates. Bradford began to micro manage Hideo's work load and it wasn't long before he was delegating work to Johnson and suggesting that he pass it on to Hideo.

Sumi didn't like the late hours her husband kept, but was proud that he was trusted with such responsibility, so she didn't complain. When Allen Bradford began to stop by in the evenings under the pretext of looking for Hideo to arrange a fishing trip or to talk about work, Sumi politely invited him in. Bradford didn't mind removing his boots during those visits, carefully placing them inside the door instead of outside where prying eyes could see them. He knew the younger boys' schedules and put Tak on the night shift so, he usually managed to find Sumi home alone.

She served him sake or tea, sometimes a beer, and was flattered that Bradford-san was interested in Hideo. When he tried to kiss her the first time, she pulled back, turning her face away. "Please, no," she said softly, her hand covering her mouth. Bradford didn't press then, but he was persistent, showing up on her doorstep often. When they finally became lovers,

Sumi was consumed with guilt, but was afraid to say no to her husband's boss. They managed to keep their affair secret from the children who were too busy to notice anything amiss and were seldom at home, anyway. It was the neighbors who noticed the regular visits by the plantation boss to the Miyamoto house and soon the whispers and rumors began. When Hideo and Sumi met with their friends, though, out of respect for him, no one said a word.

The plantation houses were old, some were built in the late 1800s and although they were painted and repaired periodically, only those reserved for upper management were remodeled. For the Miyamoto's new house, even though Hideo was only a low level supervisor, Bradford ordered the bathrooms and kitchen redone, and added an extra bedroom and bath. The lawn was tended to by company gardeners, all of whom were the Miyamoto's friends and neighbors from the Japanese camp. Before the family moved into their new home and while it was being remodeled, it was easy for Bradford and Sumi to see each other. There was always an excuse for them to be at the house to discuss the major work. Bradford went there to meet Sumi, pretending to show her how the work was coming along. They'd leave separately and meet at a vacant house at the edge of town where Bradford kept his fishing and hunting gear. Sumi took a back road, hoping no one would see her. As far as she knew, her circuitous route along the cane field which bordered the Japanese and Catholic cemeteries helped to keep the clandestine trysts secret.

Their love-making was passionate, but Sumi felt guilty and always listened for footsteps. "What if someone finds us here and Hideo finds out or the boys? And when the house is finished how can we go on? I think we must stop."

"Once you move, if the boys should come home, we'll tell them I came by to see Hideo about work and you offered me some tea. It's not that complicated, Sumi," Bradford said, as they sat on the bed in the bedroom of the house he called their love nest. He drew her to him and kissed her throat, running his lips down her chest, pulling her blouse open, kissing her small breasts. "I'm in love with you. I won't stay away and that's that. Don't worry about it." He kissed her mouth, muffling her words of protest, and laid back on the bed, pulling her down next to him.

The Miyamotos moved into the house and soon afterward Sumi became pregnant. She didn't meet with Bradford during her pregnancy and was relieved that she didn't have to see him. Hideo was surprised and overjoyed at the prospect of having another child, especially at his age. He was 57 years old. Their friends and neighbors in the camp teased him about fathering a child so late in life and they laughed with Hideo and congratulated him on his virility. Some wondered whose child Sumi was carrying. Sumi wondered, too.

What will I do if the baby isn't Japanese? she moaned to herself, imagining the shame and hurt it would cause her family. How could I save face? Never again, never again, she vowed. I will never let him in this house again.

She closed her eyes and squeezed them tightly, as if by doing so, she could shut out the image of Allen Bradford and all he stood for. She was just a young girl when she married Hideo and felt repulsed by him at first. Through the years she learned to love him for his kindness and gentleness. She couldn't forgive herself for betraying him. If only she could erase the last few years and start over without Allen in her life, but it was too late. The deception had to continue. She prayed that Hideo would never find out.

When Sachiko Ruth Miyamoto was born early one morning, she was fair-skinned like her mother unlike her brothers who were dark like their father. With straight black hair and dark almond-shaped eyes, she looked Japanese in every way. Sumi cried with relief when the midwife handed her the baby. When Hideo was summoned into the room, he cried with Sumi, but his were tears of joy.

5

WHEN THE ALARM WENT OFF, JESSIE PULLED BACK THE SHEETS and Maile's hand-stitched Hawaiian quilt. She'd been up way past midnight going over Rod's papers again and felt bleary-eyed, as if she were hung over. The bedside clock showed it was 9:30. She was going to Waikea Village to meet with Moon Toli this morning and didn't want to be late for the 11 o'clock appointment.

She headed to the bathroom, brushed her teeth, and studied her reflection in the mirror. Strands of gray were beginning to show at her temples. Peering up close, she said aloud, "I'd better find a salon and have my color done if I'm going to stay here much longer." After showering and dressing in a t-shirt and jeans, she walked barefoot down the hallway toward the kitchen and the aroma of coffee brewing.

Mary was pouring coffee and looked up as Jessie entered the room. "Good morning," she said, putting down the coffee pot and turning to the stove to flip the sunny side eggs onto a plate. "I see you worked late again last night," she said, gesturing with her spatula toward the pile of papers and the computer at one end of the kitchen table.

"Yeah, I did. I know I should be using Uncle Rod's office, but I just haven't gotten around to sorting through all the stuff on his desk yet. It's easier to work at the kitchen table," said Jessie. "Sorry for the mess. One of these days I'll clean up his office so I can work in there. I promise."

"No worry," said Mary. "I won't touch a thing. I'll just clean around everything."

Mary came to work as cook, housekeeper, and caregiver when it became evident that no amount of radiation or chemotherapy was going to save Maile. She stayed on after Maile died and it was a good thing because Rod's health began to deteriorate. Her husband, Harry, worked cowboy for Rod part time for years, filling in to help during roundup and branding. Rod didn't have to do any searching when Maile needed help. Mary was more than a caregiver and housekeeper, she was a friend. She cared for Maile and Rod as if they were family and was now doing the same for Jessie.

Jessie glanced up as Mary placed the breakfast on the table and wondered how old Mary was. Her gray hair was twisted into a bun at the top of her head and she wore not a trace of cosmetics on her faintly lined face. She looked to be in her 60s, but Jessie was to learn later that she was actually 57, just seven years older than she was. Mary was ready for anything. In the oversized pockets of her white cotton apron she stashed her phone, a dust cloth, a screw driver, a small hammer, a handful of nails and thumb tacks, Band-Aids, a tube of first aid cream, and a note pad and pen.

"I have to eat fast because I'm going to town this morning," Jessie said as she ate breakfast and gulped her coffee. "I've got an appointment."

"Going to Kahana or Hilo?" asked Mary. To her, town meant Kahana, the old plantation town. Since most of the sugar plantations on the Big Island had closed in the early '90s, the company towns that had supported them had fallen on hard times. Now many of them only had the bare essentials – a market, gas station, post office, churches, and a few other services. Kahana was no exception.

"Kahana," said Jessie. "I'm going to Waikea first. I have an errand to do there. I want to see Reverend Joe. I need some spiritual guidance." She decided not to tell Mary that she was meeting with Moon Toli. "Want me to pick up something at the market?"

"Nothing important. We are running out of a few things, though." Mary scribbled a short list and handed it to Jessie. "I'm doing laundry today. Anything special you need washed?"

"No, thanks," Jessie called over her shoulder as she ran her fingers through her curly hair that was getting more unruly every day. "By the way, do you know of a hair stylist around here?"

"There's a place in Kahana, but I wouldn't recommend it," answered Mary. "They only know how to do Asian hair, you know, real local style. Better go to Hilo or Kona. That's where the good salons are."

"Okay. I'll have to do it soon, but not today, I guess." She fished a scrunchy out of her jeans pocket and pulled her hair into a pony tail.

Jessie was sitting on the back stoop slipping on her sandals. She wasn't used to having a full time housekeeper. In San Francisco her cleaning woman came once a week, but Jessie did her own cooking and laundry. It took a while to get used to having Mary doing all the chores and coming every day.

Mary dusted everything. There was never laundry in the hamper nor dishes in the sink. She even tended the kitchen garden of herbs and a few vegetables. Jessie didn't want to let her go, thinking the issue would resolve itself when she sold the ranch and went back to San Francisco. Besides, she liked the company.

"I should be back by three or so," called Jessie. "See you later."

Driving up to the highway, she passed the old lava flow that meandered down from Mauna Loa, one of the two major mountains on the island. The flow that had erupted about 200 years ago wended its way through the Bradford pastures where it ended abruptly about halfway to the cliffs.

Although it was mostly a vast expanse of bare, black lava, thick foliage still managed to sprout up. Guava and mango trees, yellow and white ginger, bamboo, and wild grasses grew out of the craggy rock crevices.

Except for a couple of new homes that weren't there when she last visited, including a yellow, two-story bed and breakfast that looked very new and out of place, South Point Road hadn't changed much in 50 years. It was still a narrow, two-lane black-top with pasture land and thick foliage on both sides. Jessie marveled at how other areas of the Big Island had burgeoned into huge tourist Meccas. Along the Kona and Kohala coasts, new high-rise hotels filled the landscape. Shops and streets teemed with tourists wearing flip flops and wild, flowered Hawaiian shirts, while on this part of the island time seemed to have stood still. No other cars were on the road that morning.

She turned onto the two-lane highway toward Waikea Village and soon found herself parked in front of the Beachhead Inn. It appeared closed. The shades at the big picture window that looked out on the street were down. She walked up to the entrance and knocked. Moon Toli answered the door. He was tall with massive shoulders and bald with a round face. You didn't have to be a scholar to figure out why his nickname was Moon. Jessie thought he looked pretty fit for a man she guessed to be in his 80s.

He ushered her into the bar. It was dark in there even though the lights were on. He pulled up the bamboo shades and opened a couple of windows and the top of the Dutch-style front door to let in some light and fresh air. A ceiling fan whirred overhead. Moon's efforts did little to alleviate the musty odor of stale cigarettes and beer, but that didn't bother Jessie. She wasn't planning to be there long. Looking around, she thought of the hundreds of times she'd passed the place. This was her first time being inside.

A poster of John Wayne was tacked to one wall along with another poster advertising a rodeo that was held years ago. Photos of paniolo in full cowboy dress, some on horseback, others in rodeo action shots, lined the walls. Many of the photos were signed, including one of Rod Bradford on horseback holding a trophy and another of Tarzan roping a calf.

An old jukebox stood in a corner near the bar and a well-worn pool table filled the middle of the room. Tall stools flanked the koa wood bar that showed water stains and wear from many years of use by the cowboys and other regulars who stopped by through more than half a century. They came for the loud music, beer, whiskey-water-back, and the weekly fist fights before returning to the bunk house or, on some occasions, to their wives and families. The floor was scuffed and scratched. Jessie decided that she liked the place, worn and shabby as it was, although she didn't think she'd ever be one of Moon's regular customers.

Behind the bar stood a young girl of about 15 or 16, washing glasses and wiping off the counter. Moon introduced her as his daughter, Lovey Mae. Out of a back room, drying her hands with a dish towel, came a Hawaiian woman who looked to be in her 40s. She smiled shyly and asked if she could get Jessie something to eat or drink. Jessie figured she was his second wife, the first one she knew died in a traffic accident a long time ago.

"This is my wife, Noelani," said Moon. Jessie shook her hand, smiled, and said no thank you, she'd just eaten. The woman nodded and disappeared into the back room where the muffled sound of women's voices and soft laughter could be heard.

"I'm very sorry about your uncle, Miss Bradford," Moon said. "He was a good man. Here," he pulled out a chair, "please sit down." They sat at a table in a corner of the room away from the pool table and the jukebox where Merle Haggard and Willie Nelson lamented about Pancho and Lefty and the Federales. Even the music was old and musty, thought Jessie.

"So," said Moon, "you want to talk about the murder at South Point?" His voice was raspy, as if he'd been a smoker forever and that was almost the case. He smoked his first cigarette when he was 10 years old.

"It hasn't officially been declared a murder yet," Jessie replied. "They've only just begun looking into it, but I do have a few questions to ask you. This has nothing to do with the police investigation, you understand. I'm trying to satisfy my own curiosity. I was just a kid when it happened, so I don't remember much."

Moon lit a cigarette, took a deep drag, and exhaled through his nostrils. "Well, I heard he was found inside a cave on the side of a cliff with his head bashed in. Excuse me for being blunt," he said, "that seems like a murder to me."

His daughter brought him a cup of coffee. "Sure you don't want some?" he asked as he blew on it before taking a sip.

Jessie shook her head. "You probably know when my father disappeared he was presumed drowned and washed out to sea," she said. "I don't have to tell you the story. I'm sure you heard all about it back then. Do you remember if he stopped here that night? If he did, I'm wondering if he was alone or with someone."

"I told the police at the time that he came in here a couple of nights before he disappeared," said Moon. "He was alone. He drank a few beers and left. I didn't see if he went toward South Point or Kahana. That was the last time I saw him. That's all I can tell you. The police haven't been here yet this time. I'm sure they'll show up one of these days. I'll have to tell them the same thing I'm telling you." He shrugged his shoulders. "I wish I could be of more help."

Jessie plodded on. "I know he was here pretty often with my Uncle Rod and a friend of his, Hideo Miyamoto. My parents used to argue about it because my mother didn't approve of bars and drinking. She was Mormon. Anyway, what I'm wondering is did he have any problems with some of the people in here? Maybe a disagreement, a misunderstanding? Besides my uncle and Mr. Miyamoto, do you recall anyone else who came here with him?"

Moon shook his head, sipped his coffee, and drew on his cigarette. In fact, Bradford used to come in with several different women. He decided not to mention that. "They were regulars, all right, that's what I remember," he said, "him and his brother and the Japanese guy." He took another drag and exhaled through his nostrils again, the smoke curling lazily above him. "Once in a while Tom Johnson was with them. Johnson still drops in now and then, by the way. Maybe you should talk to him. He still lives in Kahana."

"Yes, I heard he lives there. I'm not going to go see him. I'll leave that to the police."

"As I told the cops when they talked to me years ago," said Moon, "nothing out of the ordinary ever happened with those guys. They had a few drinks, talked b.s. for a while, and left. They never even played pool. I'm sorry, Miss Bradford."

Jessie knew she wasn't going to get any more information. "That's all right," she said. "I figured coming here might not give me the answers I'm looking for. I thought I'd give it a try, anyway."

Moon Toli came to Hawaii with the Seabees during World War II when he was 18, drafted just after graduating from high school. He was stationed at South Point. When he was discharged from the service, he stayed in Hawaii and never returned to his hometown, Chicago. He met a Hawaiian girl, she got pregnant, and he married her. He seemed like a decent guy who married the girl he'd gotten in trouble, took care of his kids, and ran the bar. After his first wife died, he married a woman half his age and started another family. Jessie got all this news from the South Point Gazette through Maile and Mary. Moon would be surprised at how much she knew about him, that's how effective the rumor mill was. It was almost as good as the Internet. She couldn't have gotten more information if she'd Googled him.

Jessie stood, pushed back her chair, and shook Moon's hand. The juke box was now playing George Strait's "Middle of Nowhere" and that's where Jessie felt she was at that moment. She waved at his daughter who was sitting on a bar stool wearing ear buds, her head bobbing up and down to the rhythm of whatever music she was listening to while texting furiously. The girl didn't look up. Jessie opened the door and walked out to her car.

She wondered what Mac would think of her amateur detective work. She wouldn't tell him, but knew he'd find out when he got around to questioning Moon. Oh, well, I'll deal with that when I have to, she thought.

6

THE SUN WAS WARM, THE AIR WAS HUMID AND SMELLED OF honeysuckle. Jessie heard the hum of a bee. While she stood there, an old car that lost its showroom shine years ago passed noisily through town, its muffler needing repair. A dog of indeterminate breed languidly watched her from the top step of a small grocery store with a battered metal sign that read LEE'S MARKET est. 1890. The store looked its age and was sorely in need of a good coat of paint. The wooden steps leading up to the entrance needed some maintenance, too. It's a wonder someone hadn't crashed through the rotting floorboards, thought Jessie. She decided not to do Mary's shopping at Lee's, but to go to Kahana instead to pick up the mail at the post office and do the shopping there. First, she'd stop at the church up the hill from the market and see Reverend Joe.

She left the truck parked in the shade of a tree in front of the Beachhead Inn next door to the Church of Latter Day Saints. She walked the short distance toward the spire of the Hawaiian Congregational Church where Joe Kanekoa plied his trade trying to save the few souls who still lived in Waikea and some stragglers from Kahana and South Point.

In spite of its name, the congregation included very few native Hawaiians and those were mostly elderly. The others who appeared at the church doorstep on Sunday mornings were what Joe called the disenfranchised – hippies, campers from South Point, the homeless, backpackers from different parts of the world, and an occasional tourist – all in need of prayer and spiritual sustenance. Except for the tourists, most of them showed up for the hot meals that Joe and his wife, Ipo, served every Friday.

As Jessie walked toward the church, the old dog at Lee's Market peered at her through heavy-lidded eyes, not even lifting his head as he watched her pass by. He didn't move a muscle.

Waikea Village's claim to fame was a monkey pod tree that the author Samuel Langhorne Clemens, famously known as Mark Twain, planted in 1866 when he toured what were then called the Sandwich Islands. A historical marker commemorating the auspicious planting stands beside it. The tree was struck by lightning years ago and split in two. Woodworkers from all over the island came to pick through the fallen branches to find a piece of history to carve into furniture and other objects. Jessie knew this first hand because there was a coffee table at the ranch house that Rod Bradford carved out of wood from Mark Twain's tree.

The tree recovered and its branches now form a canopy over the road. Tourists stop to photograph the landmark before driving through the sleepy town, sometimes filling up at the old gas station attached to Lee's Market. More often than not, a hand-scribbled cardboard sign reading "OUT OF GAS" is taped to one or both of the two rusty, old gas pumps.

Jessie climbed the wooden steps to the churchyard. It wasn't the original church that was there when she was a child. That one burned down. This one is several years old and she donated money toward having it built. It is probably the newest building between Hilo and South Point, except for the bed and breakfast and the few new houses she'd passed that morning. Jessie guessed that Moon's Beachhead Inn was probably the second newest building in Waikea and figured it was built a few years after World War II ended, long before she was born.

When she reached the top of the stairs, she headed to the pastor's residence at the back of the church. Joe Kanekoa rounded the corner. He smiled when he saw her and they hugged. "Ey, Jessie. Good to see you. I saw you from my office window. You want to talk in my office or visit with Ipo and me?"

"I'd love to visit with both of you, if that's okay," Jessie said.

"Then, come, let's go find her," said Joe as he led her toward the house.

She and Joe were the same age. They attended the plantation elementary school in Kahana, but lost touch when she left for boarding school in Honolulu. After he became pastor at the church, she made it a point to stop and see him and Ipo whenever she was on the island. It wasn't for religious reasons, exactly, though Joe did console her through her divorce and again when Maile died. He and Ipo were easy to talk to. Jessie always felt lighter in spirit after spending time with them.

"Ipo is making lunch," he said. "Stay. There's plenty. We were just talking about you this morning. I was going to call and ask when I could go see you at the ranch. I'm so glad you stopped by." He led the way and opening the screen door off the front porch, he called out, "We have company, honey."

Ipo appeared wearing a blue and white muumuu and a red hibiscus in her gray-streaked brown hair. She was once a famous entertainer in the Islands, singing and dancing the hula, and hosted a local television talk show years ago. She was still beautiful, her green eyes still sparkled. She embraced Jessie and offered sympathy. Her voice was husky with a musical lilt to it. "I'm so sorry about your Uncle Rod," she said, "and then Joe finding your father in that cave. Oh, my goodness. How are you holding up, Jessie? You know Joe and I are always here for you. Come in. Come in."

Jessie slipped off her sandals and entered the tidy house with its rattan furniture, Hawaiian quilts hanging on the walls, and pandanus mats on the wood floors.

"I have to admit," Jessie said, "that although I'm sad and feel great loss over Uncle Rod's death, I don't really feel anything but curiosity about my father. Mostly, I just want to know what happened. We weren't close and he died when I was only 14 years old. I barely knew him." She sank back in the sofa cushions and breathed deeply. It was comforting just to be there. She felt some of the stress and anxiety she'd experienced for the last couple weeks drain out of her.

Ipo left the room and returned with a tray of glasses of freshly squeezed lemonade. The clink of the ice cubes sounded like wind chimes. Jessie took a glass and sipped the tangy liquid made from lemons plucked off the tree in their back yard. She knew that before she left, Ipo would fill a paper bag with the grapefruit-size, orange-colored Hawaiian lemons for her to take home.

Later, as they sat at the kitchen table eating beef stew over rice, Joe spoke about the archaeologist, Michael Campbell, and his search for the burial cave they discovered. "I just went along with him after my mother died," he said as he passed a small bowl to Jessie. "You want some *poi*?" he asked. She spooned some of the gray, pureed taro root onto her plate. He and Ipo ate their poi out of the same bowl, Hawaiian style.

Joe continued. "My mother said something about finding a place that was *kapu* near the cliffs, but I didn't believe her. I thought she was just talking story, you know. When we were kids, Jessie, you and Danny and I used to run all over that place. We never found anything, yeh? Not that we ever looked, I guess, but Mike kept talking about it. He said he interpreted some petroglyphs that indicated there was a royal burial site at South Point. I finally agreed to help him look.

"Once Mama died," he said, "I didn't see the harm in hiking around with him. There are some ancient relics on our land – a circle of stones, a birthing stone, some burial sites – a few with markers, others without, and cairns of lava rock and coral. Those were all out in the open for everyone to see. After talking with Mike, though, I figured maybe there was something to my mother's stories of a hidden burial tomb, after all. I should have listened to her. The land was in her family for generations. There were things she probably learned from her elders that she kept to herself. The Hawaiians didn't have a written language, so they passed down stories by word of mouth, generation to generation."

"Do you think your mother knew about the cave?" asked Jessie.

"I don't know if she knew about it. She told me she found something hidden in the cliffs. I figured she meant the gravesites that we all knew were *along* the cliffs. I didn't pay much attention. Anyway, Mike showed me maps and photographs of the petroglyphs that he said made references to the South Point area. To tell you the truth, I really didn't want to help him and that's why I didn't tell too many people about it. I put him off for a long time. Most native Hawaiians feel that these places are *kapu*, taboo, and they should be left alone, never disturbed. I feel that way, too, but I didn't think we'd find anything. It's good to know about our past and our ancestors. I just don't like all these people around. Now the different agencies are fighting with each other to get in there – the university, the museums. That's the part I don't like. It's not *pono*, not good."

He paused for a second. "Anyway, I thought, what's the harm in looking around? You hear all kinds of things and they never pan out. I figured it was going to be like that."

Ipo patted his arm, consoling. "What does this mean for Jessie?" she asked. "They did find her father in there. From what I hear, the police are sure it's him and that a crime was committed. It can't be helped that it happened in a kapu place. They'll have to investigate no matter what. Because of Michael's persistence, you found her father." She looked at Jessie. "At least now maybe you can have some closure."

"Yeh, you're right," Joe agreed.

Jessie said, "I hope the police find out what happened. John McIntire says it's complicated both because of where my father was found and because it's been so long since he died. The media is really playing it up. I can't turn on the TV without seeing something about it." She tasted the poi. It was good, a little sweet, just the way she liked it.

"How have you been through all of this, Jessie?" asked Joe. He saw the sadness in her eyes, reached across the table, and took her hand in his. "Let's bow our heads and pray to our Heavenly Father and ask for guidance in solving this crime and peace for Jessie." They all held hands and bowed their heads.

They spent most of the afternoon talking about Rod and Maile and small kid time. Later, as she was leaving, Joe said he wished he could do more. "Joe," said Jessie, "just being with you and Ipo brings me peace of mind. I feel better already." She drove away thinking that although she wasn't religious there was something about being with those two gentle people that soothed her troubled soul.

With a paper bag filled with lemons sitting on the passenger seat, Jessie drove into Kahana to pick up the mail and newspapers and do Mary's shopping. She stopped at a bakery and bought a dozen *malasadas,* the Portuguese doughnuts that are popular in the Islands. She'd eat just one before pulling out of the parking lot and give the rest to Mary and Tarzan when she got home.

The bakery was on the grounds where the plantation manager's mansion once stood, the house in which Jessie grew up. The two-story colonial had been surrounded by a spacious manicured lawn and well-kept gardens. Both the house and grounds were patterned after the antebellum cotton plantations of the southern United States. After the plantation closed, the house became a bed and breakfast. Later, it was a rooming house until it burned down. No trace of the colonial mansion was evident, not even the foundation. All that remained were the tall coconut trees and some fragrant plumeria trees in full bloom.

Her parents entertained friends and dignitaries in the beautiful home with its polished wood floors, antiques, and plush Oriental rugs. A whole way of life disappeared in a few decades. While South Point seemed to be caught in a time warp, Kahana Plantation made a 180 degree turn from prosperity.

During the 1970s and 1980s, Hawaii's sugar industry began its irreversible decline. After nearly a hundred years, labor unions were demanding higher wages and better and safer working conditions. Young people were going to college, no longer wanting to follow in their parents' footsteps working in the fields for meager pay. Women, who made up a large portion of the menial labor force, were going to college, too, wanting white collar jobs, unlike their mothers and the generations of women before them.

Developing nations were eager to fill the need for cheap labor and substandard work practices. As the Hawaiian sugar planters moved their operations to the more compliant countries, the industry died a slow and agonizing death.

When the plantations closed, the company houses and other buildings were sold to the public, mostly to people from the Philippines and other Asian countries, people who had been laborers in the cane fields. They converted the neat, American-style towns into what they were accustomed to in their home countries. Today the towns are a mixture of Asian cultures with a distinctly American hippie ambience thrown in.

In Kahana the hotdog stand in the park is now a vegetarian Thai restaurant, heavy on the curry. Some of the homes on the main street that housed the plantation's upper management are hostels. One is a hair salon and massage parlor and another is a daycare center. Others are vacant and boarded up. Even those that are occupied are in disrepair. Allen Bradford's tidy little town no longer exists. It looks like a small village in a Third World country.

Jessie remembered how her father enjoyed showing visitors the orderly little town with its company store, movie theatre, small shops, and restaurants. He proudly pointed out the neat houses and tree-lined streets, the churches and the Buddhist temple that completed the American small town atmosphere. It could have been any place in Middle America except that its industry was King Cane, as it was called in its heyday.

When he took guests on a tour, Bradford usually saved the best for last – a trip to the sugar mill where flumes and conveyor belts carried the cane for washing, cutting, and grinding. Jessie's favorite part was the end of the tour when the tanker trucks pulled up under the silo to collect the dark brown raw sugar that would be delivered to the docks. There, ships waited for the cargo that was destined for the C & H Sugar refinery in Northern California. Just as the silo was about to close, as the trucks pulled away, Allen put his hands out to catch some of the sugar so everyone could have a taste. It tasted and smelled like molasses.

Jessie took the last bite of the malasada and dusted the sugar off her hands. She pulled out of the bakery parking lot, made a U-turn in the middle of the street, and stopped in front of the post office. The old building that housed the town's civic center and post office looked run down, but at least it was still there. Using the combination Maile taught her years ago, she opened the mail box and pulled out bills, magazines, and junk mail addressed to Rodman Stephen Bradford.

After collecting the mail, she crossed the street to a small strip mall that replaced the company store. A company general store served the citizens of Kahana while the plantation was still operating. Back then in the dry goods section, cigarettes, chewing tobacco, and condoms were in the same display case as cosmetics, ladies underwear, and school supplies. The butcher shop sold plantation-raised beef and pork, and the liquor department was stocked with Canadian Club whiskey, island brewed Primo beer, and jugs of cheap wine. Today the market in the strip mall is a convenience store. Anyone with an extensive shopping list goes to the big chain supermarkets in Kona and Hilo. A gas station out front with slots for credit cards on shiny, new pumps sports a sandwich sign that reads "LAST STOP FOR GAS BETWEEN HERE AND KONA. ALOHA."

Jessie bought the few items on Mary's list and stopped outside at the newspaper dispensers for the Island Post and The Honolulu Times. She read the headlines about the mysterious and gruesome find at South Point and decided not to buy a paper. Better to get the news from Mac. She hadn't heard from him for a few days, but he said he'd call if there was any news.

She climbed into the Land Rover, took another doughnut out of the cardboard box, and bit into it. She drove out of Kahana past dusty, bare fields where sugar cane once grew, past macadamia nut trees and coffee groves, the Methodist church, and a few small houses at the edge of town, and headed toward South Point Road. She couldn't wait to get home.

7

BILLY GONSALVES WAS WAITING FOR JESSIE WHEN SHE DROVE into the yard. A tall, heavyset man stood with him and Tarzan at the hitching post where a buckskin mare was tethered. She recognized her neighbor, Frank Gomes, his usual fat, chocolate-colored cigar clamped between his teeth. The men waved as Jessie got out of the truck. "Hey, Frank," she called out as she walked toward them. Frank took off his hat and gave her a bear hug.

"I meant to come sooner, Jessie," he said, "to see how you are and if there's anything Debbie and I can do for you. Rod Bradford was a wonderful man. I loved that guy, everybody did. I'm sorry to hear about your father. It was really him they found, yeh? At least that's what they say on the news."

"Thanks, Frank. I appreciate the kind words about Uncle Rod. And yes, they think it's my father and so do I. We'll know for sure soon. The police are running some tests. How about coming in for a cup of coffee?"

"I better get home," he said. "I've been riding fences all day. Just came by to offer my condolences. Billy tells me you've been a real trooper with all that's been thrown your way. That's the tough Bradford spirit, eh?"

Frank Gomes was in his 60s with a thick graying moustache. He always wore his blue jeans hanging low, his belt buckled under his paunch, and a cigar clenched between his tobacco-stained teeth. Today he wore leather chaps over his jeans.

As he untied his horse from the post, he said, "I was telling Billy that I'd like to know what you decide to do with the ranch. I might be interested in buying or leasing some grazing land. Give me a call when you've made up your mind, okay?" He put on his hat and hoisted himself up into the saddle. "Take care," he said, waving as he rode off.

When she and Billy walked to the house he told her that he and Tarzan spent the day riding fences, too. They'd also checked the water troughs, culled two of the older calves from the herd, and put them in the weaning paddock. Jessie could hear the calves crying for their mothers and the mournful replies of the mothers from a far off pasture. Those sounds always made her sad.

"Want to finish up the paperwork tonight?" Billy asked. "I waited for you just in case. I need to call Sachi if I'm going to be late again. Besides, I have a couple of things to tell you that I think you'll find interesting." He pushed back a lock of straight, black hair from his forehead and put on his baseball cap.

Billy was thin and wiry. His broad shoulders gave him a muscular look in spite of his size. His driver's license described him as being five feet nine inches tall and weighing 145 pounds, though he seemed taller when he wore his high-heeled western boots. In his tight jeans, his legs looked skinny and slightly bowed. His olive skin showed signs of long hours in Hawaii's sun and wind and the calluses on his hands were evidence of the many years he'd spent as a hard working cowboy.

"No, you go on home," said Jessie. "We can talk later."

She walked to the truck and reached in to retrieve her packages. Billy helped with the bundles and they went around the house to the back porch. He'd brought Jack, Rod's border collie, with him. After Rod died,

Billy took the dog home to Hilo. He and Jessie agreed that if the collie and Sachi got along, he could stay with them, so Mary and Tarzan wouldn't have the added responsibility of caring for him. Rod and Jack were inseparable and the collie was inconsolable after his master's death. For days he whined and walked in circles around Rod's bedroom and spent hours lying on the carpet at the foot of the bed where Mary found Rod's body.

Billy was attached to the dog, but wondered if Jessie wanted to keep him. On the day she arrived from San Francisco, Jack went up to her, wagging his tail. Jessie leaned down to rub his ears, but he went back to Billy and stood beside him. It was obvious he had chosen his new master.

"He's yours if you and Sachi want him," she said. "You can bring him to visit any time. Uncle Rod always said that a ranch is not a ranch without a dog."

As they walked up the steps to the porch, Mary opened the kitchen door and greeted them and took the packages inside.

The air was cool and the sky turned pink and orange as the sun slowly slipped behind the clouds. Billy would be late getting home again. He sat on the porch steps with Jessie as she removed her sandals.

"I just have a few things to discuss with you," he said, "then I'll go home."

Jack curled up at their feet. They'd been sitting on this stoop since childhood. Billy's father worked on the Bradford place for years and he often brought his young son to the ranch to play with Danny and Jessie. Billy was like a brother to them. After Danny was killed in Iraq when the AH-64 Apache helicopter in which he'd been riding crashed, Billy did his best to fill the void.

"Frank Gomes isn't the only one interested in what you're going to do," he said, "but he's the first to make an official inquiry. Others are wondering what your plans are. I thought you should know. Everyone's talking about what happened to your father and why he was found in that cave. Gossip and theories are running rampant around here."

"What'd you tell Frank before I got home, about the ranch, I mean?"

"I told him you weren't sure, that if he wanted to discuss buying or leasing, he ought to call you. What are your plans? Do you have any ideas yet? We should talk about it in case someone else asks me what you're going to do."

"I don't know," said Jessie. "I'm overwhelmed. One day I'm a professor of American history in San Francisco and the next I'm a Hawaiian cattle rancher. I feel like I have multiple personalities."

Billy chuckled. "Hey, I looked over the books again today and everything is in order. There are some outstanding bills for services Rod provided – training and breaking horses, selling cattle, grazing and veterinary fees, stuff like that. Rod was a little lax about collecting from his clients. We'll have to do something about those, but it's nothing we can't handle. The property taxes are due soon. They'll be high, but again, we've got it covered. Tarzan and I made some repairs to the fences and water troughs today – everything is in good shape. The corral fence is fixed like new. If you decide to sell you won't have to do a thing to the place."

"What about the cattle and horses?" she asked. "Should they be part of the sale or sold separately?"

"I'd keep the cattle separate," said Billy. "There's about a thousand head. That's a lot of beef. You could add their market value to the sale of the ranch. With the horses it might be a little different. There's only ten of 'em left. I guess you could include them in the sale. Rod sold a couple of 2-year-olds and a quarter horse about six months ago. Someone's always looking for a good ranch pony. You might want to keep the special ones like Koa and Hoku, though. You can ship them to California, if you want."

He knocked on the railing leading up to the top step where they sat. "I'm not sure about the house. It needs new paint, some updating, and this railing is a little wobbly."

Jessie looked at the porch with its weathered wood floor and railing and the well-worn steps on which they were sitting. "I know it needs work.

If I decide to stay I'd have to make a lot of improvements. I love this place," she said, "but it's so isolated. I never really thought about it before because it wasn't in my plans to actually come back here to live. I've been a city girl for so long. You and Sachi saw my house in San Francisco. You know how it is."

Her neighbors' homes in San Francisco are so close to hers they almost share a wall on each side. Restaurants and shops are within walking distance and she hardly ever drives her car. "I've never thought of moving back to the Islands. The city has so much to offer – theatre, opera, museums. I can order pizza and Chinese take-out delivered at midnight and hail a cab to take me anywhere I want."

She tugged at her pony tail and continued, "I get my hair done just down the street from my house and my daughter lives a short drive across the Golden Gate Bridge. Then, there's my job, only an easy drive or a bus ride away. Living in the city is what I'm used to. If I fix up this house, it will probably be to sell it."

Bradford Ranch was a place of refuge for her – it was where she came after her mother died, after her divorce, and all her life's dramas in between. She couldn't imagine not being able to come here to clear her head once in a while, but knew she couldn't run it and still live in San Francisco. She didn't think she could maintain the salaries and bonuses Rod paid Billy, Tarzan, and Mary. Not even close. Rod managed financially, but in her opinion he'd been too generous. According to his books, two years ago he paid cash for two new Chevy pickup trucks that he gave to Billy and Tarzan.

As Billy said, Rod wasn't diligent about collecting on the invoices from his customers the last couple of years. He was still owed thousands of dollars for the beef he'd sold. And although he was officially retired from his veterinary work, he still provided services to his neighbors, often free of charge as evidenced by the words "No fee" written in the debit column of his ledger. Jessie figured she'd let the veterinary fees go. She'd have to send late notices for some of the other services. Still, on paper everything looked sound because there was enough in cash, stocks, and investments to cover the unpaid invoices with a substantial amount left over.

Could she run the ranch from 2,300 miles away? She didn't think so. Even with Billy as manager it would be a monumental task.

She opened her purse and pulled out the mail she picked up at the post office. There were the property tax and utility bills. As Billy predicted, the utilities weren't much, but the property taxes were high. They were waiting for the bills to arrive so they could bring the ledger up to date. These would be the last debts in Rod's name. One of the envelopes was from the Bureau of Statistics in Honolulu and it was addressed to her. She opened it and found Rod's death certificate. Cause of death: natural causes - cardiac arrest. "Here," she said, handing it to Billy.

Wiping away a tear with the back of her hand, she said, "I have something to tell you, too. Jerry Kamaka from Mauna Loa Ranch called me last night. You're right. Frank Gomes isn't the only one wondering if the ranch is for sale or lease. Mauna Loa is looking for more grazing land, too."

She looked at her watch. It was nearly seven. "Go home, Bill. Since everything is in good shape why don't you take tomorrow off? It's Friday, make it a long weekend. Tarzan and I can manage. I have a lot of thinking to do. There's some stuff I need to discuss with you, but that can wait." She gave him a playful shove. "Go on."

"Okay, okay. I'll go. Thanks. Oh, a reporter from the Island Post came by this afternoon. I told her you left the island." He grinned. "I didn't think you'd mind. Mary took about a dozen calls from the press today, one from New York, even."

"Didn't Mac call?" she asked. "I was hoping he'd have some news about the investigation."

Billy shook his head. "Not that I know. I'm sure Mary would have told me if he'd called." He headed for his truck with Jack following close behind, harnessed the dog in the back of the pickup, jumped in the driver's seat, and waved as he drove off.

Mary put away the groceries, placed the lemons in a glass bowl in the middle of the kitchen table, and put the malasadas on a tray covered with plastic wrap on the kitchen counter. "Your dinner's in the oven keeping warm," she said, untying her apron. "Need anything else before I go?"

"No thanks, Mary. Take some of the doughnuts home for you and Harry and give the rest to Tarzan. I've had my sugar rush for the day. By the way, did Mac call?"

"No, he didn't," said Mary as she hung her apron on a hook near the sink, put the doughnuts in two paper bags, and picked up her purse. "No worry," she said. "He'll call when he has something. These things take time. Everything moves slowly in Hawaii. That's why we call it Hawaii Time."

"Take tomorrow off," said Jessie. "Enjoy a long weekend. I'll see you on Monday." Giving Mary a hug, she escorted her out the door. Having the whole weekend to herself would be a treat. She'd sleep late, go for rides on Koa, pay the bills, prepare some invoices, and catch up on emails and Facebook. Thankfully, she could use her cell phone and computer. There was no Wi-Fi, but she had dial up. It was slow, but she had a lot of time and patience.

Standing at the kitchen window, she watched the lengthening shadows of the eucalyptus trees that grew along the fence in the back yard. The wind whispering through the leaves at night used to frighten her when she was a child. She wondered how Maile endured it all those years, living in this lonely place where time seemed to stand still and the only noise was the wind and the occasional call of a dove or the lowing of the cattle.

It was nearly midnight when she climbed into bed with her laptop to check her email. There were a few notes from friends sending condolences and a couple of messages from her daughter, Catherine. She felt guilty about not responding to the messages, especially the ones from Catherine. I'll do that tomorrow.

She got out of the queen-size four-poster bed and rummaged through the bookcase for one of Maile's photo albums, then settled back in bed with a quilt wrapped around her. Quilting was a craft that Maile learned from her Scottish-Hawaiian grandmother and which she perfected to a fine art. There were several quilts in a cedar chest at the foot of the bed and all of them were works of art.

Jessie opened the album. Most of the photos were in black and white and attached to the black paper pages with little black triangles at the corners. She flipped past Rod's and Maile's wedding and honeymoon photos until she came to a picture of Rod sitting on the railing of the corral he built when he first started the ranch. The fencing looked new, as though it was just finished. He was wearing a Stetson pushed back. A lock of blond hair fell across his forehead. In blue jeans, a white t-shirt, Western boots, and a cigarette dangling from his fingers, he looked young and handsome with no smile lines around his eyes yet.

Her father stood rigidly beside his younger brother with his shoulders back and his chin jutted out, looking as uptight as a bridegroom at a shotgun wedding. In his riding breeches, knee-high riding boots, and buttoned-down, long-sleeved shirt, he looked like a great white hunter. Both the Bradford men had cleft chins which were clearly visible in the photo. The cleft chin was passed down to her brother, Danny, but not to her.

She turned the pages and came to color photos of Danny and her. In one picture, he was about six or seven years old wearing cowboy boots and a holster holding a toy pistol slung around his hips. His blond hair was short with a cowlick sticking straight up in back. A cowboy hat hung down his back, the knot of its cord resting at his throat like a bolo tie.

Another picture was of her at about three or four astride Lily, the gentle mare on which she and Danny learned to ride. Maile, her head a mass of dark curls, stood next to the horse, holding the rope that was tied around the mare's neck. Jessie, her own hair curling around her face, held the reins, her bare feet dangling just below the horse's mane far from the stirrups. She was wearing a red dress with puffed sleeves. Why in the world am I wearing a dress to go riding?

It was probably one of the family gatherings Rod and Maile used to host. Her mother would have put her in a dress. Allen and Anne Bradford didn't enjoy those events, but they went anyway and made excuses to leave early. They felt Maile and Rod were too unsophisticated. Anne called them country bumpkins and Ma and Pa, though not to their faces. Sometimes they left Danny and Jessie to spend a night or a weekend or even a whole summer. There were hugs and light kisses from their parents before they drove down the dirt road while Danny and Jessie ran to the edge of the yard waving and calling goodbye. Anne and Allen usually looked back once and waved before disappearing onto South Point Road.

There wasn't a stick on the property when they bought the land, Maile told her. No house, no corral, no outbuildings, nothing, not even the eucalyptus trees. Rod and the ranch hands – Tarzan's and Billy's fathers – built the house and out buildings themselves with the help of several neighboring ranchers. "It was like an old fashioned barn-raising," Maile said, "with everyone helping each other and the wives pitching in with food and moral support and often doing some of the work. That's how most of the ranches at South Point started.

"Back then South Point was like the prairies of the Great Plains when wagon trains pushed to the western frontier and settled in the California and Oregon territories. South Point," she said, "was the last frontier only instead of covered wagons, we drove pickup trucks with all of our belongings in the truck bed. We were like Okies escaping the dust bowl in the 1930s." Jessie remembered Maile laughing as she spoke.

The area wasn't very populated in those early years. Neighbors are almost as scarce now as they were back then and most are still miles apart. Some of the original land owners sold their properties and moved to more hospitable places. Rod bought out one rancher, expanded his herd, and became successful as a cattle rancher as well as providing veterinary services to his neighbors at South Point and to other ranchers in the district. He sold beef to hotels and restaurants on the Big Island, mom and pop stores, and to private customers to fill their freezers, but mostly, he shipped his cattle to Honolulu.

Jessie turned to a picture that was taken when cattle from ranches all over the island were trucked to the beach town of Kailua in the Kona District. The cattle were unloaded from the trucks and paniolo drove the herd down the main street, Ali'i Drive, past the few tourist shops and hotels that were there during those days, and into the bay. At that time cattle were hoisted by pulleys onto barges, then to waiting ships offshore that would transport them to the stock yards of Honolulu.

Those cattle drives were exciting, Jessie remembered, with people lined up along the streets and on the piers like spectators at a parade. She found a picture of Danny and her as they stood at the edge of the crowd watching Rod and his cowboys riding herd down the middle of the street.

Kailua is a lot different now than it was when cattle were driven through the middle of town, thought Jessie. These days Ali'i Drive is crowded with high rise hotels and tourists strolling through shops and restaurants. A hotel stands at the spot where cattle were driven into the bay. Charter boats fill the bay now, hauling tourists with catches of marlin and other game fish.

Jessie put the photo album away and slipped under the quilt thinking about her brother and the two of them in their twin beds in this very room, whispering until they fell asleep. When Danny came home from Iraq in a flag-draped casket, she wondered if his blond cowlick was still sticking up at the back of his head. The casket was closed and she never found out. She visited him at the veterans' cemetery in Hilo whenever she came to the Big Island.

She clicked off the light and buried her head in her pillow.

8

Mac called from Hilo the next morning. He was going to another plantation town a few miles from Kahana on police business Saturday morning and then to South Point afterward. Since he would be down that way could he stop by? "I've got some news."

Jessie was eager to see him and hear what he had to say even though she was looking forward to being alone for the weekend. She told him to come for lunch.

She looked out the window and saw Tarzan washing the Land Rover and his pickup truck. She forgot to tell him that she gave Mary and Billy the weekend off, so she dressed and went out to join him. He waved with the water hose, pretending he was going to squirt water at her.

"Yeh, Mary told me last night that she and Billy were taking today off," he said. "By the way, thanks for the malasadas. Just like my grandma used to make."

"Tell you what, I'll feed the calves if you'll ride up and check on the cows," said Jessie. "I hear them crying for their babies."

He gave the trucks one last wipe. "I'm driving the cows further up *mauka* today because the calves can still hear them. The higher up the mountain they go the better. As long as they can hear each other they'll keep crying."

Jessie decided that she might as well give him a long weekend, too. "Why don't you take the weekend off after you check on the herd? Maybe go visit that girlfriend of yours or see your parents? Everything will be all right here."

Tarzan smiled and nodded. "Okay, I'll move the cows and when I come back, if you're sure you won't need me, I'll go. I haven't seen my family in a while. Thanks, Jessie."

While Tarzan saddled Big Red, his bay mare, Jessie went to the feed room and filled two buckets with meal mixed with supplements, a formula that Rod concocted over the years. She carried the buckets to the paddock and poured the feed into a trough. The calves came running over to her. They put their noses into the trough and started nuzzling the feed. They weren't sure what to make of it at first and started crying again, but she gently pushed their noses into the mix and soon they were eating. She patted their heads and remembered how she and Danny used to feed the newly weaned calves this way. She snapped a few photos of the calves with her phone.

Except for the cooing of a pair of mourning doves that took up lodging in the eaves of the barn, it was quiet. The sun was shining and there was no wind for a change. It was a pleasant morning with no sound of traffic, sirens, or airplanes flying overhead.

When Tarzan returned, Jessie assured him that everything was fine. "Don't worry," she said. "Just go." He left, driving his newly-washed truck down the dusty road. After clearing the breakfast dishes, she sat at her computer to answer emails and texts, attaching photos of the calves to a note to Catherine, and posted a photo to her Facebook timeline with the caption, "Feeding the babies."

She saddled Koa and headed toward the cliffs. The air cooled and the wind came up as she neared South Point and the border of Joe Kanekoa's property. After riding for about an hour, she stopped along the way to pick guavas, and ate them with relish, licking her fingers for the last drop of sweet juice that trickled onto her hands. She examined the fence line that Billy and Tarzan repaired at the far end of the property and headed home.

Riding back to the house, she saw a black Cadillac Escalade SUV parked in the front yard. A man smoking a cigarette was pacing back and forth with a phone to his ear. Who the heck is that, she wondered as she slid off Koa's back. Tying the horse to the hitching post she called out, "Can I help you?"

The man smiled, clicked off his phone, dropped his cigarette to the ground, and stubbed it out with the heel of his shoe. He handed her his card and shook her hand. "Guy Matsumoto," he said, "Big Island Real Estate."

Jessie turned the card over, reading both sides, and looked up at the realtor in his tucked-in Hawaiian shirt and dark brown dress slacks. His brown Ferragamo loafers were shiny and dust-free. "So, Guy, what can I do for you?" she asked.

He told her that he'd heard her ranch might be for sale and wanted to know if that were true. "If so, I'm the one to handle it," he said. "I'm familiar with the Ka'u District, especially the South Point area, and can bring an appraiser to give you an estimate of what the place is worth. I'd like to make an appointment to tour the property, at your convenience, of course?"

She asked how he'd heard that she might be selling the ranch and he said, "Oh, word gets around. Rod Bradford was well-known and when he died, people thought the property would probably be for sale since you live in San Francisco and there are no other heirs."

Jessie wasn't surprised that the realtor knew about Rod's death, but how did he know she was the only heir and lived in San Francisco? She was used to the anonymity of living in the city and didn't think she'd ever get used to the way news spread so quickly on the island and how people knew everyone else's business. Maile's South Point Gazette must be alive and well, she thought.

"Why don't you call me next week?" she said. "I'd like my manager to be here when you tour the property. We can make an appointment after I've talked with him."

He smiled and shook her hand. "It's a deal," he said. Jessie looked at his card again after he left before tucking it into her shirt pocket. Then, she bent down and picked up the cigarette butt the realtor left and threw it into the trash bin in the barn before she unsaddled her horse.

After working on Rod's papers for most of the afternoon, she turned off the laptop and watched the evening news. What a relief that no mention was made of the South Point mystery on any of the news channels. The media had moved on to another sensational story. A lava flow was heading toward the small town of Pahoa in the Puna District far from South Point. The flow was threatening homes in its path and reporters were covering every inch of the lava's progress. She watched for a few minutes, then aimed the remote at the TV and clicked it off.

The house was quiet and the wind picked up again. With everyone gone for the weekend, she'd experience being alone without Tarzan just a few feet away in his cottage. Is this where I want to be for the rest of my life? Tonight will be the acid test. I'll know in the morning.

Rod had recently graduated from veterinary school in California when he met Maile who was a nurse at a hospital in Honolulu. It was a whirlwind romance and they were married less than a month after they met. A few months later, Rod bought the ranch at South Point. They moved in with his parents while their house was being built.

Maile easily settled into her new life. Her nursing skills were useful when Rod needed help with sick and injured animals, mostly dogs and horses, and she'd helped more than once with the breech birth of a calf or a foal. Many cowboys came to her through the years with sprained wrists and ankles, broken ribs and bloody noses. She became fast friends with the lighthouse keeper's wife and the women from neighboring ranches. Reverend Joe's widowed mother, Loke Kanekoa, taught her the art of weaving mats using *lau hala*, the leaves of the pandanus trees. Those mats still covered the floors of the ranch house.

When Maile wasn't doing the accounting or ranch chores, she drove to Kahana to play bridge with her sister-in-law, Anne, and the other plantation wives, and belonged to a quilting group and to the South Point book club. She managed to keep busy, but Jessie couldn't imagine living that kind of a life as pleasant as it seemed. She didn't play cards nor quilt, and found book clubs boring. No, that life was not for her.

The next morning while waiting for Mac, Jessie walked through the old house. She stood in the doorway of the little guest room in which she was residing. The two small windows looked out on the barn and the other out buildings, but with its private bath and closed off hallway, it was good enough for her short stay. Rod's and Maile's master bedroom windows looked out on the pastures leading to the cliffs and the horizon and beyond. It was large, sunny, and inviting, but moving into that room wasn't an option even for a better view. That was where Rod had died. She wasn't superstitious, but she felt uneasy. She'd fix it up so no trace of him was visible. It would simply be the guest room for the remainder of her stay.

She hadn't touched anything in Rod's office yet except to get the ledgers and papers she needed to put his records in order. Shelves lined the walls, so crowded with books that many of them were stacked on top of each other like building blocks.

Every surface was piled high with papers, books and files. An ornate saddle with leather tassels and silver inlays sat on a saw horse in a corner, a gift from Allen. Although the saddle was never on the back of a horse, Rod prized it because his brother gave it to him. An original Frederick Remington oil painting hung on the wall near the saddle, another gift from Allen. A silver-framed photograph of a young Maile standing next to a vintage 1950s woody station wagon, her dark hair tousled and windblown, sat on a corner of the desk.

Faded pillows and cushions decorated the window seat against the wall in the small living room. The curtains on the bay window looked shabby. The furniture was threadbare. She needed to replace everything if she stayed, except for the monkey pod table that Rod made from Mark Twain's tree. If she sold the ranch, she'd ship it to San Francisco.

She went to the kitchen and made sandwiches from last night's roast beef, wondering how long Mac would stay when she heard his truck coming up the road. Standing on the front porch, she watched him drive into the yard. "Hey," she called, "come on in." He took off his Stetson as he walked toward her, climbed the stairs, and gave her a hug. "Boots off?" he asked, eyeing her bare feet.

"Naw, it's okay. Mary's not here, you can leave them on. It'll be our little secret."

They ate the sandwiches at a table on the back porch, sipping lemonade she'd made from Ipo Kanekoa's lemons and nibbling on brownies that Mary baked. "How's the investigation going?" she asked.

"First off," he said, "we've searched the police files of the day and didn't find anything to help us. It seems the police accepted that it was an accident from the beginning and any investigation was minimal. The Coast Guard did search for his body for a couple of weeks, but that was about it. So, we're starting from scratch. I'll let you know as soon as we have anything promising. We've got some ideas, but we don't have any suspects. It was so long ago and most of the people who were around back then are either dead or too elderly to remember anything, as I expected. Here's some news. They've completed the dental identification. Dr. Kwon's son, who took over his father's practice, kept all the files and, lucky for us, he transferred them to discs. The dental charts confirm that it's definitely your father, Jessie. It's been officially designated a homicide and the cave a crime scene."

She didn't respond. Mac leaned over, put his arm around her shoulders and asked if she was all right. "I'm fine," she said. "I've known all along it was him. It's just hearing the word homicide and knowing that someone killed him. It's so ghastly. Why would anyone murder him?" She pulled away. "I'm okay, really. Does this mean that I won't have to be tested for DNA, after all? You won't need that now, will you?"

"That's right," he said. "I'm glad for your sake. Not only would it have been an inconvenience for you, but as I told you before, we don't have the lab facilities to do really thorough testing here for such a complicated case. Now we won't have to worry about it."

He told her that her father's remains were turned over to the medical examiner and that the ME would notify her when they could be released.

"I realize this has been a nightmare for you, Jess. I want you to know that we're doing everything we can. If you have questions, I'm just a phone call away. Call me anytime. Everything's going to be all right. I know it seems slow going, but believe me, we're working on it day and night. A cold case can take years to solve sometimes. We just have to be patient."

Jessie wasn't sure how she should feel. She'd been certain it was her father in the cave from the beginning and now that it was official, she didn't know whether to cry or be relieved.

"Thanks for all you're doing, Mac. I think I need some fresh air. Let's go feed the calves. Tarzan's off today. He and Billy separated those big babies from their mothers a few days ago. They're in the weaning pen and I'm supposed to give them some feed for a couple of days until they get used to eating grass."

As Jessie mixed the meal for the calves, Mac told her that he stopped at Joe Kanekoa's church and Moon's Beachhead Inn on the way to the ranch. "They both told me you visited them. Apparently, you asked the same questions I did, so I don't have anything to tell you about them. Doing a little sleuthing of your own, Miss Marple?"

While the calves ate, Jessie explained that as long as she was going to town, she stopped at Moon's to find out if he knew anything about her father. "Moon knew him, but after such a long time he didn't remember much. I guess that's what he told you.

"As for Joe," she continued, "visiting him was more for spiritual reasons. He has some excitement of his own with the discovery of the canoe and all those relics, so we didn't talk very much about my father's case. Isn't it something that he and the archaeologist happened upon the cave? If they weren't so dogged about it, we wouldn't be talking about dental records and police investigations right now. I'd probably be selling the ranch and everything on it and be on my way back to California."

"You're planning to sell the ranch? To whom?" He pushed his hat back from his forehead and bent to look into her eyes. "When did you decide to sell? I thought for sure you'd keep it."

"A couple of people inquired. I'm not in a hurry," she said. "I have until early August to get back to school for the fall semester. That's about a month and a half from now. I'll wait until the investigation is complete. I hope you'll be done by then."

He raised his eyebrows. "I can't make any promises. As I said, investigations can take months, years, even. This one is pretty complicated. I'd like to accommodate you, but I doubt we'll be finished by the time your semester starts." He smiled. "I'll do what I can. Don't get your hopes up."

"Sorry if I seem demanding," she said. "It's just that I have a whole other life away from here and I'm eager to get back to it. I didn't plan to be here this long."

"I guess I'm surprised that you'd sell," Mac said. "I mean, this ranch has been in your family for years. I can't imagine anyone but a Bradford owning it. Who inquired about buying it, if you don't mind my asking?"

"Your brother-in-law, Jerry Kamaka, called me. He said Mauna Loa Ranch is looking for more grazing land. I think he may be more interested in leasing than buying, though. My neighbor, Frank Gomes, wants to expand his place to increase beef production for export, but, again, he seems more interested in leasing. A realtor stopped by yesterday. He's coming out to tour the property next week and bringing an appraiser with him. It'll be good to know what it's worth."

Mac was thoughtful. Jerry Kamaka, his former brother-in-law and his good friend, didn't tell him that the owners of Mauna Loa Ranch were thinking of buying or leasing the Bradford place. "Hmmm, I wonder why Jerry hasn't said anything about it," he said, idly digging the heel of his boot into the dirt. "I'm staying there tonight. I'll ask him about it."

"I'm surprised he didn't mention it to you," said Jessie, "since you spend so much time at Mauna Loa Ranch. Billy tells me there are others who are interested. They just haven't come forward yet. I don't know who they are. Everything looks good and the place is in good shape. It rained a lot this year, so it's rolling green grass until you get to the cliffs, of course. It's always dry down there. Billy thinks that I could sell tomorrow if I wanted, even without updating the house."

"Has anybody made an offer yet?" he asked.

"No. And I haven't actually made a decision. It's a strong possibility that I'll sell, though. I'm not cut out for this. I'm a history teacher, not a rancher or a business woman." She brushed a strand of hair out of her eyes. "I don't think I'm up to the challenge."

"Whatever you do, keep me posted, okay?" he said. "I'd like to know what's going on, even if it's only to keep tabs on you. I still have to go down to check with the crew at South Point today, so I'd better get going. We need to wrap up things as soon as possible."

"You must be making some progress if you're finishing up," she said.

"Not quite," said Mac. "The chief wants the investigation at the site completed ASAP so that the museum and university people can get in there. They're hounding him about it. We've probably got all we need, but I keep thinking there might be something we've overlooked. I've gotta let them have it, though. It's not my call.

"I'm going to stop and see Father Domingo at the Catholic Church in Kahana on my way back to Hilo tomorrow. I want to have a look at the church records to see if there's anyone still around who might remember something after all these years."

He faced her and lifted her chin. "Remember, if you need anything, if you have any questions, call me."

"Okay, Mac, I will."

"I'll check in," he said. "As soon as we find out anything, you'll be the first to know. Take care. I'll talk to you soon." He drew her to him and kissed her cheek. He held her a moment longer, then released her.

She felt the old attraction and thought he did, too, but she didn't want to start something that wasn't meant to be, especially if she returned to California. What would be the point? She watched him wave as he climbed into his truck and drove toward South Point Road, then she turned back to the calves and patted their heads. "All right, you guys. Tomorrow you're going to eat grass and we'll see how it goes, see? No more baby food for you."

She spent the rest of the day cleaning Rod's bedroom. She had avoided doing it for so long and brushed off Mary's offers to help because she couldn't bring herself to start throwing his things away. It seemed disloyal, somehow, and so final.

Rod's watch, wallet, change, and keys were on his dresser where he had left them. His boots stood near the foot of the bed. She suspected they hadn't been moved since the day he died and that Mary probably reverently dusted around them.

Jessie had been moving in slow motion the last couple of weeks waiting for things to happen. She wasn't able to make a decision about the ranch or anything else, always waiting to hear from Mac or asking Billy for advice. Now it was time to take control of her life. She would go to Hilo on Monday to make arrangements for her father's burial at the Mormon cemetery and, trivial as it seemed, get her hair done. Those damned gray streaks were getting on her nerves and it was getting more and more difficult to hide them.

When Mary showed up on Monday morning, she was surprised at what Jessie had accomplished. "I've wanted to do this for weeks," Mary said. "I'm glad you finally did it, Jessie. I guess you needed to do it yourself. I understand. Good job." Mary hugged her and seemed so happy that Jessie half expected to get a pat on the head.

"Thanks. I don't know what got into me. Once I started, I couldn't stop. Besides, I want my daughter to come and this will be her room. I'm going to Hilo today to run some errands and I'll probably be back late. Go home early, okay? Don't make dinner. I'll get something in town."

As she walked out the door, she said, "I'll talk to Tarzan about painting the room and I need to find a contractor to remodel the bathroom. Then, you and I are going shopping."

9

THE WINDOWS OF THE LAND ROVER WERE ROLLED DOWN SO
Jessie could enjoy the soft breeze as she drove along the highway to Hilo.
She had an appointment at the funeral home, an appointment at a hair
salon, and a date to meet Sachi Gonsalves for coffee and maybe lunch.

She passed through Waikea and Kahana and continued along the
coast to Volcanoes National Park. It was a lonely drive for most of the way.
Only a couple of cars passed her after she left Kahana. As she approached
the park, the traffic got heavy with tour buses and rental cars causing a traffic jam. The main tourist attraction in the park, Halemaumau Crater, was
spewing fountains of lava hundreds of feet into the air. She could see the
red hot fountains from the road. Madam Pele, the Hawaiian fire goddess,
was putting on quite a show. The spectacle drew crowds of tourists, most
of whom never witnessed an active volcano. Jessie saw lava shooting out of
the crater many times in her youth, so she wasn't interested in stopping for
a look. She impatiently maneuvered her way out of the crowded park and
hurried to make her appointments.

At the funeral home she learned that her father's ashes could be
interred in the same burial plot as her mother's. Since Allen was presumed
lost at sea, there was no plot reserved for him next to Anne's. Jessie was

relieved to learn that she could keep her parents together after they were separated for so long. At least she could do that for them. The funeral director said he would notify the cemetery.

She wondered how her father's remains were taken to the medical examiner. She imagined the fragile bones being lifted off the floor of the cave. Were they put in a body bag or a box? Did the bones fall apart or crumble to dust? Did they remove the belt and boots first? What did they do with them? What happened to his watch, his wedding ring? She grimaced and wondered when the police would allow her to have the remains so they could be cremated and buried.

Even after completing the grim task of planning her father's funeral, Jessie was in reasonably good spirits when she met Sachi. Sachi never seemed to age. She was pretty and petite with pale skin, a little heart-shaped face, brown eyes fringed with thick lashes, and close-cropped black hair with not a trace of gray. She looked like her mother, Sumi, except for the small cleft in her chin.

It was supposed to be a pleasant get-together, the two of them having coffee and catching up after not seeing each other in years. It started out that way – a hug, a quick kiss on the cheek, ordering lattes and biscotti at Local Grounds, Hilo's answer to Starbuck's. They sat at a table outside and watched the passing parade of shoppers and cars on Kamehameha Avenue, the main street through the city along Hilo Bay.

"I'm sorry about your uncle and your father," Sachi said after they were settled at a table. "Rod Bradford was a nice man and he was so good to Billy. I didn't know your father, but I'm sure he was a good person, too." She reached over and patted Jessie's hand. "Boy, you have a lot to deal with, yeh? Billy tells me you're handling it like a champion, though. Do they really think they found King Kamehameha's burial site in Joe Kanekoa's cave?"

Jessie didn't want to dwell on her uncle's death nor her father's. At this point she didn't care if it was King Kamehameha or King Kong in the cave, but she didn't want to brush off Sachi's condolences.

"Thanks," she said. "It was a shock at first, but I'm getting through it. John McIntire tells me this case is so complicated, it may be years before they figure out what happened, if ever. I'll be long gone and back in San Francisco by then. I'd like to put it behind me for today, though." She smiled and bit into her biscotti. "It's good to see you, Sachi. When was the last time we got together? Seems like forever."

"I think it was when Billy and I visited you in San Francisco," said Sachi. "Remember? It was, what, 10 years ago, maybe more? It was when our son, Jeff, graduated from medical school and now he's in practice in Seattle. When my brother Isaburo retired, Jeff took over his family practice. So, yeh, it's been a long time."

Except for Billy's occasional comments, Jessie knew little about his and Sachi's personal lives. He told her that his son was in Seattle, but she didn't remember if he mentioned that Sachi's brother was there, too. She made a mental note to tell Mac where one of the Miyamoto brothers was.

"I'm a tutu wahine, a grandmother," said Sachi in a sing-song voice. Billy must have told you that."

She opened her purse and pulled out a photo of her three-year-old granddaughter. "She looks just like my mother, with Japanese features, except she has blonde hair and blue eyes and the little dimple in her chin like I have. Isn't that something? My daughter-in-law is Irish, English and Norwegian, but that Japanese blood is strong. Even though Billy is Portuguese, our son looks totally Japanese. Funny, yeh?"

"It's the same with my daughter," Jessie said. "Both her father and I have light brown hair and he has brown eyes and mine are green. Cathy has red hair and blue eyes. Go figure. There must be a blue-eyed redhead somewhere in the family. You never know when genes from an unknown relative will rear their ugly heads."

After they traded stories about their kids there wasn't much to talk about. When the conversation started to lag, Jessie asked, "How's your mom? Billy told me she's in a nursing home here in Hilo."

"She's okay," said Sachi. "We placed her in the home because she's frail and she was falling a lot. We hired a caregiver to come to the house, but Mama didn't like her. With Billy and me working, we couldn't leave her alone and we couldn't take care of her ourselves."

"I'm sorry, really. I'd love to see her," said Jessie. "Can she have visitors? Do you think she'd remember me?"

"Sure, you can go see her. Let's see, I have a card with the address somewhere." She rummaged in her purse and handed the card over. "Mama doesn't get many visitors, so even though she might not remember you, she'll be glad to see you. Her memory isn't very good, though. Don't be surprised if she doesn't know who you are."

"Your mother was beautiful and gentle," said Jessie. "I remember when you and I did our homework together in your back yard and she brought us snacks and lit the candle in the stone lantern for us."

"She was really proud of that lantern," said Sachi. "My father and my brother Tak made it for her, you know. Papa ordered the granite from Oregon and they built it as close as they could to the ones in Japan. Mama always lit the candle when friends came over." She ate the last of her biscotti and brushed some crumbs off the table. "So now you know all about me and my family. What about you? Doing anything exciting these days, besides your situation here, that is?"

"Before all that's happening now, it was pretty boring, mostly work and a little play, very little play lately," said Jessie.

"Boyfriend?" asked Sachi, sipping her coffee.

"Not right now. It's been a long time since I've been in a relationship. Not everyone is lucky like you and can snag a prize like Billy. Actually, though, I like being single and having no commitments."

"How's work?" asked Sachi. "If it's anything like mine, it's probably hectic, especially in a big city."

It was easy to talk about their jobs. Since they were both educators, they compared notes and discussed class work and students. Suddenly, Sachi stood up and suggested they go to the mall. "I know it isn't much compared to what you have in California. As I told you, we have Macy's now and a couple of boutiques that have some nice things. Are you ready for shopping?"

They strolled through several stores and stopped for sushi at the crowded food court. Jessie asked about Sachi's brothers.

"You remember Tak died in the accident at the plantation mill, don't you? And Albert died in Viet Nam." She paused for a second, reflecting on the loss of her brothers, then continued. "As I mentioned, Isaburo is in the Seattle area where he's retired. He hasn't come home in years. Nobu is still living in Kahana in our parents' house. So, it's just the three of us now, Nobu, Isaburo and me."

She looked at her watch. "Gosh," she said, pushing back her chair and standing up. "I have to run some errands before it gets too late." She picked up her purse and put on sunglasses.

"It's been great seeing you. We'll keep in touch, okay?" And she was gone. Thank God that's over, thought Sachi as she made her way to the parking lot. I thought the afternoon would never end.

Sachi and Jessie were friends through elementary school and spent some of their high school and college vacations together. When Sachi and Billy were married, Jessie attended the wedding. They'd stayed with Jessie during their visit to San Francisco 10 years ago, but Sachi never felt comfortable with the other members of the Bradford family, except for Rod and Maile, and Danny, of course, on whom she'd had a crush when she was in junior high. It never led to anything. He treated her the same way he treated Jessie – like a pesky kid sister.

Both Jessie and Danny attended private high school in Honolulu and college in California, while it was public school on the Big Island and the

University of Hawaii for Sachi. That's when the friendship between the two girls began to fade.

It wasn't as if the Miyamotos and the Bradfords traveled in the same social circles. Their families never socialized and Sachi considered the Bradfords, especially Anne, to be snobs. She never liked Allen. There was just something about him. Even now, she couldn't quite figure out what it was. Maybe it was the way he looked at her whenever she was at their house playing with Jessie or when she'd run into him on the street or at the company store.

She knew Jessie wasn't anything like her parents. She was nice enough, but still it was awkward today. They were running out of things to say to each other. What do you talk about with someone you haven't seen in more than 10 years, anyway?

"Did you have a nice time with Jessie?" asked Billy when he got home.

"Not really," said Sachi. "I felt a little uncomfortable."

"Uncomfortable? Why? Jessie is so easy to talk to."

"Maybe it's easy for you, Billy. We were friends when we were really young. After she went to private school, though, we hardly saw each other except for a few times during holidays. You two grew up together. It's different for me. She's a nice person, but to tell you the truth, I couldn't wait to get away. I never warmed up to the Bradfords like you did. Besides, you're with her all the time and I only see her every 10 years or so. Today it was difficult to think of things to talk about. I'm sorry."

Sachi may not have grown up in the wealth and luxury the Bradfords enjoyed, but she'd lived in the lovely house Allen Bradford gave to her father. She was grateful to him for that. She never understood why her parents, especially her father, held the plantation manager in such high esteem.

10

When Sumi and Hideo moved into their newly remod-eled home, they were awed by what seemed luxurious to them. The house had been vacant for several years, uncared for and abandoned after the last tenants, the plantation doctor and his family, moved out.

As Allen promised, it was remodeled, painted, and another bedroom and bathroom added. The Miyamoto's new living status was the talk of the camps.

Even at the monthly bridge club meetings, sometimes the main topic of conversation among the managers' wives was the renovation of the Miyamoto house. No one mentioned it when Anne Bradford was present.

"Has anyone been inside the house?" asked Alice Johnson, hostess of one day's meeting, holding her cup of tea in one hand and fanning herself with her cards. "My maid Elsie says it's the nicest house on the plantation, next to the manager's mansion. She told me the kitchen is bigger than mine and nicer. What's that all about?"

The women at the other tables were quiet for once in their lives, lis-tening to the conversation at their hostess' table. Only one woman in the room seemed disinterested in the gossip as she concentrated intently on her cards. Her home had been renovated several years ago. Allen Bradford was very generous with his conquest of the moment.

Sumi was aware of the gossip because some of her friends worked in the managers' homes. Alice Johnson's maid, Elsie Hasegawa, was Sumi's closest friend. She filled Sumi in on the latest gossip, including the interest in Allen Bradford's friendship with Hideo.

"They say Bradford-san has very few friends and Hideo seems to be his best one. They are curious about that," Elsie whispered one day as they sipped tea in the Miyamoto living room.

"You know," Elsie rambled on, "Bradford-san has a new daughter, too. Mrs. Bradford doesn't come to parties or bridge game anymore. She stay home with the baby. Oh, they gossip about her. You should hear what they say." She giggled and covered her mouth with her hand.

"Oh?" said Sumi. "What do they say? Mrs. Bradford is a nice lady. I wouldn't believe anything those women talk about. It's just gossip."

"Hai, hai, gossip. I know, I know, Sumiko. They say she should keep her husband at home because he is like a cat, a tom cat. You know Eiko Kato, the Bradford's maid, yeh? She told me he spends a lot of time at the bar in Waikea. When he comes home, they fight. Eiko says her husband told her Bradford-san is not always at the bar, he is with his girlfriends. Eiko thinks he is handsome, so women like him too much and he likes women too much."

"I still don't believe it," countered Sumi. "He must be happy enough with his wife if they have a new baby." She looked down at Sachi who was six months old and was stroking her mother's breast as she nursed, making little gurgling sounds. Sumi was glad when Elsie left a few minutes later, letting herself out so that the nursing baby wouldn't be disturbed.

She was angry at herself for being jealous. But his new baby meant he was sleeping with his wife while he was sleeping with her and who else? A tom cat, that's what he was, all right. She wondered if she would ever be free of him and feared she might be living on the plantation forever if Hideo had his way. He planned to retire in a few years and wanted to buy some land at the edge of town and build a house there.

It was a vacant lot next to the house that was Allen's hide-a-way, where he and Sumi spent their afternoons. Hideo was going to ask his friend, Allen, to sell him that property. He was sure the answer would be yes. Why not? Allen and he were best friends. She cringed at the thought. Allen didn't come around too often after Sachi was born and for that she was glad. Sumi kissed the sleeping baby and placed her on the futon on the bedroom floor, then straightened the obi of her kimono and went to prepare dinner in her newly renovated kitchen.

The new house was a dream for the Miyamoto family. Hideo built another furo. It was big enough for the whole family. In Japanese fashion, the Miyamotos enjoyed the hot baths together.

Sumie created a garden in the back yard for which Hideo built a bamboo fence. They planted *koke*, the Japanese moss that felt like velvet under bare feet. Bonsai pine trees dotted the little landscape and a stone bench faced a koi pond that was the centerpiece of the garden.

Hideo ordered white granite from Oregon and he and Tak fashioned the stone into a lantern. They smoothed and carved the granite into separate pieces that, when fit together, formed five tiers. It was not as beautiful as the stone lanterns in Japan, but it would do. He held Sumi's hand as he led her outside to present his latest gift and she bowed to him to show her thanks.

Sumi spent mornings in the garden pruning the camellias and azaleas while watching Sachi play on the soft moss. Life was idyllic and she hoped it would last. Although Allen Bradford didn't visit as often after the Miyamotos moved into their new home, sometimes while Sumi and the baby played in the garden, he would appear out of nowhere, letting himself in through the garden gate. Sumi resented these intrusions, but knew he was responsible for her beautiful surroundings and for Hideo's success, so she'd put the baby to sleep and lead Allen to the bedroom she shared with her husband and close the door.

As the years went by, Allen found other women who interested him as much or more than Sumi and he stayed away. There was no goodbye, no breakup. He just stopped coming. When it was time for Hideo to retire, Allen gave the house to his old friend as a retirement gift for his many years of loyal service. Hideo was so grateful, he nearly cried. The ceremony was held at the community hall at the Japanese camp. Friends came from all of the camps to celebrate. They gave a *luau* for which Bradford donated a pig for *kalua* –the Hawaiian way of roasting a whole pig by digging a pit in the ground and placing it on hot rocks, covering it with banana leaves and burlap, and cooking it all day. The feast was a league of nations with food from different ethnic backgrounds – American, Japanese, Chinese, Filipino, Portuguese, and Hawaiian – placed on tables covered with ti leaves and decorated with hibiscus and orchid blossoms.

Bradford made a speech after which he handed a new set of house keys to Hideo and called Sumi to join them on the podium. Sumi feigned shyness, but urged by the crowd, she finally made her way to stand beside her husband and shook her lover's hand. She bowed like a proper Japanese wife and smiled. Sachi and her brothers joined in the cheers, proud of the honor bestowed upon their parents. Anne Bradford clapped from her seat at a table. When her husband left the stage she rose, took the arm he offered, and they strolled out of the hall to a roar of applause.

II

Sachi's abrupt departure that day in Hilo confirmed Jessie's feeling that her childhood friend couldn't wait to get away. All afternoon she felt that Sachi was preoccupied, even aloof and moody, their conversation strained. She reasoned that maybe it was because they seldom saw each other. If it wasn't for Billy managing the ranch, they probably wouldn't keep in touch at all.

After Sachi left, Jessie gathered her shopping bags, found the salon, and got her hair done. On her way out of the mall, she stopped at a Chinese deli and bought some take-out for dinner. It was nearly five o'clock by the time she got to her car and checked the messages on her phone. She found one each from Catherine, Mary, and Mac. She'd call Catherine and Mac when she got home, but listened to Mary's brief message that she was leaving and all was well.

Jessie smiled as she drove past the Hilo airport on her way out of town because she was going home to the ranch and she couldn't wait to get there. Traffic was light in the national park as she drove through. Gone were the buses and rental cars, so she sailed past the glow of the lava fountain spewing from the crater. She'd be turning down South Point Road in about an hour.

She was sitting at the kitchen table eating chow mien and sweet and sour prawns when she returned Mac's call. He was still at work and he, too, was dining on Chinese take-out, Mongolian beef he told her, hot and spicy. He said he'd called to let her know that her father's remains could be released and that she should call the medical examiner's office and tell them which funeral home would be picking them up. Before they rang off, he told her there was nothing new to report on the case. He'd call if anything came up. Jessie sighed, wondering if anything would ever come up. All she'd been hearing for weeks was that he'd let her know.

"You're still investigating, right?" she asked. "You're not going to stop, are you?"

"I'll never stop, Jessie," he assured her. "I'll investigate until I drop. That's a promise. Just because I have nothing new to report doesn't mean I'm not working the case. I'm on it every day. Look, I've got another call coming in. Gotta go. I'll talk to you soon, okay? No worries."

She reluctantly said good bye and called her daughter. They spoke briefly, making plans for Catherine's visit. After a hot shower, Jessie was in bed by 11 o'clock, a first for her since she'd been at the ranch. She looked at her To Do list and crossed off the items she'd completed, turned off the lights, and slept through the night.

The next morning she and Billy saddled the horses and scouted the ranch. Billy made an appointment with the realtor and they wanted to do a dry run before they gave him a tour. They examined the mended fences and the cattle. Billy told her that more of the calves would soon have to be transferred to the weaning pen and the two that were there now would be returned to the herd.

Jessie didn't know anything about cattle. They were all just cows to her. "What kind are they?" she asked as they sat astride the horses and watched the herd through the barbed wire fence. "What breeds, I mean? There are different breeds, aren't there, like dogs and cats? I should know more about them because I spent so much of my childhood here, but I never thought to ask."

"It's pretty simple," said Billy. "The black ones are Angus, the red ones with the white faces are Herefords, and the white-faced black ones are Angus-Hereford cross breeds. There are some Charolais in the mix. They're all good beef cattle."

"Good beef cattle. As opposed to what other kinds of cattle?" she asked, feeling out of her element.

"As opposed to dairy cattle, but that's a whole other story. You won't have to worry about that. We're not in the dairy business. Boy, for someone who was raised here, you sure don't know much about ranching, do you?" he teased.

"Uh-huh. I'm clueless," she said. "Thanks for mentioning it. Well, it's all clear to me now, as if I'm going to remember all of that. I'd better write it down in case someone asks what kind of cattle I own when I get back to San Francisco." She laughed. They moved along the fence and stopped again. Jessie pulled her foot out of the stirrup and rested her knee against the saddle's pommel.

"There are about 1,000 head in all," Billy said. "Rod was planning to cut the herd to a couple hundred to be used for beef for the ranch. He talked about getting out of the cattle business altogether, selling off most of the land and keeping just enough acreage to sustain a small herd. Said he was too old to be a cowboy and wanted me to continue running the ranch at least until he died. He planned to talk to you and see what you wanted to do after he was gone." He glanced at her. "I'm guessing he never got around to it."

"No, he didn't. Well, I'm here now and I still don't know what to do," said Jessie. "I wish I could have talked to him about it."

They brainstormed as they rode around the property, sharing ideas that they didn't want to discuss in Mary's presence, preferring to keep some information private and out of the South Point rumor mill.

"Here's what I've been thinking," she said. "I could sell the ranch and everything on it. That would leave me free to go back to San Francisco without any ties or responsibilities here. That's my first option and the easiest."

"You'd make a bundle of money and would never have any financial worries for the rest of your life, that's for sure," said Billy.

"If you decide not to sell," he continued, "you could keep the 500 acres or add to them, increase the herd, do what other ranchers are doing, including your neighbor Frank Gomes, Mauna Loa Ranch, and others. They're all becoming big beef producing corporations. Then, your job would be CEO of your own corporation. How does that sound?"

"Please, CEO of a ranching corporation when I don't even know anything about cattle? I'd rather lease some or most of the land to other ranchers," said Jessie, "and let them worry about the cows. Joe Kanekoa does that and says he makes a nice profit. We could keep a few hundred like you said Uncle Rod was going to do."

"Then, you can keep the place," said Billy, "lease the land, and come here when you get tired of the city and bring family and friends for vacations. It would still be a working ranch, only on a much smaller scale."

"Hey, what about a dude ranch? What do you think of that?" She knew that ranchers on other parts of the island did it with great success. She'd seen an ad for a Hawaiian dude ranch in the airline magazine she'd read during her flight to Kona. The photographs showed people on trail rides, eating barbecue, and driving cattle on Hawaiian ranches.

Billy did a double take. "Are you serious? A dude ranch? That never entered my mind."

"It never entered my mind either until now. It's another possibility," said Jessie. "Why, what's wrong with it?"

"There's a lot wrong with it," said Billy, his voice rising. "A dude ranch is just for show. Rod would hate it. Phony cowboys and phony ranch chores all to entertain some morons who don't know one end of a horse from the other. Next thing you'll be bringing in one of those automated bulls for the dudes to ride," he said derisively. "A real cowboy wouldn't be caught dead on one of those things. It's your ranch, you do what you want, but I say no. I never want to see the day when a bunch of yahoos invades Rod's ranch." He nudged his horse and started riding again at a fast gallop. Jessie followed. "Hey, wait up," she called.

"It seems that I've hit a nerve," she said as she caught up with him. "Okay, no dude ranch." She chuckled. "You're right, Uncle Rod would hate it." "I was…well, I guess I was just trying to be funny. Sorry. You're right, of course."

They stopped at a water trough and loosened the reins so the horses could drink. "All right, so you know some of the ideas I've been tossing around," she said, leaning over and patting Koa's mane, "excluding the dude ranch, of course."

"There's always homesteading," said Billy. "There are a lot of home-steads in this area. Small places with a house, a couple of outbuildings, a few head of cattle, some horses, you could do that."

Jessie liked Billy. He was smart. He'd learned to cowboy when his father worked for Rod. As a teenager, he spent summers doing ranch chores. That, combined with his business degree from Stanford Business School, which he paid for with his and his parents' savings, scholarships, and Rod's contributions, made him a force to reckon with. He could have become a CEO himself, but he loved ranching. He knew how to work a ranch and he knew how to handle the business end of it. She trusted his judgment, his honesty, and his eagerness to help her. Rod was lucky to have him all those years and now so was she.

"Then," he said, "there's beginning to be a great demand for Hawaiian beef not only in the U.S. and Canada, but in Asia – especially China and South Korea. I could still manage the ranch, you'd be the business manager and head of the corporation, and we'd hire more hands to work with Tarzan and me. We could do it. I'd help you. The possibilities are endless."

"In the end, I'll probably sell and walk away," she said, shaking her head. "I guess that sounds like the coward's way out, but it may be the best thing for me and for the ranch."

As they headed back, she asked, "Do you think we'll get a good appraisal?"

"Yeah, I'm sure of it. This is a great piece of real estate. It's beautiful. I'd buy it myself if I could afford it."

"When the realtor comes tomorrow morning with the appraiser, I'd like you to go with us to show him around, Bill. You know more about this place than I do. Even if I decide to stay on, we should at least know what the place is worth."

Tarzan was waiting for them at the hitching post. He helped Jessie down and began unsaddling Koa. "I'll take care of the horses," he said. "You guys go on. Mary's waiting for you. She's been baking up a storm."

Mary had baked several pies with Ipo's lemons and they were cooling on the kitchen counter. A couple dozen shortbread cookies were on a rack on the table. A fresh pot of coffee was waiting and Mary began pouring as soon as Jessie and Billy walked in the door.

"Hey," said Billy as they entered the kitchen, "something smells good!" He snapped up a cookie and began munching on it. Mary smiled. "I knew you two would like a snack when you got back. I figured I'd better use up those lemons, so I started baking the pies and next thing I knew, I was making shortbread cookies, too."

Jessie hugged her. "Oh, Mary, what would we do without you? I'm so hungry I could eat a whole pie all by myself." She sat across from Billy and sliced a piece. It was still warm. She didn't even use a fork. She picked it up with her hands and took a bite, wiping off meringue from the corners of her mouth with her fingers.

When Mary went to the laundry room to take the clothes out of the dryer, Jessie lowered her voice and said, "You know, I really like that idea of yours about homesteading. Just keep 40 or 50 acres for the horses? Maybe no cattle. Tarzan could continue living here if he wanted, be the caretaker. I could still come for vacations and bring my friends. It wouldn't require a ranch manager, though, Billy. What about you?"

"Don't let concerns about me affect your decision," he said. Dunking a cookie into his coffee, he walked out the kitchen door to the porch. Jessie followed him. He shaded his eyes from the afternoon sun and surveyed the landscape through the eucalyptus trees. "Back here, you could keep enough land around the house and yard so you wouldn't be too close to neighbors, but just close enough to be neighborly. If you ever have any neighbors, that is." He chuckled.

"The only neighbors I'll probably have down here are horses and cows," she said. "This will probably always be grazing land."

"Maybe not," said Billy. "I didn't mention this before because Rod didn't want to do it. In the last couple of years some ranch land has been subdivided and developers have begun building homes at South Point closer to the cliffs, way past Frank Gomes' property and yours. There are only a couple of homes now. From what I hear, there's going to be a lot more. You might have more neighbors than you want. Subdividing could be the way to go for you, too."

She wrinkled her nose. "I don't think so. I'd rather sell than do that, especially if Uncle Rod didn't like the idea. I'm still worried about what you'll do, though."

"Rod's not here and it's your decision to make. Whatever you decide, I'll help you settle things, then, I'll look for another job. How hard could that be? There are plenty of ranches in these islands. Surely, one of them could use someone with my talents."

As he turned to leave he said, "I'll see you first thing tomorrow and we'll give that realtor the ride of his life. We'll take the Land Rover. I doubt if he'll want to saddle up and mosey around on horseback, especially if he shows up wearing those fancy Italian shoes you told me about." He tipped his hat and grinned as he walked toward his truck with one of Mary's pies and a dozen cookies. Jessie knew that crooked grin of his since they were kids. She smiled and waved as he drove off.

She couldn't sleep that night. Her mind was on overload. Billy had given her some good ideas and combined with hers, there were more options than she'd bargained for. It was almost too much to grasp. Finally, at about three o'clock in the morning she made a pot of herbal tea and some toast and reread the email from Catherine about her upcoming visit. Jessie looked forward to having her daughter with her, but she wasn't ready for a guest. The bathroom hadn't been remodeled and Tarzan hadn't painted yet. The bedroom had to be ready and time was getting short. She'd better get on it.

12

ALTHOUGH, LIKE JESSIE, MAC HAD GROWN UP IN THE MORMON
faith, he'd never practiced that or any other religion as an adult. When he
needed information about the good citizens of Kahana and the surrounding area, he stopped in at the Catholic Church. The Catholics, he learned
during his years of police work, were more open about sharing information than the Mormons, the Buddhists, and the Methodists. In the past, he
had gotten names from the priests at Sacred Heart Church in Kahana that
helped him track down more than a few desperadoes.

Father Domingo, the young priest in residence now, had been at the
parish for about a year after coming to Hawaii from the Philippines. His
English was impeccable even though he spoke with a trace of the accent
of his native country. He and Mac went through the church's records on
births, deaths, and marriages and found several people still in town who
were probably living in Kahana when Allen Bradford disappeared.

A couple of parishioners who attended mass were about the right
age, the priest said, one of them was a Tom Johnson. Mac remembered the
name. Johnson was the plantation office manager who had gone looking
for Bradford that morning. The other people whose names the priest gave
him were laborers and almost all of them, including Johnson, were in their

80s and 90s. Mac doubted if most of them would be of any help, but he'd definitely look up Johnson. It was a start.

When he got back to Hilo, he asked his partner, Sergeant Brian Alnas, to follow up on the names the priest had given him and a couple others who were not on file at the church. The next day the sergeant handed his notes to Mac. There was an Elsie Hasegawa who used to be a maid for the office manager's household. She had the reputation of being a gossip and seemed to have a lot of information. Some of it was probably idle gossip, the sergeant told Mac, but it might be useful. Hideo Miyamoto's son, Nobu, was next, then Tom Johnson. Mac made appointments to see all of them.

"You want me to go with you, Boss?" asked Brian.

"No, I'll handle it. These people are elderly. I don't want them to feel intimidated with two cops ganging up on them. I'll call you if there's anything I need. In the meantime, do some background checks while I'm gone."

He decided to visit Elsie Hasegawa first. She and her husband still lived in a house in a neighborhood that was once a part of the Japanese camp. When she came to the door, Mac guessed she was in her late 80s or early 90s, but seemed remarkably agile. Elsie invited him in and waited, holding the screen door open while he removed his boots and lined them up with the shoes and flip flops on the porch. She led him into the tiny, neat living room and introduced him to her husband who sat in a wheel chair watching *The Price is Right* on a large, flat screen TV that took up most of the space in the room.

There was no sofa. Two straight-backed chairs stood against one wall with a low, black lacquer table between them and several tatami pillows stacked under it. Elsie offered one chair to Mac and sat on the other. Before sitting down, Mac bowed to the elderly man in the wheel chair who waved back and smiled, then continued watching the game show. Every once in a while the man yelled, "Oh boy!" at the TV and clapped his hands.

On the table was a blue and white porcelain bowl of *arare*. Elsie offered the bowl to Mac. He took a couple of the pretzel-like Japanese snacks flavored with sweetened soy sauce and ate them one by one, like popcorn. He thanked her for talking with him, opened his note book, and asked Elsie if she remembered anything about Allen Bradford's disappearance.

She said she didn't know anything about his disappearance, but she knew a lot about him. "Oh, he was like a boy cat chasing the girl cat, you know?" She laughed. "The ladies at bridge club said that he was a tom cat. He fooled around with many ladies. I think most bridge club ladies were his girlfriends, but some people said his favorite one, his pet, was my friend, Sumiko Miyamoto."

Mac didn't interrupt her, letting her speak while he took notes. She spoke broken English, sometimes throwing in some Pidgin English and a Japanese word or two, but he understood her.

"Sumiko was my best friend, *ichiban nakano* – very beautiful, very kind. But Hideo was old and she was young. I don't know for sure, but I think she and Mr. Allen love each other. She never tell me," said Elsie, getting a little excited and shaking her head, her voice rising. "It is just what I heard, you see. Everybody talk long time ago. Everybody talk story about it, not only me.

"When Allen-san drown in the ocean at South Point," she continued, "Hideo and Sumiko did not go out of the house for many days. Tak went to work and back home, that's all. Their daughter, Sachiko, stayed in the house, too. Not even go to school long time, maybe one week, I think. Hideo and Allen-san very good friends. Hideo got nice, big house. He thought the house was for him, but everybody say it is for Sumiko. I think Hideo did not know this. When Allen-san drown, Hideo was ichiban *kanashii*, very sad.

"Other husbands know about Allen-san and their wives, so some fight with him, yeh? He fire them, kick them off plantation. They divorce. This true story, everybody know this."

"What did you think about Sumiko and Mr. Bradford?" Mac asked. He couldn't bring himself to refer to Bradford as Allen-san. "Do you think they had an affair? Maybe Hideo found out about them and got jealous and angry and killed Mr. Bradford?"

"Oh, no! No!" She stood up and looked down at Mac. "Hideo was very good man. He never would do that. I don't think so!" She slumped back in her chair and wrung her hands. "They were good friends," she said softly. "Now Hideo is dead and Sumiko is in old folks' home. I never see my best friend again."

She took a deep breath and asked Mac if he would like some tea. He thanked her and said no, he had other people to see. He stood up and extended his hand, but Elsie held her hands behind her back and bowed. Mac waved at Mr. Hasegawa who was channel surfing, *The Price is Right* having ended. The old man waved and looked back at the TV, clicking away on the remote. Elsie walked Mac to the door and closed it while he pulled on his boots.

His next stop would be Nobu Miyamoto's house. He hoped he would learn a few things there. How much Nobu knew about his father was questionable. He thought of Jessie and how little she knew about her father.

When Mac drove up, Nobu was sitting on a chair on the front porch drinking a beer and reading a newspaper. He stood as Mac walked up the concrete steps leading to the porch. After they shook hands, Nobu gestured toward a chair, then offered Mac a beer from an ice-filled Styrofoam cooler that was on the floor near his feet. He was barefoot and wearing jeans and a t-shirt with a breast pocket that held a pack of cigarettes. He had a full head of gray hair, but his relatively unlined face made him look younger than his 67 years.

He pulled a Marlboro out of the pack of cigarettes in his pocket and lit it with a lighter that he picked up from the table between them. He took a long drag, inhaling deeply, propped up his feet on the porch railing, and offered the pack to Mac.

Mac shook his head. "Thanks, but I quit smoking a long time ago and I don't drink when I'm working."

"So, what can I do for you, Detective McIntire?" There was a slight edge to his voice. "You said you had some questions about my father and Mr. Bradford. That was a long time ago. I don't know if I can be of much help."

"Just tell me what you remember about your father's relationship with Allen Bradford even if it doesn't seem important and where you were when Bradford disappeared, if you can."

Nobu said he didn't start working on the plantation until after Allen Bradford was gone. He claimed he didn't have any first-hand knowledge of him or his disappearance. In fact, he wasn't even on the island when Bradford died. He was attending school full time at the U of H in Honolulu while working part time as an accountant for a small firm when the plantation manager had presumably drowned. He returned to Kahana years later because his father was ailing by then and needed help. That's when he and his wife and young son moved in with his parents and he was hired as the plantation's controller.

He told Mac that he took care of his parents until his father died, then worked for the plantation until it closed. He later worked for an accounting firm in Hilo and retired last year. A few years ago, his mother moved to Hilo to live with his sister, Sachi, and her husband, Billy Gonsalves. Now, he and his wife, his son, daughter-in-law, and two grandchildren lived in the house Allen Bradford had given to Hideo.

"Bradford and my father went fishing together, I remember that," Nobu said. "Sometimes my brothers and I went with them, but we didn't fish."

Instead, he said, they looked for olivines, the green crystallized volcanic rock that gave South Point's Green Sand Beach its name. They climbed the rocks around the cliffs, slipped through the barbed wire fence of a nearby pasture where they flew their kites, and picked *poha* berries, the tangy, tomato-like gooseberries that grew wild along the cliffs. They also visited the lighthouse caretaker who let them climb the steep, spiral staircase to the lantern room so they could look out over the open ocean.

They pretended to look for Japanese submarines even though it was long after the war had ended. "Kids, you know, always fantasizing," said Nobu with a shrug.

"That's about it," he said, crushing out his cigarette in an ashtray that was inscribed with the words "Lucky you come Hawaii." "Now, I'm reading about the cave at South Point and Mr. Bradford's skeleton that those guys found. It's interesting, but it doesn't have anything to do with me or my father or anyone else in my family." He lit another cigarette and guzzled his beer.

Mac took copious notes. He'd have to look them over later to see if anything would jump out at him. Nobu gave a lot of information, but the narrative seemed rehearsed and he appeared agitated. Was that his personality or was he hiding something? Mac asked a few more questions, scribbled some more, and asked Nobu to call if he thought of anything else, handing him his card as they shook hands. He had one more stop to make. He started his truck, and headed for the edge of town.

Tom Johnson was the plantation office manager who went looking for Bradford when he didn't show up for work the day he went missing. Johnson, whose first wife passed away soon after the plantation shut down, married a young Japanese woman whose parents were friends with the Miyamotos. He heard a lot about them from her.

Johnson lived near the Methodist Church in a small, neat, white house with jalousie windows. He answered the door wearing a big smile, an aloha shirt, shorts, and flip flops. "I don't have many visitors, so I'm happy to have some company for a change," he said, offering Mac a plastic patio chair on the front porch and sat in an old rattan rocking chair with faded cushions. He was a widower again and in his late 80s. "I'm still pretty fit in mind, body, and spirit," he said, "because I eat healthy, do 20 pushups a day, and have a shot of good Kentucky bourbon every evening."

After Kahana plantation closed, he worked for a while on another plantation and when it closed, too, he bought the property in Kahana and built the house in which he was now living. He grew macadamia nut trees on several acres outside of town. Along with his pension, social security, and the macadamias he sold, he earned enough to support himself in his old age.

"Yes, I worked with Allen Bradford," he said. "He was a good manager. This plantation was the most productive one on the island when he was top luna. He kept it that way until the day he disappeared."

"Did you spend time with him outside of work," Mac wanted to know, "fishing or hunting, maybe? Stopping in at the Beachhead Inn? How well did you know him?"

Johnson said they socialized at parties and other events on the plantation and he had drinks with Bradford and his brother, Rod, at Moon's sometimes. "I didn't know him very well, though, except for the gossip."

"What gossip?" asked Mac.

"About his womanizing," said Johnson. "That was his downfall. God, that man loved women. I mean, what man doesn't? With him it was an obsession. As long as it wore a skirt, he went after it. He made a lot of enemies because of that. He fired two of his young engineers after they confronted him about trying to fool around with their wives." Johnson snapped his fingers. "Just like that – fired them. He couldn't get away with that today. With all the laws protecting workers, if that happened now, the company would be sued and Bradford would have been out of a job. Anyway, rumor was that both couples separated before they even packed up and left town.

"Then, there was the Japanese woman, Sumi, Hideo Miyamoto's wife. Allen really had a thing for her. She was a mail order bride, very young, and a real beauty. I don't know if Hideo suspected anything. He was the nicest guy. Allen promoted him from working in the fields to being my assistant. I was the office manager at the time, you know. Hideo was smart. Best assistant I ever had."

"Wait," interrupted Mac. "Back up a little. What about the guys he fired? What happened to them? Are they still around, here in the Islands, I mean?"

"Oh, them, well, as office manager," said Johnson, "I was the one who processed their papers when they were let go. I know one of them left for the Mainland right away because I had to approve his moving expenses to Arizona." He scratched his head. "Or was it New Mexico? Anyway, it was the southwest. I don't think he ever came back to Hawaii. They did get divorced. My wife used to keep in touch with his wife, so that's how I know. We learned that he died in a car crash about a year after he arrived there, poor guy."

"What happened to the other one?" Mac asked. "Where'd he end up?"

"The other one took a job on another plantation. I forget which one, but it was near Hilo on the Hamakua Coast. I had to approve his moving expenses, too. His wife and kids went back to the Mainland and I know for a fact that they got divorced. You can imagine what the gossip was like at the time. It was a real soap opera around here."

"Do you remember their names?" asked Mac.

Johnson ran his fingers through his thin, white hair with the wispy comb over. "I think one was Mike Jameson, yeah, and the other guy, the one who stayed on the Big Island, was Ed Hampton. Nice young guys, maybe late 20s, early 30s. I don't blame them for getting riled up. Too bad it cost them their jobs."

"Was either of them mad enough to want to murder Bradford?" asked Mac.

"Oh, I wouldn't know about that. Like I said, they were nice guys. I don't know." He pondered for a moment, rocking back and forth in his chair. "No, I doubt it," he said.

"Okay," said Mac, turning the page in his notebook. "So tell me what you know about Bradford and Miyamoto's wife."

"Well," said Johnson, "Hideo and Sumi had four sons. Years later when the boys were in their teens, Sumi got pregnant and gave birth to a baby girl. There was talk that she and Bradford were having an affair. Some people thought the baby was Allen's. They were even making bets that it would look like him, but the little girl looked every inch Japanese.

"I didn't think there was anything to the rumors and neither did my second wife who was a pretty close friend of Sumi's. There was a lot of whispering about it. That's how small towns are. Everybody knows everyone else's business, or at least, they think they do." He stood up.

"Can I get you something to drink? Coke? Water?" he asked, drawing a pack of cigarettes out of his shirt pocket and offering one to Mac.

Mac said no to the cigarette and reached in his back pocket for a blue and white bandana and mopped his face and the back of his neck. "I will have some water, if you don't mind."

They'd been sitting on the porch for nearly an hour. The afternoon was hot and humid. Even the bamboo shade hanging from the ceiling to the edge of the porch railing didn't help filter out the heat from the sun's rays.

"Sure. I'll be right back," said Johnson. He went inside and returned with two bottles of icy cold water from the refrigerator and handed one to Mac. Johnson took a swig from his bottle, then, lit a Lucky Strike filter tip, turning his head away from Mac as he exhaled.

Mac held the cold bottle against his forehead for a second before opening it and taking a sip. "How did Bradford and Miyamoto get along?" he asked, hoping that he hadn't broken Johnson's train of thought.

"How did Miyamoto and Bradford get along?" repeated Johnson. "They were like this." He held up his hand and pressed his index and middle fingers together. "They fished together, drank together. It was like they were best friends."

Mac asked about the day Bradford didn't show up for work.

"Let's see," said Johnson. "I remember just like it was yesterday, it's still so clear in my mind. You don't forget something like that. I went to the Bradford house to find out why Allen wasn't at the office. No one seemed to know where he was. In fact, his wife said that she hadn't seen him since he left for work the morning before. She didn't even know if he had come home that last night. I thought it was peculiar – a wife not knowing whether or not her husband came home, but it was none of my business."

Mac looked up from his notes. "What about Miyamoto? Was he at work that day?"

"Yes, he was. I would have known if he hadn't shown up. Hideo was my right hand man, always on time, never absent. He was there, all right. I'm sure of it even after all these years."

"Did you notice anything different about him?" asked Mac. "Was he in a good mood, a bad mood, nervous? Any scratches or bruises on him? It's been a long time, but try to remember."

"It's hard to read the Japanese," said Johnson. "They're stoic, keep a lot inside. On the surface Hideo was always pleasant, worked hard, laughed at a joke now and then. But most of the time he was quiet, kept to himself at the office, a hard worker. I didn't notice anything different about him that day, not that I recall, anyway. No scratches or bruises that I could see."

"Do you think Bradford and Sumi Miyamoto were having an affair?" Mac asked.

"I don't know for sure. I wouldn't be surprised. Allen wouldn't have let on to me, of course, but everyone thought so, even my first wife. She knew all the gossip."

Johnson pointed down the road and said, "Bradford had a house. That one, two doors down. After they said he drowned and Anne was packing to move to Hilo, I asked if she wanted anything from that house. I'd never been inside, but Allen told me that he kept his fishing and hunting gear there. Anne didn't seem to know anything about the place. In fact, she was surprised when I mentioned it. She said she didn't want anything, to keep whatever I wanted, and to throw the rest away."

Mac jotted down a few notes. He stopped writing for a second, his pen poised above the spiral note book, and glanced up. "And?"

"I went over there. It was a company house, Bradford didn't own it. The front room looked like a man's place, nothing fancy, a little messy. The only furniture was a couple of chairs and a sofa that looked sort of worn. The fridge was stocked with beer. I remember there was a half-filled bottle of expensive single malt Scotch whiskey on the kitchen counter, ashtrays filled with cigarette butts on the tables, newspapers and magazines scattered all over the place – *Field and Stream, Esquire, Playboy*. His fishing and hunting gear was stored in one of the bedrooms, including a pair of rubber waders which I presumed he wore when he went fishing." He dragged on his cigarette again and continued.

"Another bedroom was a whole other story. It was fully furnished and nice, too. Curtains, double bed all made up, not frilly, but neat and tidy. There was even a record player in there. A Sinatra record was on the turntable. I kept the record. I still have it, as a matter of fact. I can't play it because I don't have a turntable anymore. Anyway, the room looked like a love nest. I figured that's where he entertained his girlfriends. I took the whiskey and beer for myself and had the rest of the stuff picked up by the Salvation Army. I never told Anne what I found in the house."

"Is anybody living there now?" asked Mac.

"Yeah, a school teacher and his family," said Johnson. "The husband teaches at the high school. He's from the Mainland, Cleveland, I think. She's a local girl, Portuguese, works at the credit union in town. Nice people. They have a couple of young kids. Several families have lived in that house off and on through the years. If you're thinking there might be something left over from Allen, I doubt it. Too many people have been in and out of there."

"Was Hideo Miyamoto the kind of man who would be jealous enough to kill someone who was having an affair with his wife?" Mac wanted to know.

"Like I said, he was quiet, stoic. I don't know. I don't think so. He was pretty mild mannered." Johnson gulped down the rest of the water in his bottle.

"What about Anne Bradford? Do you think she'd want to have her husband killed?" asked Mac. Johnson flinched, surprised. "Just askin'," said Mac.

Shocked, Johnson said emphatically, "No way! She was a real lady, very refined. Don't even think about it," he said as he stubbed out his cigarette.

Mac asked if he knew anyone from that time who was still living in Kahana. Johnson named Nobu Miyamoto and Elsie Hasegawa. He described Nobu as a taciturn guy who hardly spoke except to say hello. "He's not anything like his father. Hideo was friendly. Nobu always seemed to have a chip on his shoulder, still does. I hired him to be controller a few years after Allen disappeared. He has a master's degree in accounting from U of H. A smart guy, but he stayed pretty much to himself. Never even came to the company parties we had several times a year. Of course, Hideo was retired by then. Anyway, Nobu still lives in his parents' house up the hill from here."

"Yeah, I know," said Mac. "I just came from there."

"Elsie Hasegawa was friends with my second wife and Sumi Miyamoto," said Johnson. "She worked as a maid at our house when I was married to my first wife and also at the homes of several other managers. Elsie didn't mind telling people what she learned about all of us. Not that we ever did anything exciting enough for people to gossip about, but I'm sure she thought of something."

"And Miyamoto's wife?" Mac asked. "What was she like?"

"Sumi was quiet, but really nice, sweet, you know? Beautiful girl, a real doll. You might try talking to her. I don't know what shape she's in nowadays. I heard she's at a nursing home in Hilo, Paradise Senior Care, I think it's called. That's about all I can say about her." He became pensive.

"There are a lot of newcomers here in Kahana," mused Johnson, "immigrants from Micronesia and the Philippines, even some from Southeast Asia, hippies. Most of the old ones from my time are gone." He sighed and dragged on his cigarette.

"It'll be my turn one of these days. I bought a plot at the Catholic cemetery right up the hill from this house. I'll be with my first wife when the time comes. Isn't that a kick?" He laughed. "My second wife is buried at the Japanese cemetery farther up the hill. She died 10 years ago. Cancer. She was young, too young to die. I don't have any kids, so there won't be anybody to mourn me when I'm gone." He shook his head sadly and drew on his cigarette again before grinding it out. Mac noticed the yellowing of his fingers from countless years of holding cigarettes. Probably started smoking when he was still a kid, he thought. That's what they did in those days, started early.

Mac remembered that the Japanese cemetery was flooded years ago while the plantation was still operating. The flash flood brought raging waters through the old grave yard, upending tombstones and monuments. Skeletal remains were dredged up out of the ground and laid out in the open for weeks until cleanup crews could complete the job of reburying the corpses and reinstalling the headstones. They were never able to identify all of the remains and most were buried in mass graves. Those were the days before DNA testing.

He was a just a boy at the time and had seen it from the back seat of the family station wagon as his father drove by the macabre scene. He passed the cemetery this morning on his way to Johnson's home after meeting with Nobu. The place is now as beautiful as a Japanese tea garden. Mac guessed that Johnson's wife was there amid the stone lanterns and other Japanese ornaments. He stood, ready to leave, but he had one more question for the old man.

"I have to ask," said Mac. "What about you, did you have any problems with Bradford? Where were you when he was murdered?"

Johnson seemed to expect the question and didn't hesitate to answer. "We got along fine. No axe to grind between us," he said. "My first wife was a wonderful woman, but she wasn't Bradford's type, if you know what I mean, so there was no problem as far as that was concerned. I was home the night before he went missing and went to work at eight o'clock the next morning like always. Allen usually showed up around 8:30. When he didn't come in by 10:30, I wondered where he was. Sometimes he'd ride his horse through the fields early in the morning to see how the work was going, so I checked at the stables and the stable hands said the horse was in its stall and they hadn't seen Allen. That's when I went to the house and spoke with his wife."

"Okay," said Mac, closing his notebook and slipping his pen into his breast pocket. "I guess I have all I need. Thanks for your time, Tom. Here's my card. Give me a call if you think of anything else."

He left Johnson sitting on his porch smoking another filter tip. Johnson smiled and gave the *shaka* sign - the Hawaiian version of the hand signal for hang loose. As Mac got into his truck he made the hang loose sign back. When he got to the highway at the end of Johnson's driveway, he debated whether to go to South Point to see Jessie or head back to Hilo. He turned left toward Hilo.

As he drove off, he wondered how much he would tell Jessie. He didn't want her to know about her father's alleged womanizing right away. He'd have to tread very carefully on that one. He hated to be the one to give her the news, but knew he would be.

He called Brian Alnas and asked him to look up Mike Jameson and Ed Hampton.

13

THE BRADFORD INVESTIGATION WAS TAKING UP MOST OF Mac's time. It was becoming an obsession. He was relieved the dental records confirmed that it was Allen Bradford's remains that were found even though it was no surprise. There were still a lot of unanswered questions, mainly, who the hell had killed him and why?

Although he told Jessie that he didn't have any definite suspects, he was seriously considering Hideo Miyamoto and possibly one or more of his sons. Then, there was Ed Hampton, one of the guys Bradford had fired. He even began to suspect Tom Johnson, but had to admit that idea was far-fetched.

He needed to go to the site at South Point again and try to figure out how the body got there. Was Bradford lured to the cave and murdered there or was he killed somewhere else? The medical examiner said he had received two blows to the back of the head with a blunt object, the first one probably stunned him and the second one crushed his skull. Mac figured that any of the large rocks in the cave could have been the murder weapon. When he asked the ME about that, he was told that the object was smooth with no jagged edges as a lava rock would have.

If Bradford was murdered somewhere else and carried to the cave, it would have taken more than one person to carry his body down the trail. Mac wanted to retrace the steps based on what Nobu Miyamoto told him. Something Nobu said nagged at him.

When he got back to the office, he read through his notes and found what he was looking for. Nobu said that he and his brothers didn't fish with their father and Bradford, that they "…climbed the rocks around the beach, slipped through the barbed wire fence of a nearby pasture where they flew their kites, picked poha berries near the cliffs…" That's what Mac wanted to check out. He was sure those kids were playing in Joseph Kanekoa's pasture where the cave was located.

Mac saw the poha berries near the cliffs as he walked down to the crime scene. The boys could have found the cave while flying their kites and picking berries. There were berries growing along the trail about half-way down the cliff. He figured that when the boys reached that point, they probably got curious about the big rock standing free on the ledge and when they went to investigate, they found the cave.

Hideo Miyamoto was in his 70s when Bradford was murdered. If he did it, he couldn't have disposed of the body by himself. Someone, maybe one of his sons, probably helped him put the body in the cave. If Bradford was killed there, Mac couldn't imagine how Miyamoto alone could over-power him. Bradford was six feet two inches tall and weighed 180 pounds according to the meticulous medical records from the files of the old plantation hospital. Miyamoto stood five feet six inches tall, weighed 130 pounds, and was 15 years older than Bradford. Someone else had to be involved, someone bigger and stronger than the old man. Tomorrow morning Mac and his partner, Brian, would try to recreate the crime. They had a test in mind that might prove his theory.

Mac envisioned a scenario that had the Miyamoto kids discovering the cave. Kids are like monkeys, he thought. They have no fear and if they were picking berries and found the path leading to the cliff ledge, they'd have no qualms about climbing down to see where it led no matter how precarious it was. They may have told their parents about it, but kept it a secret from anyone outside the family. Or maybe they kept it a secret even from their parents and when the murder occurred, knew just where to hide the body.

Perhaps Miyamoto learned about Bradford and his wife and lured Bradford to the cave to kill him. Or someone waited for them and helped with the murder. Who could that be? A friend? One or more of the sons? Two of the boys were dead. The surviving sons were Isaburo, a doctor who was living in Seattle, and Nobu. If it was a friend, was it someone from the Japanese camp – Elsie Hasegawa's now wheelchair-bound husband, for instance? Tom Johnson, maybe, or Ed Hampton seeking revenge?

He was focusing on the Miyamotos because he felt they were the most likely to be involved. It wouldn't be the first time a jealous husband killed a rival for his wife's affections. Mac had a hunch.

The next morning, Sgt. Brian Alnas drove to Mac's house near Volcanoes National Park with two large, black coffees in the drink holders of the Expedition. He parked on the street, blew the horn, and waited for Mac to come down the steps of the vintage cottage that had been in the McIntire family for nearly a century. After the divorce, Mac moved out of the house in Hilo that he'd shared with his wife and sons and had lived in the cottage ever since. His youngest son was in college in southern California, the middle son was a fire fighter on Maui, and the eldest was a lawyer in Honolulu.

Mac pulled on his hiking boots instead of the cowboy boots he usually wore, grabbed his fleece-lined denim jacket and a baseball cap, and ran down the steps to the street where Brian was waiting in the truck.

Brian started to get out of the driver's seat so Mac could drive, but Mac waved at him to get back in. "You drive," he said. "Let's go straight to South Point. Did you bring Archie?" he asked, sipping the steaming black coffee.

"Yep," replied Brian. "He's back there." He jerked his head toward the back seat.

Mac looked over his shoulder and saw the mannequin the police department used to train recruits in CPR stretched out on the back seat.

"By the way, Boss," said Brian, "I looked up those two names you gave me, Jameson and Hampton? Both of those guys worked at Kahana Plantation, lost their jobs, and Jameson returned to the Mainland shortly after being terminated. Both got divorced. As far as I can tell, Jameson never came back to the Islands and he died in a car crash in Arizona a year later. He was nowhere near Hawaii when Bradford was killed."

"What about the other one, Hampton?" Mac asked.

"After he left Kahana," said Brian, "he worked on Kehei Plantation on the Hamakua Coast. He retired from there in the late '80s. He never remarried and now he's at a nursing home on Oahu. He's in his 70s and has Alzheimer's. His daughter lives in Honolulu and his son works construction for the county here on the Big Island. Both are in their mid 50s. Do you think Hampton could be a suspect?"

"Just want to cover all the bases," said Mac. "Apparently, Bradford had affairs with their wives, they confronted him, and he fired them. We can eliminate Jameson as a suspect, of course, but, yeah, do more digging on Hampton. He was around when Bradford was murdered and he had motive. For starters, talk to the son."

"Okay, I'll keep checking on Hampton. I'll track down his son and see if he knows what his father was up to back then." Brian turned off the highway at the water tower where South Point Road began. When he reached the end of the pavement near the light house foundation at South Point, he started to turn the SUV toward the locked gate that led through the pasture to the cave.

"Wait," said Mac. "Stop here and let's get out for a minute. I want to get a look at the fishermen." Several people stood on the rocks with their fishing lines in the water. "How do they stand on those rocks without falling in?" Mac wondered aloud. "One guy is wearing rubber boots, but the others are just wearing flip flops, must be slippery. I've never fished here, have you?" he asked.

"No, not here," said Brian. "I've fished from my cousin Fernando's boat. I'm not much of a fisherman, though. I like to hunt. Shootz! Those rocks look slippery, yeh?"

"Johnson told me he found a pair of waders at the house where Bradford kept his fishing gear," said Mac. "I bet he wore them when he came here. If he was fishing that morning, why wasn't he wearing them?"

As they walked onto the beach, they stopped and watched. Up close, it didn't look too dangerous. Maybe it was risky if someone were wearing leather boots with smooth soles. Mac squatted down and sifted a handful of green sand through his fingers. Green olivines shimmered in the sunlight through the sand.

"You know what," he said, "we never examined those boots Bradford was wearing to see if there was green sand on the bottoms. Even after all this time there might be traces and if we do find some it could mean that he walked on the beach that day and he was here to fish. If we don't find any, it could prove that he never set foot on the beach and the whole thing was staged to look like he was fishing. Let's look into it when we get back. I've never thought it was a robbery and a random killing."

He didn't believe Bradford would have worn his expensive boots to go fishing no matter what Jessie said, and he didn't think he was murdered on the beach. "He was either killed somewhere else and brought to the cave or killed in the cave. Let's go take a look."

Mac opened the padlocked gate with his key and paid no attention to the "NO TRESPASSING" and "KAPU" signs hanging on the fence. No one was standing guard. A large metal sign that read "ARCHAEOLOGICAL DIG DO NOT ENTER DO NOT DISTURB" was planted nearby and spray-painted with graffiti. There were bullet holes through all the letter Os, as if that letter was chosen as a bull's eye.

Brian drove through and stopped to wait as Mac closed and locked the gate. Mac got back in the truck and they started the bone-jarring drive through the pasture. Although a crude track was formed by vehicles going to and from the site since the discovery, it was still a rough ride. A few handwritten signs discouraging intruders from entering the dig area were placed at various points along the track. Near the site they saw vehicles parked in the grass.

They stopped, Mac pulled Archie out of the back seat, and as they headed toward the cliff, a young woman who was texting on her phone, blocked the way. Before she could ask who they were, they flashed their badges. She shrugged, let them pass, and continued texting.

Carrying the 120-pound mannequin by the arms and legs, they made their way down the ledge to the boulder that shielded the cave's entrance. The dummy was bulky, but they had no trouble even with the wind gusting around them. Brian went first, holding onto the arms, while Mac held the legs. They showed their badges to the people working on the dig and said they were finishing up their investigation of the crime scene and needed to go inside for a few minutes.

Once in the cave, they were met with bright lights and a flurry of activity. The canoe was still on its catafalque of boulders, but most of the artifacts – the bowls, lamps and tools – were gone. Workers were on their knees sifting through sand and dirt with brushes and other tools. They looked up at the two cops, saw their badges, and went back to work.

Mac and Brian studied the corner where Allen Bradford's skeleton was found. Together they carried Archie in and out a couple of times. They dragged him by his legs, by his arms. They threw him over their shoulders, laid him down where Allen Bradford had lain all those years. The dummy was five feet six inches, about the same height as Hideo Miyamoto, so they pretended he was the assailant, and with Brian manipulating him, had the dummy simulate hitting Mac with a rock. Mac was about the same size as Bradford. Then, they dragged Archie back to the cave's opening.

They looked at each other and nodded. "Could have happened," said Brian. "The first blow probably stunned him, he fell, and the second one finished him off, just like the ME said."

'Seems that way," Mac agreed.

They carried the dummy back up the ledge, passing the berry bushes that were picked clean, nodded at the young woman standing lookout with her hands now jammed into the pockets of her hooded, woolen jacket. They put Archie back in the truck and drove off.

They didn't speak as they headed out. A sentry was at the gate now. He opened it for them. They waved, drove through, and turned up South Point Road. Once on the paved road Brian said, "I thought either of your theories could have worked, Boss. Someone had to know that cave was there beforehand. I don't think it was a coincidence that when they needed a place to hide the body, they just happened to find it. What do you think?"

Mac agreed. "I'm sure the kids found it while they were playing. They were probably scared and never told anyone, except their parents. And you're right, when they needed a hiding place, they knew just where to go."

"Yeh," said Brian, "and it was the perfect spot for 36 years."

Mac nodded. "But I don't think the murder took place there," he said. "I think it happened somewhere else and the body was brought here, but one person couldn't have done it. Especially not an elderly man as slightly built as Hideo Miyamoto. Bradford was a big guy. If Miyamoto did it, he needed the help of one or more other people, probably his sons. It would have taken at least two people to carry the body down to the cave."

"We know Nobu was in Honolulu when Bradford was killed," said Brian. "If it was his father who did it and only the one son, Tak, was here, Nobu could have caught a plane to Hilo or Kona, rented a car, driven to Kahana, helped dispose of the body, and hopped on another plane and flown back to Honolulu without anyone noticing. Or he might know who helped."

"Too bad we can't check with the airlines to see if he flew that day, but after nearly four decades there wouldn't be any record of it," said Mac.

"Still, we have a pretty good theory, Mac. Shootz, I think we're on to something."

"Maybe," said Mac. "Let's not forget about Ed Hampton. Remember, he had motive, too, and he was a big guy, about my size. As far as I'm concerned, everyone is a suspect."

"I just don't see Bradford being lured here by a man he fired from his job," said Brian. "Considering he was having an affair with the guy's wife, I think he'd be wary of going anywhere with him. My money's still on the Miyamotos."

"Yeah, mine, too. Bringing Archie was a great idea, by the way. Wish I'd thought of it," said Mac.

"That's what I get paid for, right, Boss?" said Brian. "Now what?"

"Let's go back to Hilo. You go look at those boots of Bradford's and see what's on the soles. I'm going to interview Miyamoto's widow at the nursing home."

"Wow! She's still alive? How old is she, a hundred?"

"She's in her 80s or 90s, I think. I hope her mind is still sharp and that she feels like talking today."

"In her 80s or 90s!" said Brian, shaking his head. "Shootz!"

"Hey, don't knock it. Haven't you heard that 90 is the new 70?"

"Seventy? Man, that's old, too. How old are you?"

"Never mind."

14

After dropping off Brian at the police station, Mac drove to the nursing home on the outskirts of Hilo and turned into the parking lot of Paradise Senior Care at 1:30. He knew the patients would have finished lunch and were probably watching television or taking naps. He was familiar with the routine because his father was a patient at the same nursing home until his death a few years ago.

He stopped at the reception desk and asked to see Mrs. Sumiko Miyamoto.

"Oh, yes," said the receptionist. "She's in the sunroom overlooking the koi pond." She pointed. "See? Over there, that's her."

Sitting in a wheel chair, looking at the koi pond through the floor-to-ceiling windows of the sunroom, was an elderly Japanese woman wrapped in a colorful patchwork quilt. Mac walked over to her and removed his hat. Sumi shaded her eyes from the afternoon sun with her hand and squinted at the tall stranger. Mac nodded at the aide who was sitting beside her.

"I just want to talk to her for a little while, in private," he said and showed his badge. The aide left, saying he'd be back in a few minutes.

"Okay, this won't take long," said Mac. He squatted next to the wheel chair and smiled. Her eyes were clear and seemed pretty alert for someone so elderly, he thought.

"Mrs. Miyamoto, I'm from the police. Do you understand?"

"Yes," the police," she said. "I understand. Hai."

Mac decided to just say it straight out. "I would like to ask you a few questions about Allen Bradford. Do you remember him?"

He watched for some reaction, but there was none.

"Mr. Allen, hai. He died, you know. Ichiban long time. He was Hideo's boss."

"Yes," he died a long time ago," said Mac. "Do you know how he died?"

"Oh, he drowned. Hideo told me. At South Point. Hai, South Point."

"What did Hideo tell you, Mrs. Miyamoto?"

Sumi was quiet for a few seconds. "What did he tell me? Oh, yes, now I remember," she said. "Hideo told me Mr. Allen drowned at South Point. Hideo died, too, you know, ichiban long time, long time." Her voice was fading. She closed her eyes and slumped down in the wheel chair. Wait, did she nod off? For Christ's sake! Mac stood up and watched for a few seconds, wondering if the old lady had really fallen asleep. What the heck? He was still staring down at her wondering what to do when the aide returned. "It's time for her nap, Detective. Sorry, I think she's had enough excitement for today. She doesn't get many visitors."

Mac reluctantly stepped aside and watched as the aide unlocked the wheels of the chair and pushed it down the hallway and out of sight. He left wishing he'd had more time with Sumi, but figured that he probably got all the information he could, anyway, and wouldn't bother her again. He called Brian as he drove out of the parking lot.

"She appeared to be a little senile," he groused. "All she seems to remember is that her husband and Bradford are dead and she kept repeating that it was a long time ago. I wanted to ask about her sons, but she fell asleep while I was talking to her."

"She fell asleep? Hmmm…and here I've been thinking that you have such an electrifying personality," said Brian. "Guess I was wrong about you, Lieutenant. Me, I've never had a woman fall asleep while I was talking to her."

"I guess I'm not as electrifying as you are, Sergeant," said Mac. "By the way, did you get a chance to look at the boots?"

"Yeah, I did, with a magnifying glass. There doesn't appear to be any green sand on them and no material from the floor of the cave either. Just traces of red dirt like he would have picked up walking around the cane fields. I think you're right, Mac. He was killed somewhere else and his body was taken there. He never walked on the beach or in the cave wearing those boots, not that day, anyway."

Jessie arrived at the nursing home shortly after Mac left. She didn't know what to expect. Because of her father's close friendship with Hideo Miyamoto, she hoped Sumi might remember if the two men were together that last day. Maybe there was a clue that the police missed or that Sumi forgot to tell them. Perhaps Mr. Miyamoto knew who'd want to hurt Allen and told his wife about it. Jessie remembered how gossip flowed around the plantation in the old days. Her mother was always complaining about it.

She told the receptionist that she was there to visit Mrs. Miyamoto. "She's down the hall on the left, number 116," the young woman said. "I don't know if she's awake. Another visitor just left. I think an aide took her back to her room for a nap."

"That's all right," said Jessie. "I won't disturb her if she's asleep."

The door to room 116 was open. Jessie found a tiny woman sitting in a wheel chair, her thin white hair pulled back in a bun. She was wearing wire-rimmed eye glasses that had slid a little way down her nose. Her hands were folded in her lap as she looked out the window at the profusion of flowers in the garden. Sumi looked up at the woman who entered her room, but didn't recognize her.

If Jessie hadn't seen the name Sumiko Miyamoto on the door, she wouldn't have recognized this woman either. Sumi was young and beautiful those many years ago with a porcelain-white complexion and long, lustrous black hair. This old woman's skin had an unhealthy, sallow look to it. Jessie extended her hand and Sumi hesitated, then reached out and clasped the outstretched hand. Jessie felt the dry, parchment-like skin and feared that if she gripped too firmly, the fragile, thin, bird-like fingers might break.

"Hello, Mrs. Miyamoto," said Jessie. "It's so nice to see you again."

Sumi smiled. She withdrew her hand and cocked her head to one side. She tried to remember who this person was who was so glad to see her again. Was she a nurse, a social worker? They were always checking on her. "Hai," she said, "yes, so nice to see you, too."

"I'm Jessica Bradford, a friend of Sachi's. Do you remember me? Sachi and I went to school together on Kahana Plantation. I visited your home many times."

The sound of the name Bradford startled her. Sumi shrank back in her chair, clenching her hands tightly under the quilt. "Yes, I remember you," she said. "You and Sachi did your homework in the garden small kid time. I used to light the candle in the stone lantern for you girls." Jessie smiled. "That's right," she said. "May I close the door, Mrs. Miyamoto?"

"Yes, please close the door," said Sumi. So, she thought, this is Allen's daughter, the same age as Sachi. She remembered her very well, a nice, quiet girl. But why was she here? She had pushed Allen Bradford and all he stood for so far back in her memory that it was a shock to hear his name again, twice in one day – first the policeman and now the girl. What did she want, this daughter of his?

"Hai," she said. "You and Sachi were always together."

Jessie said, "We still see each other. I had lunch with her just the other day."

Sachi never mentioned that she was still friends with the Bradford girl, thought Sumi. Was this a friendly visit? She avoided looking into the eyes of Allen Bradford's daughter at first. She had tried to forget him, but the memory was always there. Adjusting her glasses and squinting to get a better look, she wondered if she should pretend to be senile and fall asleep as she did with that policeman or should she allow Jessica Bradford to stay a while? She decided to let her stay. After all, she seldom had visitors and the girl seemed nice and looked so much like Allen with her light brown hair and green eyes.

They talked for nearly an hour, longer than Jessie intended. She noticed that Sumi was beginning to look pale and tired and decided that it was time to leave when a nurse knocked and opened the door. "Good afternoon, Mama," said the nurse in a cheery voice. "It's time for your meds."

"I was just leaving," said Jessie. She reached for Sumi's hand and held it gently. "Thank you, Mrs. Miyamoto. Thank you very much for letting me spend time with you. I'll visit again, if you'd like. "

"Thank you, too," said Sumi. "I am very happy to talk with Allen's daughter. Yes, please come again."

Jessie smiled at the nurse and left the room. Sumi dabbed at a tear on her cheek and took a deep breath as she watched Jessie walk out the door. Since Hideo died she'd had two wishes – to visit Japan one more time and to die with a clear conscience. She knew she wasn't going to get the first wish, but the second one seemed within reach. Ah, now I can die easy, she thought.

Jessie drove to the ranch wondering if she should tell Mac what Mrs. Miyamoto told her. She'd think about it. She'd have to tell him sometime, but not now.

15

WHEN MAC GOT BACK TO HIS OFFICE AFTER VISITING THE nursing home, he found a message from Moon Toli in Waikea. Brian told him he tried to find out why Toli was calling, but the bar keeper wanted to speak only with Mac. "He said he had some information that Detective McIntire might find useful in the investigation of the Bradford murder," said Brian.

Mac returned the call, but Moon didn't want to talk over the phone. "Can you meet me at my bar tomorrow around noon?" Moon asked. "There's someone I think you should meet. It's about the Bradford case." Mac agreed. Since he was going to be out that way, why not stop and see Jessie, he thought. Maybe take her to dinner. He could spend the night at Mauna Loa Ranch.

He called Jessie. "Detective, are you asking me out on a date?" she teased. "I thought you'd never get around to it."

"Yeah, well, I thought it was about time," he laughed. "How about I pick you up at five o'clock for dinner and a show at one of the resorts on the Kohala Coast?" When he clicked off the phone, his palms were sweaty. He felt like a school boy. He hadn't been out with a woman in a couple of years.

It wasn't really a date, he tried to convince himself. It was just Jessie, two old friends having dinner. No big deal.

Mac met with Moon the following day. When he walked into the Beachhead Inn it was quiet. There was only one customer in the place and the juke box wasn't playing. Even with the windows and door open, the odor of stale beer and cigarettes hung in the air. A man with a military-style haircut wearing a red t-shirt emblazoned with the words "Hawaiian Native" across the chest, sat at the bar drinking a beer. The image of the Eagle, Globe and Anchor, the U.S. Marine Corps emblem, was tattooed on his left forearm. He looked to be in his late 30s or early 40s. Mac thought he knew everyone in Waikea, but he'd never seen this guy before. Moon introduced Master Sergeant Nick Mahuna who was on leave from his third tour of duty in Afghanistan and was in Waikea visiting relatives. He'd only been in town for a few days and didn't know about the discovery of Allen Bradford's remains at South Point until the day before when his family told him about it.

"It might not be important," said the Marine, "but Moon felt I should tell the police what I saw the morning Mr. Bradford disappeared." He sipped his beer and continued. "I grew up here in Waikea. We lived in a house on the right hand corner as you enter town coming from South Point. The house burned down years ago and both my parents have passed away, but I still have family here. I come to visit whenever I'm back on leave."

He was nine years old and was walking to the school bus stop in front of Lee's Market that morning when he saw a car speeding through town. Hideo Miyamoto was driving a white sedan and Tak was in the passenger seat. "I knew them because my uncle and Tak were friends and I recognized the car. Tak came to our house many times," he said. "I waved and he looked right at me, but he didn't wave back."

School started at eight o'clock, he said, so that would have been about seven. The bus usually stopped at Lee's around 7:10 and it came a few minutes after the Miyamotos drove by. It meant nothing to him back then.

He never gave it another thought even with all the excitement later about Bradford missing and presumed drowned.

He felt foolish telling Mac about it now because Tak and his father were probably going home from fishing. When he mentioned it to Moon yesterday, Moon told him about the police investigation and thought he should tell Mac what he had seen that morning. "So," he said, "that's all I have to say." He looked a little sheepish. "Can I buy you a drink, sir?" Just then Mac's cell phone rang. It was Brian calling from Hilo.

"Mac, you'd better get to Kahana and fast. Nobu Miyamoto is shooting up the place. We just got a call from Sgt. Karen Souza. She and another officer are there now. They've cleared the roads leading up to the Miyamoto place and ordered people to stay inside their homes. Nobu is asking for you. He doesn't want to talk to anyone else. I'm leaving now. I'm taking Keith Ikeda with me. Sgt. Bill Vickery and some other guys from Kona are on the way. See you there."

"Okay, got it," said Mac, clicking off. "I'll have to take a rain check on that drink, Sergeant, but thanks for the information. It may be more important than you think. Every little bit helps. Good luck to you." He shook hands with the Marine and Moon and hurried out to his truck.

As he sped away from Moon's, Mac called Jessie to cancel their date and Jerry Kamaka to tell him he wouldn't be stopping at Mauna Loa Ranch that night. Both of them said they were watching the news on TV. The local television stations sent crews with cameras to the site and most of the reporters were spewing pure speculation because nobody was allowed near the Miyamoto house. That didn't stop them. They kept repeating the same information over and over. A crowd was gathered on the main road near the civic center hoping for any bit of news. The usual helicopters were circling above like birds of prey.

"It's the biggest thing to happen in Kahana since President Harry S. Truman passed through in 1953 and stopped to give a speech right here in front of the post office, on this very spot," said old timer, Tom Johnson, looking straight into the camera. Johnson was interviewed by just about everyone with a microphone and a camera. He was on all the news channels and was getting more than his 15 minutes of fame.

Kahana was a quiet town where every day seemed like a Sunday. People seldom walked along the main street and those who did strolled as if they had no place to go and weren't in a hurry to get there. As Mac drove through town, he passed the small crowd in front of the post office. News crews stood near the cluster of civic buildings – the community center, the mayor's office, and the small auxiliary police station. A police car with flashing red and blue lights blocked the road that led up the hill to what were once the plantation camps. Wooden barriers were placed along the way to keep people from slipping through the roadblock. Yellow police tape cordoned off the area like a ribbon at the grand opening of a new shopping center.

Mac sped through town with his siren blaring and lights flashing. He passed the small strip mall, the bakery and snack shop, the park with the vegetarian restaurant, and turned up the long-neglected potholed gravel and dirt road that led to the Miyamoto home. A police officer moved the wooden barriers at an intersection to let Mac through. He passed old camp houses, most in disrepair, some boarded up.

A couple of boys were kicking a soccer ball in the middle of the road. He slowed down and motioned for them to get out of the way. They scattered like chickens as he drove by and stopped playing as they watched the white SUV go up the hill. A police car was parked across the road from Nobu's house.

Mac stopped and got out of his truck. "How's it going, Bobby?" he asked the officer standing beside the open door of the police car. "Anyone come out yet? Anybody talk to him?"

The officer shook his head. "No, Detective. It's been pretty quiet since he asked for you."

"Anyone in the house with him?" asked Mac.

"I don't know. We haven't seen or heard from anyone except Miyamoto."

"Where's Sgt. Souza?" asked Mac.

"She's at the other end of the road," said the officer. "We've sealed off all the streets, advised people not to leave their homes. So far everyone's staying away."

"Okay," said Mac. "Brian Alnas is on his way from Hilo. He should be here soon with Keith Ikeda. We've called Miyamoto's son. He's coming from Kona, said he'll get here as fast as he can. I'm going up to the house. Let's handle this without anyone getting hurt, okay? No shooting. Pass that on to the others. This isn't Hawaii Five-O, just sayin'!"

Mac pulled away and continued up the road to the house with the bamboo fence in the back. He parked in the driveway, got out of his truck, opened the door, and stood behind it. He gripped his Glock semi automatic revolver, but didn't take it out of its holster.

"Nobu," he called, "Its John McIntire. Put your gun away and come out and talk to me."

Nobu fired a shot through an open window, but the aim was high.

"Thanks for the warning shot, Nobu. Now put the gun down before you hurt somebody. Come on out so we can talk. You asked for me and I'm here."

Another shot rang out, this one closer. Mac could feel it whiz past. He ducked behind the open truck door. "Damn it!" he said softly. "I'm not kidding, Nobu," he yelled. "I'm telling you to put that gun down and come out of there."

"McIntire," called Nobu, "I'm not coming out."

"Nobu, why are you doing this? Let's talk about it before somebody gets hurt. Where's your wife and your daughter-in-law, your grandkids? Are they in there with you?"

"Never mind about them, they're here and they're okay. What do you care, anyway? Why am I doing this? Because my mother is dead and it's your fault. She died last night. A nurse from the home called and told me that you and the Bradford woman were there. My mother died because of you and that bitch. I don't know what you did or what you said to her, but whatever it was must have upset her. You couldn't leave her alone, could you? After all this time, why couldn't you just leave her alone?"

Mac was stunned. He didn't know that Sumi had died nor that Jessie had visited her.

"Look, Nobu, I'm sorry about your mother, okay? I didn't know. This is the first I've heard of it. If your wife and kids are in there with you, send them out. Put the gun down and come out with your hands in the air where I can see them. Then we can talk. You asked for me, remember?"

As Mac waited for a response, he heard a car slowly driving up the hill toward the house. It was Nobu's son. He stopped at the roadblock and was shocked to find his home surrounded by police and his family held hostage. He got out of his car and before the officers could stop him, ran to stand beside Mac behind the open door of the Expedition. He called to his father, but couldn't get Nobu to give himself up.

Finally, after another hour of negotiating and yelling back and forth, Nobu relented and the women came out crying hysterically with their hands in the air. Two boys who looked to be about 9 and 10 years old walked beside them.

Nobu continued to hold off the police for several more hours. Finally, after a couple of shots in the air, he agreed to give himself up. He came out of the house with his hands behind his head. "You're in a lot of trouble, braddah," said Mac, as he patted him down.

He handed him over to Sgt. Souza who read Nobu his rights and handcuffed him before placing him in her patrol car. Another officer retrieved the rifle from the front porch where Nobu had dropped it. Mac laid the weapon on the back seat of his truck and locked the doors. He told the other officers to remove the roadblocks, but to leave the yellow tape surrounding the Miyamoto yard.

Nobu's son, Albert, and his family, waited outside while Mac and Brian went into the house along with several officers. The police were in there for about an hour before they started the long drive back to Hilo.

16

MAC CALLED JESSIE AT SEVEN O'CLOCK THE NEXT MORNING. He knew he didn't say anything to upset Sumi Miyamoto. What had Jessie said to her and why did she go to see the old woman in the first place? He'd been up most of the night and was at his desk at 6 a.m. He already emptied the coffee pot once, had a fresh one brewing, and hadn't had any breakfast. Dammit! Jessie could derail the investigation if she didn't stop playing amateur sleuth. He didn't have a chance to say hello when she answered the phone because she saw his name on her caller ID.

"Hey, Mac, what's up? Mary and I were just talking about you. We're eating breakfast and reading about the hostage crisis in Kahana last night. We were just saying it's probably the biggest news since the discovery in the cave at South Point. Your name is all over the front page under the headline 'Police Make Arrest Over Gunfire in Old Kahana Town.' Have you seen the papers yet? "

It was annoying to hear her sounding so chipper and perky this early in the morning and not letting him get a word in. He interrupted her. "When did you go see Sumi Miyamoto?" he asked. "Did you know she died the other night?"

Jessie got up from the table and walked out of the kitchen as far from Mary as she could, stepped into her bedroom, and closed the door. "What? She died? I didn't know. No wonder Billy called yesterday and said he wouldn't be in for a few days. He didn't say why, only that he needed some time off. He probably thought I already knew. I figured it was because of the ruckus Sachi's brother caused. What was the shooting about?" she asked. "They didn't say on TV why Nobu Miyamoto was shooting up his neighborhood and the papers aren't giving a reason either. What happened?"

"Let's just say he was a little tense," said Mac. "I visited his mother two days ago. According to Nobu she was upset after you and I spoke with her. He blames us for her death. I know I didn't say or do anything to disturb her. In fact, she was so relaxed she fell asleep while I was talking to her. When were you there and what did you say to her?"

"It was the day before yesterday, same as you, I guess. Sachi said it was okay for me to go see her. Mrs. Miyamoto and I chatted for about an hour. She was fine when I left, I swear, Mac. In fact, she seemed glad to see me and I kissed her when I said goodbye. She remembered me from when Sachi and I were kids. I was going to tell you about it the next time I saw you." Jessie felt guilty about not being completely forthright with him, but she didn't want to tell him everything Sumi told her, not yet, anyway, and not over the phone.

"Okay, okay," said Mac. "But Nobu thinks that something we did or said caused her death. Apparently, a nurse called and told him we'd been there. According to the nurse I spoke with this morning, Mrs. Miyamoto died peacefully in her sleep that night, but she didn't give me a cause of death. I hate to think that one of us is the reason she had a coronary or something. I was only with her for a few minutes and asked a couple of questions, nothing to cause a heart attack. She was 84 years old and senile, for Christ's sake! It couldn't have been anything I did."

"Nor I," said Jessie, defensively. "She was in a pretty good mood when I left and even invited me to visit again. She certainly didn't seem senile."

"Nobu was agitated when I talked with him a while ago about your father's case," said Mac. "That probably set him off and he must have snapped when he learned that his mother died after we were there. I was planning to go back to Kahana to talk to him again, but I won't have to now. He's sitting in the county jail just down the street. I can see him anytime I want. It's very convenient."

Jessie ignored the sarcasm. "What'll happen to him?" she asked. "How long will you keep him?" She stammered, "Is he, did he, I mean, does he know anything about what happened to my father?"

"He didn't say anything about your father, Jess. We're still checking on the whereabouts of Miyamoto and his sons during that time. What do you know about the Miyamotos' possible involvement, anyway? I've never mentioned to you that they might be suspects."

"I thought they might be witnesses," said Jessie, "not suspects. That's why I went to see Mrs. Miyamoto. I figured she might know something because her husband and my father were pretty good friends. You know, she may have picked up on a little detail that didn't seem too important, but could shed some light on what happened, something she may not have wanted to share with the police, but might have told me. Perhaps something her husband mentioned to her. Anyway, what about Nobu? Is he going to be in jail for a long time because of what happened yesterday? Sachi and Billy must be devastated."

"Well, did she?" Mac asked impatiently.

"Did she what?"

"Tell you something that she might not have wanted to tell the police," he said, exasperated.

"I don't think so." She quickly changed the subject and asked again, "Is Nobu going to be in jail for a long time? Is he a suspect in my father's case?"

"We'll talk to him today and get a psychiatrist to see him. He has no prior arrests, so that's in his favor. We have to keep him at least 72 hours for the psychiatric evaluation. Then, he'll be arraigned. The judge will probably set bail, but that depends on what the shrink says. After that, it's up to his lawyer and the DA. If he makes bail, he can't go home unless the doctor says it's okay. He'll be charged with reckless endangerment and probably kidnapping and false imprisonment for holding his family hostage. We'll need to keep an eye on him. And, no, he's not a suspect in your father's case, not exactly, not yet."

"Well, you're making quite a name for yourself, aren't you, Detective McIntire? First there was South Point, now the shooting and hostage thing with Nobu Miyamoto. You're in the news all the time these days. You're getting to be a real celebrity." She laughed.

"It's not funny," said Mac. "We handle a lot of the usual stuff like cock fighting and domestic abuse and we have our fair share of drug and alcohol problems, crimes that are hardly mentioned on the news and get maybe a last page notice in the papers. Robberies are on the rise along with sexual assaults and murders, unfortunately, and those get more notice. This is my first shoot-out and hostage crises and it ain't like the movies. The news outlets apparently are eating it up, though."

"I don't remember crime being a big problem here," said Jessie. "We never even used to lock our doors, remember? What happened?"

"This isn't the Hawaii you and I grew up in, Jessie. Times have changed. What happened to your father 36 years ago? That was an isolated incident. But today it wouldn't be considered too much out of the ordinary. Hawaii is just like any other place. Sorry to be such a downer, but it's true. I may be a bit jaded, but I'm a cop, I see it all. By the way," he said, "we are making some progress on your father's case. Nothing definite yet, so don't get your hopes up. We're still trying to put the pieces together. I'll let you know when I have more info. I understand that you want this to be over before you go home. Jess, do me a favor and stay away from little old ladies in nursing homes. Let me do the investigating. I mean it. This amateur detective work of yours could backfire on you, just sayin.'"

"Okay, I promise I won't play detective anymore. I'll leave it to you. Do you think you're closer to finding out who murdered my father?"

"Like I just said, we have some ideas. We don't have a suspect yet. It was so long ago and most of the people who were around back then are not around today. We're following some leads. Your father had enemies, Jess. I hate to say this, but there may have been more than a few people who wanted him dead." There were some things he didn't want to discuss with her until he was sure. She'd have to learn about Allen Bradford's reputation as a philanderer sometime. It could wait. No telling how many irate husbands there were whose wives were the targets of Bradford's affections.

"Okay, keep in touch," said Jessie, "and call me when you know something, anything. My daughter Catherine will be here soon. She's staying a couple of weeks and I'd like for you two to meet. I hope to be making some decisions about the ranch by the time she goes home and I may even leave with her."

Mac was quiet for a few seconds. "Okay, see you later," he said.

After clicking off the phone, Jessie sat on the edge of the bed. Mac knew she'd visited Sumi. What would he say if he knew what they'd talked about? The poor woman might still be alive if I hadn't gone to see her and dredged up all those old memories. She buried her face in her hands.

Mac said that her father had enemies who had wanted him dead. Why and who were they? She never suspected anything. Her parents weren't the most affectionate couple. When she was a kid, Jessie figured that was the way married people were. Now, she wondered about the separate bedrooms and the fact that her mother hadn't even known whether or not her own husband had come home that night. What kind of a relationship was that? Her mother never talked much about her father once they moved to Hilo. Dammit! What did Mac mean when he said her father had enemies?

She couldn't dwell on it now. She had to pull herself together, go finish breakfast, and face Mary as if nothing had happened.

Mary was standing and leaning against the kitchen counter sipping her coffee and reading the front page of the Island Post. The Honolulu Times was spread out at Jessie's place at the table. The headlines for both papers were about the shootout in the old plantation town. The articles were short on facts. As usual, Mary seemed to know more than both the newscasts on TV and the newspapers combined. The South Point Gazette was fully mobilized. The rumor mill just about had Nobu Miyamoto tried and convicted for Allen Bradford's murder and for any other crime that was committed during the last 36 years. "Otherwise, why would he freak out?" wondered Mary aloud.

When Jessie said that Mac called to tell her that Sumi Miyamoto, Billy's mother-in-law, had died, Mary looked as though she'd been slapped, she was so stunned. It was the first time Jessie told Mary something that she didn't already know.

Jessie chuckled to herself and felt a perverse satisfaction in passing on some news that wasn't already in the South Point public domain. She should feel a little guilty at being gleeful, but she couldn't help it. As much as she liked Mary, she enjoyed the moment immensely.

Breakfast was cold and she wasn't hungry anymore, but finished eating for Mary's sake. She needed to be alone to think about what Mac had said. While Mary cleared the table, Jessie made a peanut butter and jelly sandwich and put it in a paper bag along with a slice of mango bread. "I'm going riding, Mary. I have some decisions to make and I need a place to think. I'll be back in a couple of hours and I won't need lunch. Thanks for breakfast, it was delicious."

17

Jessie saddled her horse and rode toward the cliffs wishing Billy wasn't away now when she needed him. Shame on me for worrying about my own problems, she chided herself. It was probably my fault that his mother-in-law died. She felt sorry for Billy and Sachi, but the realtor had received several offers for the ranch, all of them for less than the asking price and she needed Billy's opinion. Should she accept the best offer and just be done with it and go home to San Francisco?

Guy Matsumoto said the bids weren't as high as he'd like. He told her to be patient, the prospective buyers were trying to outbid each other and he expected them to offer even more than the amount listed if they kept it up long enough. "You know how people are," he said. "Everyone wants something for nothing. I'm not going to let that happen. Trust me."

Trust him? Was he leading her on? Did he really have buyers? She worried about depending on him. She'd have to rely on her own instincts if Billy didn't get back soon. The only property she ever sold was a condo in San Francisco, not that San Francisco real estate is cheap. Her two-bedroom condo in the Richmond District of the city sold for close to a million dollars a couple of years ago and she had a nearly million and a half mortgage on the house she was living in now. A five hundred acre ranch was a whole other matter. It was not just a small city lot with one building on it. There was all the land, the livestock. It was a big deal to her. She may have to figure it out for herself. She wanted to leave soon and didn't have time to waste.

Jessie was so deep in thought that she didn't realize how far she had ridden. She reined in the horse at the boundary of the Kanekoa and Bradford properties near the cliffs and saw a rider on horseback near the lava rock fence that separated the adjoining ranches. The man was on the other side of the fence with his back to her. He didn't hear her ride up until she called to him. "Joe, is that you?"

When he turned around and saw her, he smiled. "Ey, Jessie!" He was wearing a black cowboy hat, jeans, boots and a faded denim jacket over a Hawaiian shirt. She was used to seeing him in his pastor's uniform – white cotton, short-sleeved shirt usually open at the neck, and black slacks. Sometimes he even wore a tie. Joe was handsome, dark-skinned with wavy, black hair. He had a lean, chiseled jaw and perfect white teeth that showed every time he smiled, which was often. He proudly proclaimed to whoever would listen that he was "one of the last pure Hawaiians, a true son of the 'aina, the land."

"I almost didn't recognize you dressed like that," said Jessie. "You look like a real paniolo." She rode over to the stone fence and he met her on the other side.

He laughed. "Yeh, sometimes I get the urge to be a cowboy. What are you doing down here?"

"I needed to clear my head. This is where I come to do that. What about you?"

"Same as you. Even a servant of God has to get away to think once in a while. I come here to God's country for spiritual guidance."

"Did you hear what happened at Kahana last night?" asked Jessie.

"Yeh, I heard about it this morning," said Joe. "On the news they said the man did it because his mother had just died. They said Mac is the one who talked him into giving himself up."

Jessie nodded. "Mac does have a way about him. He's not trigger happy and he seems able to calm people down. It's a good thing he was there."

"He's good at handling some of those folks who live life on the edge," said Joe. "This isn't the first time he's diffused a situation that could have ended badly. I've read in the papers that he's done it before. Not a hostage situation like yesterday, but domestic disturbances, fights, things like that. He seems to have an innate sense of how to talk to people in a crisis. You know, Jessie, in my job I hear and see all kinds of things about the human condition. After more than 20 years as a pastor, I still don't know what drives people to do some of these crazy things."

"I'm sure you've seen it all, Joe."

"Not so much the criminal element, like Mac," he said. "Sometimes I get them before it becomes criminal. I listen to everyone who comes to me for guidance and I try to help them find peace and the answers they're searching for. In the end I'm just a man trying to do the Lord's work. All I can do is listen and try to steer them right. Sometimes I succeed and when I don't, that's where Mac's work often begins."

"What happened last night may have been my fault," said Jessie. "I went to see Nobu Miyamoto's mother to ask her about my father and her husband. They were friends. She and I had a long talk and she told me things I guess she's kept secret all these years. Maybe bringing up those old memories caused her to have a heart attack or something."

"It was her time, Jessie. They said on the news that she was in her 80s and in ill health. Why did that man think that shooting up his neighborhood and threatening people would help in any way? I don't like to question our Heavenly Father's methods, but sometimes I wonder, what is He thinking?"

"Mrs. Miyamoto seemed at peace after we talked and I thought she was glad to get some things off her chest," said Jessie. "She even thanked me for visiting her. I kissed her goodbye when I left. She died that night. Now, I wish I'd never gone to see her. Maybe she'd still be alive if I hadn't tried to play amateur detective. Mac warned me about that. I feel like the grim reaper."

"Don't blame yourself," said Joe. "Like I said, it was her time. I believe that everything that happens to us on this earth is predestined."

Jessie wasn't convinced of the predestined explanation and she still felt guilty.

She looked toward the cliff where the cave was. From where she sat astride her horse, she could see in the distance that people were still at the site and vehicles were parked in the pasture. "So, how's the dig coming along? I see they're still working at it. I know Mac is finished with his investigation there and my father's remains have been removed. Mac said last time he was here quite a few people were still digging around. Do they have any idea whose tomb it is?"

"Well, Jessie," said Joe, "it wasn't King Kamehameha or any other king, as we thought. They believe it was a chief of the people who landed here in the olden days, maybe some of the first people to come to this part of Hawaii Island about a thousand years ago. You know what? It's an ancestor of mine. Apparently, my ancestors settled on this dry, windswept plain. It must have been a shock to them to find such an inhospitable place after their long sea voyage from Tahiti. But this is where they landed and this is where they stayed and I am a part of this land and those people."

Michael Campbell told him he was like Cheddar Man, a caveman whose remains were found in a cave at Cheddar Gorge, England. Scientists compared the caveman's DNA with the DNA of the people living in that area in modern times and they found that he was the ancestor of some of them.

"It's the same with the person whose bones we found in the canoe in my cave," said Joe. "He and I share the same DNA. Michael said he must have been a great chief because of the way he was laid to rest, with all the trappings of someone important. I feel humble. I always knew my ancestors had settled here long ago, I just didn't know how far back it was."

"Joe, that's incredible. What are you going to do? I mean, aren't you afraid of people, even vandals, tramping around looking for the cave on your property? I'd hate to think of graffiti desecrating the burial ground of your ancestor. Look what they've done to some of the old buildings and the signs near the beach and the cliffs. Everything is covered with graffiti and bullet holes. How are you going to keep people away now that everyone knows where it is? All they have to do is hop over your barbed wire fence."

"They have it guarded 24/7 for now and there's not much left in the cave, anyway," he said. "They've shipped almost everything to the university. The canoe is still in there, though. They have to take it apart to get it out and rebuild it at the university or wherever they plan to display it. It was built inside the cave, probably long before the chief died. That's what they did in the old days. They prepared everything in advance. So, when the time came, there was no waiting. I'm thinking of cementing the opening so there'll be no way to get in. I haven't thought it out yet. You're right. I'll have to come up with something to keep intruders away. There will always be the curious, and, of course, vandals."

He requested that the university return the chief's remains when they were finished studying them. "I want to bury him on the land, to keep him with my family already buried here. Not just my parents, but my grandparents and other relatives before them. Some of the markers are just cairns of lava rock or coral with no names, nothing written. I guess it was before the *haole*, the white foreigners, came. This is our *ohana*, our family place. Someday Ipo and I will be buried here, too. Whoever he is, he should be with us."

"I don't see why they wouldn't let you bring the remains back here, Joe. You have a right to them, don't you? If I were you, I wouldn't want them displayed in a museum. I have an idea, though," Jessie said. "You should ask whoever leases your land to put a big, fierce-looking bull in the pasture near the road. That should keep trespassers away."

"Frank Gomes leases it," he said, laughing. "I'll ask him to do that."

"What about Michael Campbell," asked Jessie. "Is he going to continue looking for another big find?"

"Mike is going to quit," said Joe. "He followed what the petroglyphs told him and found what he was looking for, although it wasn't exactly what he expected. He's in his 80s, you know, and has been following this trail since he was a young man. I didn't know this at the time, but he visited my mother several times asking for permission to search our property. She always refused. That's why he dogged me after she died, thinking I'd be a softer target than she was and I was, but he's content now and planning to retire."

Jessie shared her sandwich and mango bread with him as they sat on the lava rock fence. When it was time to go, she said, "I'd like to come by the church before I leave for San Francisco. I need the kind of spiritual guidance that one can't get from riding horseback in God's country. Can you fit me in?"

"Any time you want. When are you leaving?" he asked as he jumped down from the fence and dusted crumbs off the front of his jacket.

"In a couple of weeks," she said. "I have to be at school for the new semester which starts in mid August. I need to be there early to prepare. Something is weighing heavy on my soul, Joe, and you're the only one I can tell my story to, at least for now." They hugged and got back on the horses. "I'll call you soon to make an appointment to stop by. Give Ipo my love, will you?"

On her way to the house, she rode to the spot where Maile's and Rod's ashes were scattered and stopped for a moment. "If you guys only knew what was going on down here," she said. "On second thought, you probably wouldn't believe it." Nudging the gelding, she headed home and found Tarzan unsaddling his bay mare.

"Howzit, Jessie? Where you been?" he asked as he helped her unsaddle Koa.

"Down at the cliffs talking to Joe Kanekoa. What about you?"

"I was up mauka checking on the cows. I drove them further up the mountain. It's time to rotate pastures. The calves are good now and back with the herd. They're all weaned and nobody's calling for their mamas anymore. Jessie, I've been meaning to talk to you. Do you have a minute?"

"Sure. What's up?" They sat on a bench in the tack room. Jessie took a deep breath. She loved the smell of saddles and leather and horses.

"Coupla things," said Tarzan, hunching over, elbows on his knees, hands cupping his chin. "Billy says you're planning to sell the ranch and I've been wondering when I'll have to leave. I've never worked any place else, been here since I was a teenager. I'll stay as long as you want me to, but I'll have to start looking for another job if you won't need me anymore. The other thing is I'm getting married and I thought we could live here. My girlfriend is a nurse. She works at Memorial Hospital in Pahala. The commute wouldn't be too bad, less than an hour and it's an easy drive from here. The cottage is big enough for the two of us now. We might need a bigger place later on. If you sell, we're going to have to find somewhere else to live, near the hospital probably or maybe near my folks. I'm not sure what to do. Any ideas?"

Jessie couldn't believe how self-absorbed she'd been. It had been all about her and Billy. She didn't think about Tarzan and how any decision she made would affect him. She stood and paced around the small room where saddles, blankets, and bridles took up most of the space.

"I'm sorry I got so lost in my own problems, Tarzan. It's true I'm thinking about selling, but I haven't decided yet. I have a realtor looking for a buyer. If I do sell, the new owner might want to keep you on. If I keep the place, I hope you'll stay and work for me just like you did for Uncle Rod. I'm trying to figure out what's best for all of us. Congratulations on your coming marriage, by the way. That's exciting news."

As with Billy and Mary, he was like family. Jessie didn't want to lose him, but he had to do what was best for him and his new wife. Of course they could live in the cottage, she told him. She'd even hire a contractor to remodel it for them and add more rooms.

"Tarzan, you know all the ranchers around here and they know you. Any of them could use someone with your skills and experience. You won't have any trouble finding another job. Mac could put in a word for you at Mauna Loa Ranch if it comes to that. As you know, Jerry Kamaka is his former brother-in-law and they're still good friends. I hear Mauna Loa has great benefits for their employees, including housing."

Tarzan still looked worried. "I'll take care of you as best I can," she said. "Don't worry, okay?"

"Thanks, Jessie. You're right. I'll ask around, see what's out there. Like I said, I'll stay until the very last day, no matter what, as long as you need me."

18

Jessie was driving to Kahana to pick up the mail and do some grocery shopping when her phone buzzed.

It was Mac. "Hey, sorry for the short notice. Do you have plans for tomorrow night? I thought we could go on that date Nobu Miyamoto interrupted the other day if you're free. How about it?"

"You're in a good mood," said Jessie. "What a difference from the last time we spoke."

"Well, that's what not enough sleep and too much coffee do for you. Sorry."

"Okay, you're forgiven. What about Nobu? Is he still in jail?"

"His son made bail, but he'll have to face charges. He's been seeing our shrink and is on medication. He could get jail time. It depends on what the DA and his lawyer work out. Didn't Billy tell you?"

"Billy's been pretty quiet since he got back. He's coming around slowly," said Jessie. "He doesn't seem to want to talk about it, so, I'm leaving him alone."

"They've had a tough time, that's for sure. Better let him sort things out. Anyway, what about our night out? Are we on?" asked Mac.

"Sure, I'm looking forward to it. What time and where are we going?"

"I thought we'd go somewhere along the Kohala Coast. When was the last time you did the tourist thing? You hardly ever leave the ranch. I think it's time for you to have a little fun. I'll pick you up at five o'clock, okay?" Jessie heard him take a deep breath. "We can walk on the beach and soak up some salt air. See you then."

So, Jessie mused, she had a date with Mac, her high school sweetheart. Life had come full circle. They were seniors in high school when they last dated and now they were 50 years old. She didn't know about Mac, but she was already receiving mail from the American Association of Retired Persons and ads for hearing aids. If that wasn't enough to make a girl feel old, what was? I hope it isn't too late for a little romance, she thought, because I could really use some. She felt her cheeks redden. It's just dinner and salt air. What am I thinking? Romance? She laughed out loud.

There were more important things to think about now that Billy was back. He returned to the ranch a week after his mother-in-law's funeral. Jessie had called and asked if she could attend the service. He said it was only for the family – him, Sachi, and Nobu and his wife and kids, thanks, anyway. His brother-in-law, Isaburo, was ill and couldn't make the trip from Seattle. Just immediate family, he reiterated, at the Buddhist cemetery in Kahana. Jessie sent flowers.

On Billy's first day back he told Jessie it was sad, but a relief that Sumi died. "She was sick for a long time and her kidneys finally shut down. The doctors warned us about it. Sachi's taking it pretty hard. It'll be a while before she recovers."

"It was kidney failure?" Jessie asked, incredulously. When he said yes, she was so relieved she nearly hugged him. If he'd said it was a heart attack, she would have felt responsible for Sumi's death. She'd be sure to tell Mac it was kidney failure, not a coronary, thank God!

His mother-in-law's mind wasn't always clear, Billy said. Half the time he didn't think she knew where she was or even who she was. "But she always recognized Sachi. It was amazing. Whenever Sachi walked into the room, Sumi's eyes lit up, even on her bad days. Because of her dementia, she rarely recognized anyone else."

Jessie didn't comment. Sumi recognized her and seemed pretty clear-headed the day she was there. Why did people think the poor woman was senile?

She gave Billy a few days to settle in, then, told him about her talk with Tarzan. "Don't worry, I'll speak to him," he said. "Right now, I have some catching up to do. I'll be in my office if you need me." He felt like telling her that he just wanted to be alone to get some work done. They weren't playmates anymore and she was his boss now, so, he didn't.

Jessie caught the hint. She wondered if there would still be the cozy coffee klatches at the kitchen table as they'd had the last couple of months. He was still grieving and she'd let him be until he was ready to join Mary and her again for those few minutes they all enjoyed every morning.

"I'm glad you're back," she said. "We've missed you. Mary and I tried to rope Tarzan into joining us for coffee while you were gone, but he opted out."

Billy chuckled. "Tarzan was smart to say no. You guys are too much of a distraction. Just let me get some of this stuff cleared up and I'll be back for your morning gossip fests, all right?"

"Okay, we'll keep the coffee hot."

Billy and Sachi had been through a lot lately with Nobu's arrest and Sumi's death. If he wanted some space, she'd let him have it. She, of all people, knew what it was like to deal with so much adversity at one time and was glad to be past that stage and moving on.

Billy was eager to catch up after his week away. He called Guy Matsumoto and warned him not to play games, there were other realtors on the island they could hire when his contract with them expired. "Just come up with a buyer and the asking price and quit fooling around," he said. "Property in this area goes for at least $10,000 an acre and we're only asking eight thousand. It's not negotiable."

"Just happens that I have some clients who want to view the property," said Guy. "Can we set up something for next week? There are two of them and I was thinking Tuesday and Wednesday around 10 a.m. each day. Will that work for you guys?"

"Sounds good to me," said Billy, "the sooner the better. I'll check with my boss and get back to you."

He called Frank Gomes and Jerry Kamaka. Both said they were interested in leasing, not buying. He told them Jessie wanted to sell. If she changed her mind, she'd definitely consider leasing to them. He knew Jessie would be disappointed. She'd been hoping one of them would buy at least some of the land.

After giving Billy an hour to settle in, Jessie knocked on the open door of his office while he was still on the phone. He had staked out a small space near the tack room for his office when he first became manager of Bradford Ranch. He sat on a swivel chair at an antique roll top desk on which rested a laptop computer and neatly stacked papers and ledgers.

"May I come in?" she asked. He was holding the phone to his ear. He nodded and pointed to a chair next to his desk. "You'll be the first to know if she changes her mind, Frank. I'll keep in touch," he said into the phone and clicked off.

He turned to Jessie. "I have some good news and some bad news, bad news first. Both Frank Gomes and Jerry Kamaka are only interested in leasing. The good news is Guy Matsumoto wants to bring a couple of clients to see the ranch next week. I told him that I'd have to check with you."

"Tell him yes," she said. "It's about time, but you give them the tour, Bill. You'll know exactly what to tell them and how to answer their questions. I'll make myself scarce and leave it to you, okay?"

She took a deep breath. "Finally," she said, leaning back in the chair and stretching her legs. "I hope we get an offer, a good one. What do you think?"

"We'll see," said Billy. "Okay, I'll give them the tour. Let's keep our fingers crossed and hope we get lucky. I'll do my best."

Jessie stood up and looked around. A framed photograph of a horse and rider on a grassy hill hung on the rough, natural wood wall above the desk. A tall, four-drawer, antique oak file cabinet stood in a corner. She hadn't been in his office since she arrived at the ranch. "I've always liked it in here," she said. "It's neat and organized, unlike Uncle Rod's office. I should visit you more often. It's so...Zen-like."

As she turned to leave she said, "All right, set up the appointments with Guy and let me know how it goes. I want you to know how lucky I feel to have you helping me, Bill. Really, I appreciate everything you do."

He looked embarrassed and fiddled with the papers on his desk.

"Okay," said Jessie, "I can tell you're busy. I'll leave you alone. I'm sorry to bother you so soon after I told you I'd give you some space. I wanted to know if you'd heard from Guy. Now that question has been answered, and I, uh...well, see you later."

The following week Billy took Guy Matsumoto and his clients on tours of the ranch.

The first client was a studio executive from Los Angeles who was looking for an island get-a-away. He liked the location because it was remote and private, but even before they started the tour, he said the shabby house would have to be torn down. His guests would be Hollywood A-Listers and he couldn't entertain them in a shack like that. The place needed a complete overhaul. He'd have a main house built, a big one, and some guest cottages, put in a swimming pool and tennis courts, maybe a 9-hole golf course. All the other buildings on the property would have to go, too. He didn't want the cattle and he intended to bring a string of thoroughbred horses to replace the nags that were there.

Billy disliked the man the minute he stepped out of the realtor's Cadillac SUV. All it took was one look at his hair implants, his phony salon tan, and his alligator hide cowboy boots. Billy sneered at the shiny, new boots. Probably cost a couple thousand bucks and they wouldn't last one day on the range. He made up his mind that no matter what the offer was, even if it was for the asking price of $4 million, he would advise Jessie not to accept it. The guy was not worthy of Rod's ranch. He was planning to turn it into a resort.

When Billy heard the client whisper to Guy that he'd pay $3.5 million, he could barely contain himself, he was so happy. He knew Jessie would refuse it.

They were near the cliffs when the client got out of the truck, looked around one last time, and asked where the beach access was. Guy tried to stammer his way out of that one as he explained that there was only rocky coastline and no beach at the bottom of the jagged cliffs. Billy chuckled to himself as he listened, turned the Land Rover around, and headed back to the house, deliberately hitting every bump along the way. He wanted the annoying guy from Hollywood to be as uncomfortable as possible. What a jerk.

The next day they took the second client out. The man was a rancher from Kona looking for a wedding present for his son and new daughter-in-law. His plans were a bit simpler than the studio executive's. He wanted to raze the old house and build a new one for the newlyweds, otherwise, the place was fine. They could make more improvements later. He offered $3.2 million, $800,000 less than asking. Too bad, thought Billy, Jessie wouldn't accept that either. The man seemed like a nice guy and at least he would keep the place as a ranch and not a playground for movie stars. He'd talk to her and see if she'd negotiate this one and tell Guy to try to get the client closer to the price Jessie wanted.

When Guy called a few days later and learned that Jessie rejected both offers, he said he'd keep working on it. "If he can come up with something before his contract expires next month, great," Billy told her, "otherwise we'll hire another realtor, Jessie. We'll find a buyer. You might have to negotiate a little bit if you really want to sell, though. You know that, don't you?"

19

JESSIE WAS READY FOR A NIGHT OUT. HER DILEMMA WAS TO decide what to wear for an evening with Mac. She'd been wearing jeans, denim work shirts, and t-shirts since arriving at the ranch. Was anything in her closet appropriate for a date? She looked through the few things hanging haphazardly from wire hangers and found the pickings were sparse. Having a social life when she was packing for the trip to Hawaii was the last thing on her mind. It was supposed to be a quick visit to settle her uncle's affairs and here it was nearly two months later with no end in sight.

She decided on a white blouse she'd bought during her shopping trip with Sachi, a beige knee-length cotton skirt, and sandals. Nothing dressy, but it would do. The big resorts were on the Kohala Coast. If that's where Mac was taking her, people would be wearing flip flops and shorts. She'd fit right in.

Mary left early for a dental appointment, so Jessie didn't have to explain why she was getting dressed up, putting on makeup, and shaving her legs for the first time in two months. It didn't matter what Billy and Tarzan thought. Still, she was glad when Billy knocked at the kitchen door and said he was leaving for the day. Shortly after he left, Tarzan drove out of the yard. Probably going to Moon's Beachhead Inn or to see his girlfriend, she figured.

She went into the bathroom, propped up her foot on the sink, and began shaving her legs. She didn't have her electric razor and used Rod's safety razor. She nicked herself a few times, but it was way past due.

She was ready when Mac drove up the road ten minutes early. She looked out the window and saw him park a blue BMW. A BMW? Macho Mac with his cowboy boots and faded jeans? She smiled and watched him get out of the car and reach in the back seat for a bouquet of flowers.

"Pink roses, my favorite," she said when she met him at the door. "Thank you, how sweet." He kissed her lightly on the cheek and she went into the kitchen for a vase, came back to the living room, and placed the flowers in the middle of Mark Twain's monkey pod table.

"The florist told me pink is for friendship and red is for romance," Mac said. "I wanted the red ones, but I thought that might scare you off, so I settled for friendship. That can change at any time."

"I love the pink ones," she said, picking up a sweater and her purse. "I'm ready, shall we go?"

As they drove toward South Point Road, she said, "I like your car. I never figured you for a Beamer, though. I have a red one at home."

"It's my son's," he said. "I drive it sometimes while he's away at school, you know, to charge the battery."

They were quiet as they headed to the main highway. Finally, he glanced at her, looking her up and down. "You look nice, beautiful, in fact. Great legs. I'd forgotten. You should wear skirts more often."

"I do in the city. Skirts aren't exactly practical when doing ranch chores and riding horses." She laughed.

He was wearing a blue aloha shirt and khaki slacks. "You look good, too, Mac, very handsome. I haven't seen you without your denim jacket and jeans since I've been here. And not even cowboy boots tonight," she noted, checking out his brown loafers. "Very nice."

"Yeah, well, I may not be able to play cowboy detective much longer. The chief is talking about having us plain clothes guys dress up, although he hasn't decided yet whether he wants us to dress alike, like the Secret Service, or to wear coats and ties, like on "Law and Order" on TV. He thinks we look scruffy and unprofessional. Personally, I think he watches too much television."

She smiled. "I kinda like the rugged cowboy look myself. I'd hate for that to change," she teased, leaning back in her seat. "So, tell me about Nobu Miyamoto. Anything new?"

Mac said there would be a trial unless there was a plea bargain. "No one was hurt and there was no property damage, but he scared the hell out of the neighbors, most of whom had only seen action like that on TV or in the movies. He put his family through hell. In nearly 25 years of police work, that was my first shoot out. Nobu's a senior citizen with a clean record, until now, that is. You never know what the district attorney and the judge will decide. I hear Billy has hired a very pricey defense attorney from Honolulu. I wouldn't be surprised if Nobu got off with only a slap on the wrist. I think he should get some jail time, just sayin'.

"Here's something else," he said. "Billy Gonsalves' uncle is a criminal court judge in Hilo. Did you know that?" He glanced at her. Jessie shook her head and said, "I had no idea."

"I've known Judge Gonsalves for years," said Mac. "I never knew he and Billy were related. He wouldn't be allowed to preside over a trial involving a relative, even one by marriage, conflict of interest and all. He could have some influence, though. You never know."

"Billy and I just about grew up together, him and Danny and me," Jessie said. "But I've realized lately that I really don't know that much about his personal life anymore. We talk about Uncle Rod, the ranch, local gossip, stuff like that, but not much else. I've never met anyone in his extended family except his father who worked for my uncle. I never even met his mother. Of course, both his parents have passed away."

"It turns out that Judge Gonsalves and Billy's father were brothers," said Mac. "Getting back to Nobu, it was interesting going into his house. I expected it to be like the Hasegawa home. I interviewed an Elsie Hasegawa a while ago. She was Tom Johnson's maid way back when and a friend of Sumi Miyamoto's. Her place was pretty bare, with only two chairs and a table in the living room and a couple of tatami pillows like the ones you sit on at Japanese restaurants. She did have a giant flat-screen TV, but it was the only modern thing I saw in that house.

"Nobu's home was different, really upscale, with nice furniture, pictures on the walls and rugs on the floors. There were some antiques and artwork, a porcelain vase that looked expensive – the kind you see in Asian art galleries. The back yard is enclosed with bamboo fencing. It's shut off from the other camp houses, sort of like a private retreat. There's a koi pond and all kinds of flowers, bamboo, ferns, ti leaves, and moss that looks like velvet. Near the koi pond is a stone lantern made of white granite like they have at Japanese tea gardens, really beautiful. It was surreal being in there."

"I remember that garden," said Jessie. "I used to go there with Sachi when we were kids. We'd do our homework on a bench near the koi pond. Her mother lit a candle in the stone lantern for us, it smelled of incense. Mr. Miyamoto made that lantern and gave it to his wife as a gift. Sachi told me he ordered the granite shipped from a quarry in Oregon. The garden was beautiful, an oasis in the midst of the ramshackle camp houses with their postage-stamp-size yards. I never went in the house, though."

Mac continued, "I told the investigators not to ransack the place, to put everything back the way they found it. We didn't find any other guns. He had just the one shotgun and some ammo, which surprised me because it seems that everyone owns an assault weapon these days even with Hawaii's strict gun laws. He was about to run out of ammo, that's probably why he quit when he did. A lethal-looking antique Samurai sword was hanging on the wall. We also found a bow and arrow. There were no drugs or paraphernalia."

"Hmmm, Nobu must be a hunter," said Jessie. "A lot of hunters use bows and arrows here on the Big Island."

"Yeah, looks that way or maybe his son. We confiscated all the weapons. He'll probably get the sword and the bow and arrow back eventually, but not the rifle."

They turned onto the highway and were driving toward Kona on their way to the Kohala Coast. "How's the sale of the ranch going? What are your plans when and if you sell?"

"Actually, I've decided to sell. I can't run a ranch, don't even want to. If it weren't for Billy handling things, it would be a mess. I was in a panic when he was gone for only a week after his mother-in-law died. I just want to go back to San Francisco."

"Any offers?"

"We've had a few inquiries. The problem is no one wants to pay the asking price. I'm not budging, though. We're already asking several thousand dollars less per acre than some of the other ranches around here. It's only been on the market for a few weeks. I thought things would move faster than they have. Guy Matsumoto, my realtor, tells me it could take months."

"You don't have to run it by yourself," Mac said. "You have Billy and Tarzan. You'd just keep track of everything. You could do it. I hate the thought of you selling."

"Billy has shouldered a lot of the responsibility for the last couple of years," said, Jessie, "including keeping the books and paying the bills in addition to running the ranch. I never realized that my uncle had given him so much responsibility. He's done a great job, but he can't do that forever. Besides, he needs to move on to a bigger operation than Bradford Ranch. He only stayed this long out of respect for Uncle Rod.

"Your brother-in-law, Jerry, by the way" she continued, "put Mauna Loa Ranch on our list of possible buyers, but they changed their minds and decided they want to lease instead. My neighbor Frank Gomes backed out of buying, too, and is only interested in leasing grazing land. So, they're both out of the picture. I'm disappointed. I was depending on one of them offering to buy at least some acreage."

Mac was quiet for a while. "Jerry didn't tell me that the Mauna Loa Ranch Corporation was thinking of buying your place. After you mentioned it, I asked him about it. A lot of ranches have gotten into the export business as well as providing beef to the Islands and the Mainland, that's why they need more land. It's cheaper for them to lease than buy."

"I know," Jessie said, "but that doesn't help me because I want to sell."

"Are you sure you don't want to be a rancher in charge of your own corporation?" Mac asked. "You Mainlanders probably don't know it, but Hawaii is one of the biggest beef producing states in the country. That's why so many ranches are becoming incorporated."

"I wasn't aware that Hawaii was such a big beef producer, but I don't want to be a rancher. I just want to go home."

"What about the cattle?" he asked. "How many head do you have? Will the herd be part of the deal?"

"Aren't you the inquisitive one," she teased. "Are you interested in becoming a rancher, Detective? To answer your question, there's about a thousand head. Billy thinks we should sell them separately. I don't know anything about cows. I'd probably end up naming them and keeping them as pets. It's better for Billy to handle it."

"That would be a first," said Mac, "giving them names. Rule number one – never name anything you're going to eat."

20

MAC TURNED OFF THE HIGHWAY AND INTO A DRIVEWAY WITH a sign that read Kohala Coast Beach Resort. The man at the guard shack asked if they were guests at the hotel. When Mac said they were just having dinner, he handed Mac a temporary parking permit and waved them through.

"The Kohala Coast Resort is one of my favorite places," he said. "I hope you like it. Have you been here before?"

"No, I don't think so."

Jessie had never been to this resort, but her big, white wedding was held next door at the Lani Kea Hotel. She wondered if Mac was married at the Kohala Coast. She didn't ask.

When they pulled up to the entrance, a valet opened her door and helped her out of the car, while another took the keys from Mac, got behind the wheel, and sped off like he was trying out for NASCAR. Mac shook his head as he watched the BMW race away.

"If he knew that you're a cop," Jessie said, laughing, "he wouldn't be speeding like that."

"It probably wouldn't make any difference," said Mac. "Cops get no respect. I shoulda been a fireman. Now, those guys get respect." He took her hand as they walked into the hotel lobby.

A trio was performing at the Beach Lounge while they sipped Mai Tais. They sat on a sofa, Mac seated slightly behind her. He pulled her close and wrapped his arms around her waist. Jessie leaned back, her arms resting on his forearms. It felt natural, as if the years hadn't passed and they were young and carefree. They pretended to listen to the music, but neither of them was concentrating on the musicians strumming their guitars and ukuleles. Each was thinking about how intimate this was, wrapped in each other's arms and trying to be casual about it.

"Let's not talk about the ranch or the investigation or Nobu Miyamoto," said Jessie after they were seated for dinner. "Let's pretend we don't have a care in the world and enjoy a great dinner." She raised her wine glass. "Here's to old friends."

"To old friends," said Mac, looking into her eyes over the rim of his glass.

Later, as they walked barefoot on the white sand beach, it was too dark to see Mauna Kea, the highest peak in the Hawaiian Islands, looming in the distance, but they could see the twinkling lights along the coast across the wide expanse of ocean. During the day, the views of the sea and the snow-capped mountains were an awesome sight. At night, illuminated by the lights of the resort and gas-fueled tiki torches on the beach, the ambience was more romantic than awesome. A light breeze rustled the leaves of the tall coconut trees near the hotel behind them. Jessie looked up at the star-studded sky.

"We can't see the stars this clearly in San Francisco," she said. "There's too much fog and too many lights. This is what draws the tourists to Hawaii, the spectacular views, the ambience. It's so romantic. I guess everyone is looking for a little romance."

Mac cleared his throat and asked, "Uh, speaking of romance, are you, uh, seeing anyone in San Francisco, anyone serious?"

"Not right now and I'm not looking, really. I've had a few relationships through the years. Somehow nothing seemed right. What about you?"

"Same as you, nothing seemed right," he said.

They walked to the water's edge and let the waves wash over their feet. The water felt almost warm. He turned and took her in his arms. "You know how I feel about you, don't you? It's not just me is it? Am I picking up the wrong signals?" He kissed her.

She leaned into him and breathed in his scent, it was fresh and clean. He wasn't wearing cologne or after shave. "I've wanted to do this ever since that first day at South Point," he said, pulling her closer. "Me, too," she whispered. They kissed again. She knew this was bound to happen, imagined what it would be like, and it felt good, but she'd be leaving soon and… She pulled away. "I think we should be getting back, don't you? We have a long drive ahead." He let her go, but they held hands as they walked to the hotel.

They waited for the valet to swing by with the car. It came to a screeching stop in front of them. The drive along the highway toward the South Point turnoff was quiet, with each of them wondering how the evening was going to end. Would they just say goodnight at her door and he'd drive off to Mauna Loa Ranch? Would it be awkward? Should she ask him in? What then? Dammit, I'm acting like a kid. This isn't my first time around the track.

Mac broke the silence. "Jessie, I know you didn't want to talk about anything serious tonight. There are a couple of things we need to clear up and we may as well do it now."

"Like what?"

"Like the investigation into your father's death. We have to be realistic. The case may never be solved. We have a few leads we're working on, and as I told you before, I thought we were making progress and we were, but things are at an impasse now.

"I've interviewed some people who were around at the time who knew your dad. There are only a few of them, most are elderly, and they have some information, but nothing on which to build a case. None of them knows what happened that day. Even old Tom Johnson doesn't have a clue."

"I know you've worked hard, Mac, and I'm grateful. Don't worry. I can live with whatever the outcome is."

"The best I might be able to offer you," he said, "is that at least you know what happened to your father even if we may never know who did it or why. Now you can give him a proper burial. I hope I'll have some news for you before you leave for San Francisco." He glanced at her. "If you do leave, that is."

"I'll be leaving," she said, "and soon. That's the plan."

About halfway to the South Point turnoff, it started to rain. It began with the plop of a single raindrop on the windshield. Within seconds it was falling in sheets so that by the time they turned off the highway and were driving toward the ranch, it was pouring so hard they could hardly see through the windshield. That's the way it is in the tropics, one minute the weather is balmy and mild, the next minute a storm of monsoonal proportions was beating against the window panes and then a few minutes later the sun comes out again. When Mac pulled up in front of the house it was still pouring.

"We can wait in the car until it lets up or make a run for it, you choose," he said.

"Let's make a run for it," said Jessie. "You're coming in, aren't you? Wait for the rain to stop before going back to Mauna Loa. I'll worry about you driving in this downpour. At least come in for a brandy until it eases up."

Mac shifted in his seat and faced her. "If I come in, Jess, I'm staying the night. It's up to you."

She was quiet for a moment. "We'll see. I'll make some coffee for the brandy," she said, opening the car door.

They were dripping wet by the time they reached the front porch. As they entered the living room, slipping out of their wet shoes, she gestured toward the fireplace. 'You start the fire and I'll go make some coffee. It'll warm us up."

Mac stopped her as she started to walk across the room. "Jessie, do you really think we need a fire and coffee to warm us up? Come here." He pulled her toward him and kissed her. Later, as they lay in a tangle of sheets and Maile's quilt on the four-poster bed, they saw that their clothes formed a trail all the way from the living room.

It was still raining. The downpour sounded like someone was pelting the corrugated metal roof with a bucket of marbles. "I'm glad I didn't drive back to Mauna Loa tonight," said Mac. "The rain sounds fierce, but that's not the reason I stayed. I drive in rain storms like this all the time. It's my job. I stayed because I wanted to make love with you, Jessie. I've been waiting a long time for this."

"I'm glad you're here," she said, nestling in his arms. "What took us so long? We wasted a lot of time this summer and I'll be leaving soon."

"I've been hoping that you wouldn't sell the ranch," he said, "so you'd have to stay longer to figure things out and hoped that you'd realize you liked it here so much you couldn't bear to leave. I'm just a small time cop. I can't compete with the big city and the sophisticated life you live. We got sidetracked years ago, but we're here now." He sat up and turned to her.

"Look, I'm not any good at this. I'm a straight talking kind of guy, so I'll just say it – I love you. I've loved you since we were kids. I want you to stay. Marry me. We could live together for a while if you want, try it out, then get married. Either way, it's up to you. I don't care, I just want to be with you. Now you know how I feel. Can you see yourself making a life here with me? This is your home, after all. This is where your roots are. I know we could make it work."

"Mac," she said, reaching for his hand and holding it against her cheek. "San Francisco is my home. My work is there. I can't think about falling in love. I'll admit I've thought about you through the years and wondered what might have been. I do have feelings for you. Making love with you tonight was all I thought it would be. It was wonderful. Is it love? I don't know.

"I'm going to sell this place and go back to my life, my job, my daughter. I'm not cut out to be a rancher or a CEO like you and Billy said, or anything close to that. I'm not even sure I want to be married again. I didn't like it the first time. And living together? Are you kidding? Here, with all the gossips?"

"You analyze things too much, Professor. Its love, all right," he said, kissing her again. "Don't make it sound so complicated. Who cares about gossip? It's just talk."

As the rain pelted the window panes, they lay side by side under the quilt. Jessie rested her head in the crook of his arm as she ran her foot along the length of his leg, enjoying the feel of him. She hadn't felt so comfortable, so trusting, with a man in a long time.

"I know it's just talk," she said. "I'm not used to living in a place where people know everything about you. In the city I can be anonymous. Here everybody knows what you had for breakfast. What would they say if we lived together? I hate to think. And for your information, my life is not as sophisticated as you imagine. It's pretty mundane, actually, teaching, grading papers, and holding office hours. That's my life in the big city."

"The heck with the gossip," he said. "We could have a good life together. I'm crazy about you, Jess. I always have been. That's all that matters." He pulled her on top of him. They made love again, only this time it was more urgent, as if it might be the last time.

Before they fell asleep, Jessie whispered, "Rain or shine, you'll have to leave early before anyone comes because if they find out you spent the night, it'll be all over the grapevine. I'll set the alarm for six o'clock. That'll give you enough time to get dressed and leave before Billy comes at seven. Mary usually shows up around eight. Sometimes they get here earlier."

"Why are we whispering?" he asked.

"I don't know," she said. "I guess I was thinking this is probably the first time, ever, that sex happened in this room."

Jessie woke to the sound of a truck coming up the road and bright sunlight streaming through the window. Had she dreamed about the rain storm? She glanced over at Mac who was still asleep, lying on his side facing her, his arm outstretched as if reaching for her. It was nearly seven o'clock. They'd slept through the alarm! "Oh, no, dammit!"

"Mac! Mac! Wake up! Someone's coming." She looked out the window and saw Tarzan getting out of his truck. "It's only Tarzan. He must have spent the night at his girlfriend's. It's okay."

Mac was up and dressed and looking for his shoes. He slipped his bare feet into his loafers. "Jessie, I don't get it. What do you care what they think? You're the boss around here and we're consenting adults."

"You wouldn't understand. Thank God it's Tarzan. But you'd better go because if Mary gets here before you leave, we'll be in the headlines of the South Point Gazette before you reach the main road."

"The South Point _what_?"

"I'll explain later. Hurry!"

"About last night," she said as she pushed him toward the door, "we'll talk about it later, okay? I was awake most of the night thinking about us."

"I haven't slept so soundly in years," laughed Mac, "but I'm thinking about us now." He reached for her.

She rolled her eyes and pulled away. "Just go. Please. Mary will be here any minute. We'll talk later about…things."

"Things?" he said. "You're nuts, you know that? I bare my soul, declare my love for you, ask you to marry me, and you call it things?"

"Not now, Mac. Please."

"Okay, okay." He put his arms around her waist, pulled her toward him and kissed her on the mouth. "I'll take the back road so I won't run into Mary," he said. He was out the door in seconds.

Jessie made the bed and tidied up the room, making sure there were no signs of Mac having been there. She put on a t-shirt and jeans and walked down the hall to put the coffee on.

Mac was right. She was the boss. Why should she care what they thought? She was too old to behave like a teenager. She just didn't want to be the topic of conversation the next time Mary made a phone call to one of her friends. As kind-hearted as Mary was, not only was she a gossip, she was the Hawaiian version of Sherlock Holmes. Jessie was sure Mary would spot something, some clue, that Mac had stayed the night. She didn't have time to worry about it now. She poured a cup of freshly brewed coffee, sat down at the table, and opened her laptop.

Her cell phone buzzed. "I just saw Mary in my rear view mirror as I drove down the back road," said Mac. "She was going through the gate toward the house. She didn't see me. Your reputation is safe." He laughed as he clicked off.

Jessie was sitting at the kitchen table reading her email and pouring her second cup of coffee when Tarzan knocked on the kitchen door. He handed her a newspaper. "Thought you'd be interested in the headlines," he said. Jessie asked him not to mention to anyone about Mac being there.

"No worries, Jessie. I know how it is, been an item myself a coupla times. If you change toothpaste around here, everybody knows about it." He smiled and said, "I'll keep your secret."

"Want to come in for a cup of coffee?" she asked.

"Nah, thanks. I'd better get started with the chores. Billy will be here soon. See you."

Mary came in with more newspapers. She saw that Jessie was already reading one, so she spread hers out on the table, poured herself some coffee and sat down across from Jessie. The headlines were about Joe Kanekoa's cave at South Point. One headline read "South Point Cave Burial Site of Ancient Hawaiian Chief." Another blared "Archaeologist Discovers Royal Tomb at South Point."

Mary read aloud to Jessie. "It says here that the cave is not the tomb of King Kamehameha." She glanced up at Jessie, shook her head, and rolled her eyes. "Of course, we already knew that, didn't we? Kamehameha wasn't from around here. His tomb is probably in Kohala where he was born. These reporters, they never get anything right. I hope they never find him, may he rest in peace, poor soul. They'll dig him up, put him on display. It'll be just awful." She shook her head and clicked her tongue.

She added more sugar and milk to her coffee, looked down at the newspaper and continued reading aloud. "It is thought to be the burial site of a high ranking chief of one of the first groups to arrive in the Hawaiian Islands about a thousand years ago."

"Get this," she said, her voice rising. "It also says that DNA testing proved the ancient chief is an ancestor of the owner of the property on which the cave was found, Reverend Joseph Kanekoa of the Hawaiian Congregational Church at Waikea on Hawaii Island. Jessie, can you imagine that? Joe is *ali'i,* royalty."

Mary was so excited about the news that Jessie didn't have the heart to tell her that she already knew all about it from Joe Kanekoa himself.

21

"Boss," said Brian as he and Mac sat at their desks. "I looked up the whereabouts of Ed Hampton, one of the guys Bradford fired. According to his son, Junior, Hampton was laid up at Queen's Hospital in Honolulu with a bad back when Bradford disappeared. I checked and sure enough, the guy was having back surgery at the time. I also found out where the Miyamoto sons were when Allen Bradford died." He handed some papers to Mac.

"Looks like Nobu was at the university on Oahu, just like he said. Isaburo, the doctor, was in medical school at UCLA, and the youngest son, Albert, died in Viet Nam in 1972, six years before Bradford was murdered. So that clears them of any involvement. The oldest son, Takeshi, known as Tak, was the only one still here and working at the plantation mill and that explains why the Marine sergeant saw only him and his father driving through Waikea that morning."

He handed more notes to Mac and continued. "I double-checked everything and except for Tak, the brothers were nowhere near South Point or Kahana or even on the island. And listen, I also learned that Tak had black belts in jiu jitsu, judo, and karate. Turns out he was a stocky, muscular guy and pretty strong. Maybe strong enough to bear most of the load helping Miyamoto carry the body down the cliff to the cave, if that's what happened. He might have been able to do it by himself. So what do you think?"

"It fits with our theory that it took only two people. As for the other sons, maybe they weren't involved in the murder, but how about the cover-up? Just sayin'."

"Even if Nobu knew about the murder and we can prove it," said Brian, "since he wasn't here when it happened, what do we do? Arrest him? He wasn't involved in the murder. I'd bet on it. He may have learned of it later and kept quiet. So, his crime is that he didn't tell. He's pretty old and in enough trouble as it is, don't you think?"

"Sixty-seven is not considered that old these days," said Mac. "Anyway, it looks like it was Hideo and Tak, all right, but everything we've got is circumstantial. We need something definite or we'll never know for sure who killed Bradford. The captain told me today that Chief Lindsey wants us to close the case. They think we've been spending too much time chasing down leads that take us nowhere. I'm not ready to let it go yet."

"We've been working our asses off," said Brian, "and we haven't been on the case that long, not even two months. We need more time. I was hoping the Ed Hampton angle would lead us somewhere and that if he wasn't the one who killed Bradford, maybe he helped put the body in the cave. He wasn't even around, though, so that eliminates him. Now, we're back to square one with the Miyamotos."

"I hate to admit it," said Mac, "we'll have to send it to the cold case file if we don't come up with some hard facts soon." He shuffled the papers Brian gave him and put them in Allen Bradford's case folder.

"If it was them, you know, Hideo and Tak," said Brian, "they're dead, and with Mrs. Miyamoto dead, too, and no other witnesses, we don't have much to go on. No one is left besides Nobu and I don't think he'd talk even if he did know something." Mac didn't respond. Brian looked sideways at him. "What? You want to close it now?"

"No, but let's think about it for a while before we meet with the chief again," said Mac. "He wants to keep it quiet until we officially designate it a cold case. He doesn't think it'll ever be solved and doesn't want us talking to the press until he's ready to make a statement. I doubt if the news media is interested, anyway. They're covering the lava flow that's heading toward Pahoa, so our case is finally off the front page."

"It's not even in the back pages of the papers these days," said Brian. "We're probably the only ones who care about it, except for Jessie, that is."

"I know," said Mac, "but we've overlooked one last member of the Miyamoto family who I'm sure was not actually involved, but probably knew what was going on. Someone who might be that elusive witness we've been looking for."

"There's another person in the Miyamoto family that I don't know about? Who would that be?" asked Brian. "I thought they were all deceased except for Nobu and the doctor in Seattle."

"I'm talking about Sachi Gonsalves," said Mac. "She's Nobu's sister. Let's give it one last try before we call it quits."

"You mean Professor Gonsalves, Billy Gonsalves' wife?" Brian stood up, a look of disbelief on his face. "She's a Miyamoto?"

"Yeah, she was just a kid – same age as Jessie, about 13 or 14, when Bradford died. She probably doesn't know much, but they were a pretty close family from what I've been told. They were all cooped up together after Bradford went missing. Some of them didn't leave the house for days, maybe weeks, after he disappeared according to several people I've talked to. If she was in there, cloistered with the rest of the family, she must have heard or seen something. It's worth a try."

"Huh," said Brian. "She was my Econ 101 instructor at U of H here in Hilo. You want me to go talk to her?" He paced around the office, leaned against the door frame, crossed his long legs at the ankles and jangled the keys in the pocket of his khakis. "If I go alone she might open up to me since we know each other. It hasn't been that long since I was in her class, only a couple of years. She probably remembers me. She gave me an A. Professor Gonsalves," he mused. "Wow, I never made the connection."

Mac nodded. "Yeah, and I hate to admit it, but I should have thought of this a long time ago, damn it. By the way, I have some personal business in Kona today. Why don't you give her a call and make an appointment to meet with her? You're right, it'll be better if you go alone. When you see her, though, go easy. We don't want to spook her. She may be our last chance to solve this thing."

He headed for the door. "I just need a couple of hours this afternoon and I'll be back. Anything happens, call me. Let's hope there won't be any re-enactments of the OK Corral while I'm gone," he said over his shoulder.

He was meeting his brother, David, about selling his share of the McIntire ranch. If David would buy him out, he'd be able to make a stake of his own. He'd thought of making an offer on Jessie's ranch, but he didn't know how she'd feel about it. He'd put that on hold for now.

David was against Mac becoming a police officer because he planned for both of them to work the family ranch. "If you're set on being a cop, then I'll run the ranch as I see fit with no interference from you, understand?" he'd said years ago. As the older brother, David was always the one in charge. That's the way it was when they were kids and that's the way it is now.

When Mac called about selling his share, David said, "Good. It's about time. I've been waiting for you to come around." He was the one who ran the family business after their father died. It was only fair that he should own it outright. He and his sons worked the place together for many years with no help from Mac. He'd be glad to get Mac's name off the deed and would pay him half of whatever the appraisal was.

Mac hoped his brother was in a good mood. He wasn't easy to get along with on a good day and was even more abrasive and short-tempered on a bad day. David said he'd have an appraiser look over the ranch so they'd know what the 50-50 split would be. Mac wasn't sure how the transaction would be handled. He figured they'd sign some papers and transfer funds as directed by their lawyer - simple, with no drama.

22

WHILE MAC WAS QUIBBLING WITH HIS BROTHER ABOUT SIGN-ing over his rights to their family ranch, Jessie was driving to the airport to meet her daughter, Catherine. She thought of the last time she spoke with Guy Matsumoto. He said the Hollywood executive was now looking at property on Kauai and the other client was still haggling over the price. The realtor had no new prospects. She was beginning to think Billy was right. When the contract with Guy expired, they'd hire someone else.

At first, Guy said it would be a quick sale, but it was nearly two months since they'd put the ranch on the market. When Jessie told him she was getting nervous, he said that sometimes it took months, even years to sell a property, but he didn't think that would happen with her place.

She hoped he was right and that they'd get a solid offer before she left for San Francisco. Guy suggested she give power of attorney to someone, so she asked Rod's lawyer to draw up the papers giving that task to Billy. It would be difficult for her to handle the sale from 2,300 miles away and she'd feel more at ease if Billy had the authority to make decisions in her absence. Rod had depended on Billy for so much. Now, he might have to help her sell the ranch. She reasoned it would probably be the last time he'd have to do anything for the Bradfords.

A few weeks ago she considered taking a sabbatical, skipping the fall semester at the university and staying until everything was settled, but decided against it. She couldn't wait to get home, but there was always Thanksgiving weekend or winter break if it became necessary for her to come back to finalize the deal. For now, she and Catherine could catch up after not seeing each other for several months. In a couple of days they would go to the cemetery in Hilo for her father's interment. It was comforting to know that her daughter would be with her and that she wouldn't be alone.

She bought two orchid leis at the airport flower stand and waited for the flight from San Francisco at the baggage claim area. She opened the notes app on her phone and read her To Do list again. It ended with a note that read "What about Mac?" Just when it seemed that she had it all figured out and was crossing items off the list, here was another complication, Mac. What about him? They danced around each other from the day he came to the ranch after the cave was discovered. The other night was spectacular. She cared for him. Was she in love with him?

He wanted her to give up her job and her life in California and live in Hawaii. He was a dyed in the wool Hawaiian. He'd never leave the Islands. If she wanted to be with him, she'd have to be the one to make a change. What if it was only a sexual attraction, a one night stand? They were worlds apart, it would never work. Would it? She had so many questions and so few answers.

She still hadn't decided what to do about her conversation with Sumi Miyamoto. When was she going to tell Mac what she learned from Sumi? Did she have to tell him at all? Did it even matter anymore? So much time had passed and Sumi had died. She'd decide after she talked with Joe.

The arrival of Catherine's flight was announced. Jessie held the fragrant flower leis up to her face and breathed in their scent as she watched for her daughter. Suddenly, there she was. Jessie waved and ran toward the slender young woman with the unruly curly red hair, hugged her, placed the leis around her neck, and kissed her cheek, her neck, and her cheek again. "I'm so glad you're here, Cathy. You have no idea." She felt like crying.

Catherine traveled light. Her only baggage was a purse slung over her shoulder and a wheeled carry on. Soon they were in the parking lot looking for the Land Rover. Tarzan had cleaned it inside and out and it was shiny from the wax he'd used. He wanted the old truck to look its best.

"How are you doing, Mom?" Catherine asked when they were heading down the highway toward South Point. "You look tired."

"I am tired. It's been a tough time with all that's happened. I'm stressed out because there's still so much to do before we leave in two weeks. But you know what? I feel better now that you're here."

"So, you're still planning to go back with me?"

"Yes. I don't think I'll have all the answers I want regarding your grandfather, but I can go home knowing that at least he'll have a proper resting place. It would be great to sell the ranch before I leave, although, I don't think that'll happen. I may have to come back to settle things if and when we find a buyer. Billy will probably be working someplace else by that time. He says he'll handle things for me and I know he means well. If he got another job, I wouldn't expect him to take the time to do it. Just to be safe, I'm giving him power of attorney."

"What about Mac, the detective? Can't he help you out?"

"He could help in a pinch, but I'd rather not ask him. He's got his job, too, you know. I don't want to have to depend on him."

"Weren't you and he an item before you married Dad?"

"That was when we were in high school," said Jessie. "A lot of time has passed since then. Don't start making anything out of it, girlie. We're just two old friends who enjoy each other's company and he happens to be assigned to your grandfather's case. That's all. The only reason we've been spending time together, really, is because of the investigation."

"Sure. That's what you said in your emails and phone calls," Catherine teased, "but I can read between the lines, and I know you better than you think. It seems to me that he's more than just the investigator on Grandfather's case."

"Don't be silly," said Jessie.

When they arrived at the house Mary, Billy and Tarzan came out to welcome them. Catherine hadn't been at the ranch in more than 10 years. She remembered Billy and Tarzan, but she hadn't met Mary before.

"Call me aunty," said Mary, hugging her. "That's Hawaiian style. The young ones always call their elders aunty or uncle in Hawaii."

After Catherine was settled in her newly painted and decorated room, Jessie suggested they go for a ride. It'll be good to get out the kinks after the five-hour flight, she said. "I asked Tarzan to have the horses ready."

Tarzan had saddled Ruby, one of the gentle ranch spares, for Catherine. She'd taken riding lessons one summer at Golden Gate Park in San Francisco when she was in fifth grade. She knew the basics of how to handle a horse and had ridden a couple of times at the ranch years ago. She hoped she still remembered how to stay in the saddle.

They rode a while, stopping at the burial mound on the way back so Catherine could pay her respects to Rod and Maile. They laid Catherine's orchid leis on the mound, then, headed to the house for Mary's vegetarian chili and homemade bread. When Mary learned that Catherine didn't eat meat, she went through Maile's vegetarian cook book and marked the recipes she planned to prepare while Catherine was there. The chili was her first attempt at cooking a meatless meal.

"Ranch people eat a lot of meat, especially beef," said Mary as she put the bowl of chili on the table. "This is the first time I made chili without beef. I hope it turned out all right."

"Just delicious!" exclaimed Catherine as she filled her bowl again.

Two days later Jessie placed the cardboard box containing the empty wooden urn on the back seat of the Land Rover. It was a gray, cloudy morning at Bradford Ranch and was muggy and raining steadily when they got to Hilo. They stopped at the farmers market and bought some flower arrangements for the graves. By the time they got to the cemetery, the rain had stopped, but it was still damp and overcast, a gloomy day for a funeral. An attendant put the ashes into the wooden urn.

Jessie had requested that the usual formal Mormon funeral service be waived. Under a large, white tent, Jessie and Catherine stood with their heads bowed as the elder from the Church of Latter Day Saints said a solemn, brief prayer and blessed the burial site. Jessie placed her father's urn in Anne's grave and laid the flowers beside it. As they walked to the car afterward, instead of feeling sad, she felt relieved. It was finally over. Now she understood what Billy meant when he said it was a relief when Sumi died.

She honored her parents and they were together now as they should be, no matter what happened when they were alive. Was she supposed to feel closure, that word she heard whenever someone's loved one passed away? She didn't feel it when her mother and Danny died, nor more recently with Maile and Rod. The last step in the life cycle, the memorial service, didn't bring her any closure this time either. Maybe she'd feel it when she knew what had happened to her father. She requested that his name be added to the granite gravestone next to her mother's name. That task wouldn't be accomplished for several weeks. She'd be long gone by then.

After the service, they went to the veteran's cemetery where they placed red and white anthuriums at Danny's grave. A small plastic American flag honoring his service was planted in the ground next to his simple, government-issued gravestone. It was raining again as they walked to the Land Rover. Jessie asked if Catherine wanted to do anything in Hilo before they started back. "Lunch? Shopping?" Catherine shook her head. "Then, let's go home," said Jessie.

23

AT THE HOUSE, JESSIE AND BILLY GATHERED EVERYONE IN THE living room and she let Billy do the talking. Since Mary and Tarzan already knew that she had decided to sell the ranch, they weren't surprised when Billy told them Jessie was returning to California in less than two weeks and that he would stay on until he found another job. "Tarzan will take over for me until the place is sold and Mary can come several times a month to tidy up the house and tend the kitchen garden out back, you know, to keep up the place." He glanced at Mary. "Is that all right with you, Mary?" She nodded. "Any questions or comments, you can call me or Jessie any time. Okay?" He glanced at Jessie.

She took a deep breath. "Thanks for everything you've done, all of you. Uncle Rod couldn't have done it without you and neither could I. You have my cell number, so, as Billy said, call anytime." She looked at the three of them, her eyes lingering on each face for a few seconds. "I love you all. You're my family, my only family now, along with Catherine."

She had gone through Rod's belongings and set aside some of his things. She took Billy into Rod's office and pointed to the ornate saddle that Allen Bradford gave his brother years ago. "The saddle's for you, Billy," she said. "I know Uncle Rod never used it, but he loved it. He'd want you to have it and his dress up Stetson, too." She picked up the white hat and handed it to Billy. "Is there anything else you want?"

Billy asked for the trophy Rod won for bronco riding at a long ago rodeo and a framed photograph of Rod and him that sat on the bookshelf behind the desk. In the photo, Rod had his arm around Billy's shoulders. They were wearing sun glasses and their western hats pushed back from their foreheads. A cigarette hung from Rod's lips. Jessie thought he looked like the actor James Dean. Billy remembered the day it was taken. He was 16 at the time and his father snapped the picture.

Jessie gave Mary a heart-shaped diamond pendant with a platinum chain that belonged to Maile, one of Maile's Hawaiian quilts, and Rod's well-worn everyday Stetson. "The hat is for Harry," she said as she handed over Rod's favorite hat. She gave Rod's gold pocket watch to Tarzan and asked if there was anything else he wanted. He pointed to a steel guitar that rested on a stand in a corner of the room. "I'd love to have that. I'll think of Rod every time I play a Johnny Cash song," he said, as Jessie handed it to him. Well, that went well, she thought, as they joined Billy in the living room, then she gave each of them an envelope.

Except for most of Maile's jewelry, the Hawaiian quilts, the monkey pod table, the Frederick Remington painting, and the photo albums, Jessie was leaving nearly everything else behind. Guy told her it would be easier to sell the ranch if the house was furnished and looked homey even though things did look a bit worn and shabby. He said the new owner might even want to keep the old furnishings until they could give the house a much needed make-over or even tear it down.

The next day, Catherine and Jessie went through Rod's office thinking it would take only a day to clean it out, but it took three days to dispose of more than 50 years of Rod's business and personal life. The shredder was working overtime as it gobbled up tax forms, invoices, and letters.

Finally, when they finished they could see the top of the desk, the file cabinets were empty, and the book shelves were nearly bare. Jessie left some of the books, a few by Louis L'Amour, Zane Grey, John Muir, Jack London, Mark Twain, and an anthology of John Steinbeck's.

After they closed the last of the boxes, Jessie sat down on one of them and said, "Guess what? Tomorrow we're getting away from the little house on the prairie and we'll spend a couple of days at the Lani Kea Resort. How does that sound?" Catherine's face lit up. "Great!" she said, plopping down in a chair. "I'm ready for some beach time." They sat for a few minutes. There were no sounds, not even a bird chirping or wind through the trees. Just quiet.

"Mom, this place is so isolated," said Catherine. "Without Mary, Billy, and Tarzan it would be really lonely. I don't know if I could live here. I understand why you're not keeping it."

"It is isolated," Jessie said. "That's why I'm trying to sell it. I never planned to live here. Once it's sold, I'll probably never come back. It makes me sad because I've had a lot of happy times on this ranch, so many wonderful memories, but I can't see living here. When we get back from our beach jaunt, by the way, I have a couple of errands to run," she said. "Billy and I are going to Hilo to sign the power of attorney. Will you be okay spending a few hours here with Mary? You can go with us if you want, but it's going to be a quick trip and I think you'd be bored."

"Don't worry about me, Mom. I came to help you out. A few days at the beach will more than make up for my being alone here with my iPhone, iPad, and Aunty Mary's shortbread cookies. Do what you have to do."

Before they left for the beach the next morning, Jessie called Joe Kanekoa and made an appointment to see him the following week. "By the way, Joe, I have some things of Rod's – clothes, books, and things. Shall I leave them with you to give to the needy in your congregation?"

"Thanks, Jessie, we have a food pantry at our church," he said, "but the Mormons up the road next to Moon's have a clothes closet. Better give clothes and books to them. We split things up between us when it comes to helping those in need. Ipo and I supply the food and the LDS Church provides everything else."

She thanked Joe for the tip, gave Mary three days off, told Billy and Tarzan she was leaving things in their capable hands, and threw two overnight bags into the back seat of the Land Rover.

The time at the beach was just what they needed. They swam and snorkeled at Hapuna Beach, lounged around the pool, drank Mai Tais, shopped at a nearby mall, slept late, and had breakfast in their suite.

For both of them it was like coming out of a fog – Catherine because of her full time job, her heavy class load, and her MBA finally within reach and Jessie because of the emotional roller coaster she was on for the last couple of months.

On the last day at the beach, they packed their belongings and reluctantly checked out of the spacious suite with ocean view, as the hotel room was described online. The valet loaded their bags into the Land Rover and they were off. There was still a lot to do before they left for California. They had to, as Rod would say, shake a leg and get a move on.

As they drove out of the resort's grounds Jessie said, "Cathy, did I ever tell you that the Lani Kea Resort is where your father and I were married? We said our vows back there on the beach under those palm trees. It was a beautiful wedding."

24

JESSIE FELT RELAXED FOR THE FIRST TIME IN WEEKS WHEN SHE and Catherine returned to the ranch. They had a good time at the beach, but now her arduous journey of the last few months was reaching its conclusion and there was only a short time to do everything she planned. One of the last items on her list was meeting with Joe and that's where she was going today.

Mary and Catherine were in the kitchen baking mango bread and planning another vegetarian dinner, this time with tofu. Jessie sat on the top step of the porch and pulled on her boots, grabbed her purse and felt in her jeans pocket for the car keys. As she was getting into the truck, Mary ran out with a paper bag of home cured coffee beans and a box of her famous shortbread cookies.

"For Ipo and Joe," she said, handing the bag to Jessie.

While she was driving to Waikea, Jessie thought about how she was going to start her conversation with Joe. She wasn't sure if she should tell him all she had learned from Sumi Miyamoto. Maybe some things were better left unsaid. By the time she got to Waikea and had parked in front of the church, she decided to leave out a few details. No use giving him more information than he needed. She hoped Joe could help her. Even if he couldn't, it would be a relief to get it off her chest where it weighed as heavy as the anvil in the ranch blacksmith shop.

He was waiting for her in his office when she knocked lightly on the door. "Jessie, come in. You look upset. Hard times, yeh?" He offered her a chair, then sat beside her instead of sitting behind his desk.

Sitting in the straight-backed wooden chair, she turned to face him. "Hard times? Joe, you have no idea. Before I start, I want to make sure that what I tell you today will never be repeated to anyone, not even Ipo. Please promise me. I'm talking to my pastor, not a friend. Will you promise?"

"I promise."

"I just wanted to know what happened to my father," she began, "so I visited Mrs. Miyamoto at the nursing home in Hilo. As I told you the other day, her husband and my father were friends and fishing buddies. I thought she might know what happened the day my father disappeared. Mac told me he was going to interview her, but I wanted to hear for myself. When Mac found out I went to see her, I told him it was more of a social call. I didn't want him to think I was butting into his investigation. I guess I was hoping she might tell me things that she wouldn't tell him and to my surprise, she did."

Jessie thought back to the day she visited Sumi. She told Joe what Sumi Miyamoto had said, holding back only a few details.

"I walked out of there thinking, oh, my God! It was an accident, well, maybe not an accident, exactly, but killing him wasn't intentional. Joe, it was a misunderstanding that got out of hand. Mac thinks it was murder, but it wasn't, not really. I can barely think of anything else. It's always on my mind. I don't know if I should tell him. I don't know what to do.

"To make matters worse, Mrs. Miyamoto died that night after I spoke with her. I feel responsible for her death even though I know that she died of kidney failure and not a heart attack as I feared. I stirred things up.

I'm the one who made her remember things she probably never wanted to think about ever again."

Jessie didn't want to leave Hawaii without knowing who was responsible for her father's death. Now she knew, but at what price? Did Mrs. Miyamoto die because she had relived that terrible time? Was remembering what happened just too much for such an elderly person to live with? Did Sumi Miyamoto regret revealing that she and Jessie's father were in love and had an affair and that was the reason he was killed?

Joe didn't speak and wondered how he was going to advise her. He was a pastor and she confided in him. No matter what she told him, he was bound not to break that trust.

"I promise you, Jessie, this is just between us. You're very troubled. What do you want to do about it?" he asked. "Are you angry with Mrs. Miyamoto because she had an affair with your father? Do you think that perhaps if not for her, he might be alive today? Are you angry at your father for being an adulterer?"

"I'm angry at myself, Joe. I want to tell Mac, but I don't know how. Besides, I've asked myself a million times now that Mrs. Miyamoto is dead, what difference does it make? But Mac's a police officer. Who knows what he'll do? It was an accident. I can understand what happened, why it happened. Would it be wrong for me to keep it from him? He says he'll continue to work on the case. He really wants to solve it. If I tell him what I know, people would be hurt, people close to me. I feel so guilty."

"You have to tell him, Jessie. If it was an accident, Mac will figure out how to deal with it. If you don't tell him, you'll always feel guilty. I've got a feeling that you aren't telling me everything, though. You've left out something. You haven't told me who killed your father. Do you know? Did Mrs. Miyamoto tell you who did it? Was it her? Is it someone who has died and whose reputation you want to protect? Is it someone who is still alive?"

"I can't tell you, Joe. I think it's best that you don't know. I'm just glad I know what happened and that it wasn't deliberate," Jessie replied. "You're right. I don't want to ruin anyone's reputation, dead or alive. Mac tells me the case may never be solved. I could solve it for him in a minute, in a second. If everything Sumi Miyamoto told me is true, there was a witness and now I'm a witness, too. I just don't know if I can tell Mac."

Her voice softened. "I buried my father yesterday. Now that I know what happened, I can let him go. But yes, I guess I'm angry with him. I don't like some of the things I've learned about him. But still, he was my father."

Joe reached out to hold her hand. "Only you can make the decision, Jessie. I have faith that you'll do what's right. It may take a while, but you will tell Mac. Trust him. I believe that once he has all the facts he'll know what to do and you'll feel much better. You'll be free."

"I need to go home to San Francisco, so I can think clearly. I'm leaving soon and I can't wait to get on that plane and get away from here," said Jessie.

She knew there wasn't an easy answer and Joe hadn't offered one, but she felt better having talked to him. She needed to get it out of her system and she did. "I'll keep it to myself for now," she said. "Someday I'll tell Mac, I promise."

She stood up. "I'd better be getting home. They'll be wondering what happened to me." As Joe walked her to the door, she turned and said, "Did you know that I put Bradford Ranch up for sale? I needed to lighten my load and the ranch is the first thing to go. It was a difficult decision, but I think it's the best one."

"Yeh, I heard about it. Mary called Ipo the other day. You know how word gets around. I understand what you mean about needing to lighten your load. I wish I could do that sometimes, divest myself of those several hundred acres of mine, but my family burial plot is there and the cave. I'll never sell, I can't. Since Ipo and I have no children, though, I plan to donate the property to the Hawaiian Conservancy. It's in our will. They'll take care of it. The old homestead is still there – my mother's house and the few acres fenced in around it. I feel a bond with the place even though

I rarely visit anymore. That day we ran into each other at the cliffs was the first time I'd been down there since Mike Campbell and I found the cave."

He walked her to the top of the wooden steps leading down to the street, and hugged her. "Aloha, Jessie. A hui hou, until we meet again."

"Aloha, Joe and mahalo, thank you. Take care of yourself, my friend. Give my love to Ipo, will you? Tell her I'll see her next time."

If there is a next time, she thought as she went out to the truck. I may never come back. She slid behind the steering wheel, turned to look up at the church spire one last time and found the coffee beans and cookies from Mary on the passenger seat. She started to open her door and looked up at the top of the stairs. Joe wasn't there. Oh, never mind, she thought. She closed the door and took a cookie out of the box and bit into it as she drove toward Kahana to pick up the mail and the items on Mary's shopping list. She made a mental note to send a check to Joe's church when she returned to San Francisco.

25

SEVERAL WEEKS LATER, JESSIE DROPPED OFF A DONATION AT the Church of Latter Day Saints next door to Moon's Beachhead Inn in Waikea. The young missionary who accepted the boxes and bags of clothes and household goods helped her unload the truck, said the things would be put to good use, and thanked her profusely. "Are you LDS?" he asked.

"You're welcome," she said, shaking his hand, "and no, not really LDS."

At the ranch, Billy put Rod's saddle in the back of his pickup and covered it with a tarp, ready for the ride to Hilo. He wasn't sure where Sachi would let him put it or if she'd even want a saddle in the house, but he was proud to have it. He'd find a place for it for the time being and when he had another job, he'd use it for special occasions. The strains of guitar music came from the tiny front porch of Tarzan's cottage. The ranch house was as ready as it would ever be. As Guy suggested, Jessie left some of the furnishings. A shipping company packed up the monkey pod table and other things that were to be shipped to San Francisco. Her To Do list was getting shorter as she ticked off things one by one.

It was Wednesday afternoon and she was finishing packing and putting things in order for the flight to California on Monday morning. She hadn't planned anything for her last weekend at the ranch.

With a few days left before Jessie and Catherine were to leave, Billy was back to his morning routine with Mary and Jessie, drinking coffee, nibbling on Mary's baked goods, and listening to the latest news. Mary and Jessie never referred to their chats as gossip, they called it news. It was like old times. Even Tarzan joined the coffee klatch during those last days, stopping in for a quick cuppa. Catherine enjoyed being a part of it. She watched her mother and wondered why she was in such a hurry to leave it all behind. Yes, the place was isolated, but she seemed so happy here. What about John McIntire? Did he have a place in her mother's future? When am I ever going to meet the guy?

Tarzan said that he and his fiancée, Sophie, would be married in December. "You'll be getting an invitation," he told Jessie. She didn't think she'd be back for the nuptials, but kept that to herself. "I'd love to come," she said. "I'll try to make it, really, I will try."

"By the way," Billy interrupted, "the Hamakua Rodeo and Paniolo Days festival is this weekend. What do you think about going, Jessie, one last time for the road?" The Hamakua rodeo was a big deal on the island and attracted cowboys young and old from as far away as Montana, Wyoming and Texas, as well as the other Hawaiian Islands.

The idea took Jessie by surprise. She couldn't remember the last time she'd been to a rodeo. She and Danny went with Rod and Maile when they were kids. They watched Rod win the trophy in bronco busting. Billy's and Tarzan's fathers and Harry Chin won trophies back then, too. Later, both Billy and Tarzan rode the bulls and competed in the calf roping contests. It was a Bradford tradition to pack a lunch and stake out a wide swath in the bleachers. Rod hadn't participated in years. Rodeo was a young man's sport, he said, but he still went and watched Tarzan and Billy win their trophies, and hung out with the other old cowboys behind the bleachers, talking stories about their glory days.

Jessie wasn't sure she wanted to spend her last weekend in Hawaii at a rodeo, but upholding a longstanding Bradford tradition might be a good ending before the ranch was sold. She looked at Catherine. "What about it?" she asked. "Are you game for a rodeo?"

Catherine looked stricken. As a vegetarian, she preferred not to be a spectator at a sport where animals were used and abused, but she'd never been to a rodeo. How bad could it be? "Okay, I guess I'll give it a try."

"Great!" Billy said. "I was talking to Mac the other day and asked if he'd like to join us if we went and he's in." He glanced at Jessie. "Do you mind?"

"No, not at all," she said, casually shrugging her shoulders.

Catherine smiled at her mother. "So, he does exist," she said. "I was beginning to think he was a figment of your imagination."

"What about you and Harry?" Billy asked Mary. "And you and your girlfriend, Tarzan? We could make it a Bradford Ranch holiday, just like old times. How about we go on Saturday? That's the day of the parade and the opening ceremonies." He looked at Jessie. "Then, you and Catherine can finish packing on Sunday for your trip back to the coast on Monday. That'll work, won't it?"

"Okay, sure," she said. "Let's do it."

Mary offered to make a picnic lunch, but Jessie said they would buy food and drinks at the kiosks. "That way we won't have to lug coolers and stuff to the bleachers."

Later, after everyone left, Catherine said, "So, I'm finally going to meet the great Detective McIntire. I can't wait. Mary says he's a hottie."

"Really? A hottie? That doesn't sound like Mary. He's a nice guy and he is handsome, I suppose. I'm glad you're going to meet him, but don't make such a big deal out of it," Jessie chided. Still, she couldn't help herself when she asked, "What else did Mary say about him?" They were curled up in front of the fire wrapped in a blanket, Maile's quilts having been packed and on their way to San Francisco. A bowl of popcorn sat between them on the sofa.

"Oh, not much, just that he's crazy in love with you and you are just plain crazy to let him get away." She popped a kernel into her mouth.

"God, I hope that's not what she's spreading around. Don't believe everything she says. Mary's sweet, but she does tend to exaggerate. And don't get caught up in the gossip of the South Point Gazette."

"Hey! I will never be a contributor to nor a fan of Aunt Maile's imaginary tabloid. Well, I'm already a fan, but don't worry about that, Mamacita. I'm just interested in my mother's love life or lack thereof, mostly lack thereof, apparently."

"Mac's a childhood friend," said Jessie. "Besides, what would be the sense in my getting involved with him when I don't plan to come back?

"You're not coming back, ever?" Catherine asked. "Not even for a visit? I don't believe it."

"I don't know, maybe someday. I told Tarzan I might come to his wedding in December. I'd like to, but I don't think I will. Once the ranch is sold, that'll probably be it. There's no reason for me to return. Remember why I came here, Cathy. It was to settle Uncle Rod's estate. Never in my wildest dreams did I think I'd be staying as long as I have and that I'd be involved in a murder investigation, of all things. The only reason Mac and I have been spending time together," she said, "is because of your grandfather's case." She thought of the night they spent together and felt herself blush. She hoped Catherine didn't notice.

"Do you think the police will ever find out who did it?" asked Catherine.

"That's a good question. They're working on it hard enough. We'll see. I really don't care anymore. Well, I do care but, there's nothing anyone can do about it now. The police may never find out and I have to accept that. I've taken care of everything I needed to and I can't wait to go home. That's what I'm concentrating on now."

She stood up and closed the fireplace screen. "C'mon, let's go to bed. We have a couple of busy days ahead of us. We haven't even begun to pack yet."

26

AT A MEETING WITH THEIR ATTORNEYS, MAC AND DAVID SET-
tled the split of the McIntire ranch. Mac sold his 1,500 acre share to his
brother. Now he could buy a place of his own, even the Bradford Ranch, if
he wanted to, something he couldn't have done on a cop's salary even with
the trust fund money and his share of the profits from the family ranch he
received each year.

He called Jessie's realtor, Guy Matsumoto, and asked him to keep
an eye out for ranch land on the Big Island. He wasn't planning to make a
career change yet, but he wouldn't be a cop all his life. He might as well plan
ahead. "I have just the place for you," said Guy. "It's a beautiful property at
South Point. I'll arrange a tour and get back to you."

Meanwhile, Brian Alnas had an appointment to meet with Sachi
Gonsalves who agreed to see him after her last class of the day. He hoped
the meeting would turn up something to help solve the Bradford case.
It was late afternoon when he arrived at the Gonsalves house in the hills
above Hilo.

Sachi figured the police sergeant wanted to talk about Nobu who was
out on bail awaiting a court date. When she last saw her brother, he seemed

contrite about what he'd done. As far as she knew he was behaving himself. She didn't know what else the police wanted, but she'd help if she could.

She hoped the defense attorney from Honolulu that Billy hired would be worth the exorbitant fees he charged. She heard he was working on a plea bargain to ensure Nobu wouldn't serve any prison time. She didn't know what charges, if any, would be brought against him, but Billy said he was confident everything would turn out well for Nobu.

Now this police officer wanted to talk to her. She remembered Brian Alnas from her economics class. He was a good student and she felt comfortable meeting with him. It would be nice to see how one of her former students was doing, although she doubted he was using what he learned in her class at his job on the police force.

She answered the knock on the door. "Hi, Mrs. Gonsalves," Brian said. "Thanks for seeing me."

"Hello, Brian. It's nice to see you again. Please come in."

Brian spoke with Sachi for nearly an hour. Afterward, he couldn't wait to talk to Mac, so he called him as he was pulling out of Sachi's driveway. The first thing he said when Mac picked up was, "Boss, she knows something, but she's not telling."

"What'd she say?" asked Mac.

"It's not what she said, but the way she said it."

"I'm already half way home," Mac said. "Why don't you come to my place? We'll have a couple of beers and talk about it."

While drinking a beer and eating roasted macadamia nuts in Mac's kitchen at the cottage, Brian said that Sachi seemed surprised, shocked, as a matter of fact, when he told her he wanted to discuss Allen Bradford's case. "She thought I wanted to talk about Nobu.

"I told her Nobu's attorney was still working on the plea deal, but that I needed some background information for the Bradford file. When I asked her where she'd been on the day Bradford disappeared and if she remembered anything, I tell you, Mac, I thought she was going to faint. You know how pale she is. Well, she got even whiter. My instincts tell me she knows more than she's letting on. I think you're right when you say she couldn't have been in that house and not know what happened. Go talk to her yourself and see if you get the same vibes I got."

"What exactly did she say?" Mac put down his beer can and leaned forward. "So?"

"She claimed that she didn't remember much about that time. I guess it's as you said, Mac, just like Jessie. It was her demeanor that got my interest. She seemed, um, scared, worried. Shootz! I don't know how else to put it!"

"Very interesting," said Mac. "Scared? Worried? That's a good sign. We must be on the right track if she's scared and worried. It means that all wasn't well in the Miyamoto household, especially if Hideo knew about his wife and his boss."

"That's what I think," said Brian. "I guess I shouldn't be surprised at her reaction. After all, we suspected that she probably knew what was going on. I'm convinced now that she did. She may seem delicate and fragile, but I think she's tougher than she looks. It won't be easy to break her."

"Well, we know it's not Nobu," said Mac. "He wasn't on the island when it happened. Everyone else is dead except for the brother in Seattle, and he wasn't here either. So, maybe she's protecting the memory of someone who died. That's the custom, isn't it, what they call saving face?"

"Could be," said Brian sipping his beer. "That's an Asian thing, but we Filipinos don't have to worry about stuff like that. We're just like you guys in that department."

"What do you mean 'you guys' – you mean a hapa haole, hapa Hawaiian like me?"

"No," said Brian, laughing. "I mean a hapa Filipino, hapa Hawaiian like me. But maybe you're right, it could be something like that saving face thing."

"Okay, okay. I'll call Sachi and see if I can talk to her, but not right away," said Mac. "I don't want to scare her. She may not want to see me, but too bad. I'm just going to ask her the same questions I asked Jessie. That should calm her down. Want to share a frozen pizza?"

"Thanks, Mac, but I've got a date. I'd better be going." He stood up, snapped his fingers, and did a dance step. "Goin' dancin'."

After Brian left, Mac put the pizza in the oven and popped open another beer. He listened to the rain tapping on the windows for a while, and then turned on the 20-inch television that sat on the counter between the toaster and the coffee pot and watched the San Francisco Giants lose to the Los Angeles Dodgers. He muted the sound because he didn't like listening to the sports announcers. Sometimes he wondered if they were discussing the same game he was watching or even if they were watching the game at all. It was better not to hear them. He'd rather listen to the rain. It was getting dark, but he didn't turn on the lights. He just sat there drinking his beer.

As he ate the pizza, he thought about the rodeo on Saturday. He was looking forward to going because it meant he would see Jessie again and it would probably be the last time he'd see her before she left for California. He realized that the rodeo was not the most appropriate place to discuss anything personal, but it might be his only chance. He'd have to try to get her alone, but first things first. He called Guy Matsumoto again. "What's the asking price for the Bradford Ranch?" he asked. "Just curious."

"That's the property I was talking about the other day," said the realtor excitedly, "the one at South Point. You're interested in it?"

"I am."

"Right after we talked, I left a message for the ranch manager to call me about giving you a tour," said Guy. "I haven't heard back yet. I'll try again in the morning and let you know. There are a couple of other clients interested, so you'd better act fast. Oh, they're asking $4 million."

"Fine, that's about what I thought they were asking. I already know that ranch pretty well," said Mac. "I don't really need a tour. I knew Rod Bradford." He paused for a moment. "What the hell. Okay, set it up as soon as possible. You can tell those other prospects to get lost because I'm serious. I'm not just shopping around. I'm buying it."

27

SATURDAY ARRIVED WITH A FLURRY OF ACTIVITY. TARZAN left early to pick up his fiancée. Jessie dressed in her Durango boots, jeans and denim shirt. They had to search for something for Catherine. She ended up wearing jeans, a t-shirt and a pair of dressy high heeled, knee high boots that were more appropriate for the streets of San Francisco than a rodeo, but at least they were boots. Jessie wore an old hat of Rod's that hung on a hat rack in the kitchen and handed Catherine one of Maile's straw hats that sported a red bandana for a hat band. "I think I look like a cowgirl, don't you?" Catherine asked, pulling the hat brim down over her eyes and doing a line dance step around the kitchen. "Where'd you learn to line dance?" asked Jessie. "You've always been a rocker girl."

"Oh, I like variety," Catherine teased. "Actually, I'm taking a class with a guy I'm dating. He's into Country Western music. You aren't the only cowgirl around here, you know."

"And, this guy is…?"

"Greg. He's someone new. Studying for the bar exam. You'll meet him when we get back, don't worry."

"Is it serious?"

"Not yet. I'll let you know if it ever gets serious."

Jessie's phone buzzed as she was pulling the Land Rover out of its parking spot in the back yard. It was Mac. "Hey," he said, "how about stopping by my place at Volcano? You can leave the Rover here and we can go to the rodeo together. No use taking two cars. What do you think?"

"Uh, okay," said Jessie hesitantly. "I have Catherine with me."

"Great. I'd like to meet her," he said. "Just blow your horn and I'll run down. You know where my house is, don't you? It's the cottage on the right with the wrought iron gate. You've been here before, but it's been a while."

"I remember. Thanks. See you there. We're just leaving, so it'll be about an hour."

Mac was waiting for them on the front porch. Catherine was all smiles as she watched him come down the steps to the street. He was just what she expected. Mary's description couldn't have been more accurate. He was as good looking as Mary said, and in his cowboy boots and hat, jeans, denim jacket, and sun glasses, she thought he looked pretty hot for an older guy. Jessie introduced them.

"I've been looking forward to meeting you," said Catherine. "Same here," said Mac, shaking her hand. He smiled at Jessie. "Hey, cowgirl," he said and kissed her on the cheek. He opened the doors to the SUV. "Ladies," he said and bowed, making a sweeping motion for them to get in.

They drove along the Hamakua Coast, headed to the cowboy town of Honokaa. The scenery along the way was much different than the dry, arid landscape of South Point. Jessie loved this drive. It's lush and green with waterfalls on one side of the road and small streams and rivers on the other side with deep gullies reaching out to the Pacific Ocean. It's like one of those travelogue videos PBS airs during their fundraising programs only it's close up and real. The drive is almost dizzying with all the twists and turns. Around each zigzag curve is a different and more beautiful tropical, jungle setting. The colors are so vivid that Catherine quipped it looked as though the scenery was photo shopped. Mac stopped several times so she could take pictures.

He and Catherine chatted all the way to the rodeo grounds, asking questions, learning about each other. Jessie liked the easy way the two of them got along. She could tell her daughter was trying to find out all she could about the man in her mother's life, as she referred to Mac. Jessie didn't say much, just sat back and listened and enjoyed the ride.

They found Billy waiting for them at the gate with their tickets. Mac pulled out his wallet, but Billy said, "My treat, a going away present."

He led them to the bleachers where Mary, Harry, Tarzan and his fiancée, Sophie, were already seated. Billy noticed Jessie scanning the bleachers. He touched her arm and pulled her aside. "Are you looking for Sachi? She didn't come," he said, softly. "She really doesn't enjoy rodeo. It's better this way. She'd be miserable after the first bronc threw its rider, believe me."

"Too bad you missed the parade," Mary said to Catherine, moving over to make room for them. "It was so beautiful. Some of the riders on horseback wore beautiful silk costumes in the colors of the different islands."

Harry joined in. "And the governor is here from Honolulu. He rode in a Cadillac convertible with Miss Hawaii," he said, "and the mayor from Hilo rode a white stallion. I bet it was the first time he ever rode a horse." He laughed. "He looked nervous and so did the horse. The paniolo who'll be in the rodeo rode in the parade, too. A lot of them are from the Mainland, even some from Canada and Australia. This rodeo is world famous, you know."

Harry was in his 60s, with thinning gray hair and a gray beard, slightly built and bow legged, and he, too, showed signs of many years riding horseback and working cowboy in the Hawaiian sun. His skin was brown as chocolate and deeply lined like a road map. Like Mary, he was Chinese with some Hawaiian thrown in. "We're island mix," Mary once told Jessie. "You can tell Harry has plenty of Hawaiian blood in him because he talks with his hands, real Hawaiian style, almost like hula."

Mary turned to Catherine. "Of course, our parade is nothing like the Rose Parade you have in California, but it's a big deal to us local folks."

"Darn, I wish I'd seen it," said Catherine. "I'd love to have taken some photos."

"Mary held up her camera. "No worry. I took lots of pictures. I'll send you some." She turned to Jessie. "Oh, I'm so glad we came." She clasped Jessie's hand. "It's just like the old days. I wish Rod and Maile were here."

"Me, too," Jessie said. She gave Mary a hug. She regretted that they'd missed the parade, especially for Catherine's sake. "We stopped a couple of times so Cathy could take photos along the Hamakua Coast road. I'm sorry we're late, next time we'll be early." Then she realized that they were leaving in two days and there might not be a next time. She and Mac were sitting next to Tarzan and Sophie who were holding hands. Mac slipped his hand around hers and squeezed gently.

"Harry's niece is the rodeo queen this year," said Mary. "Did I tell you that she won the queen contest?" She pointed across the arena at a young woman wearing a white Western hat and sitting astride a palomino, the horse's blond mane a sharp contrast to the rodeo queen's nearly waist-length dark hair.

The high school band played the national anthem before the master of ceremonies introduced the queen, Carol Ann Chin. Carol Ann waved as the palomino pranced to the center of the arena. As is customary for the rodeo queen, she performed a barrel race routine to great applause from the crowd.

By the time the calf roping and bucking bronco competitions were over, everyone was hungry. Jessie took orders, and accompanied by Mac and Catherine, headed to the food kiosks. Mac asked Catherine how she liked the rodeo so far. She wrinkled her nose. "I feel sorry for the animals."

Mac stopped on the way to the kiosks located behind the bleachers to talk to a couple of cop buddies dressed as cowboys, while Jessie and Catherine continued to the food venders. Hot dogs and hamburgers were the order of the day for their group, with a couple of teriyaki chicken skewers and one teriyaki beef sandwich. Jessie asked Catherine if she wanted anything. Catherine had packed some celery and carrot sticks and a hard-boiled egg in her purse, suspecting that vegetarianism hadn't yet reached that part of the world. She was right. A cowboy town and a rodeo catered to meat eaters, especially home-grown beef. There would be no veggie burgers nor carrot and celery sticks at the food stands. "Just some fries and an energy drink, if they have it," she said.

As they stood in line waiting to place their orders, Jessie heard someone call her name.

"Jessie! Jessie Bradford!" Wending her way through the crowd was a woman with short, straight, mousey blonde hair and a sunburned face who Jessie recognized from her days at boarding school. "Oh, no, Patsy Sherman," she said under her breath as the woman approached her. "I knew it was you," said Patsy. "How are you? Oh, my God! I haven't seen you in ages! You look great!" Jessie stood with her arms at her sides as Patsy threw her arms around her and hugged tight, as if they were long lost friends.

"Fine, fine," said Jessie, pulling out of Patsy's grip. She introduced Catherine.

"I heard you were back," said Patsy. "Are you here to stay?"

"No, we're leaving for San Francisco on Monday. We only came to settle my uncle's estate."

"I'm so sorry about your Uncle Rod and we're all still waiting to hear what happened to your Dad in that cave. It really is him, isn't it? We've read about it in the papers and watched the TV newscasts.

"So, do you live in San Francisco or are you just stopping there to change planes headed for somewhere else?" asked Patsy. She didn't wait for a response. "My husband and I lived in California for years. But we were down south in Newport Beach. We're back in Hawaii for good now. We bought the old Austin mansion in Hilo and we've turned it into a bed and breakfast. We live there and run the B & B."

"I know the Austin house," said Jessie, avoiding saying where she lived. "It was beautiful. Good for you. How's business?"

"It's still beautiful and business is great," said Patsy. "Wait a minute, aren't you related to the Austins?" She wrinkled her brow. "No, that must be someone else." Actually, Jessie was related to the Austins. Her mother was an Austin, but again Patsy didn't wait for an answer and rambled on. "Anyway, we fixed it up. We cater to a high-end clientele – no locals or unacceptable guests. You know how it is here. You have to be so careful." She smiled slyly, as if she were sharing a private joke. "By the way, where are you sitting?"

Jessie pointed to the bleachers where the Bradford group was seated. "Over there," she said vaguely. She never liked Patsy and didn't want to risk having her insinuate herself into joining them. In high school, Patsy was head cheerleader and the leader of the most popular clique on campus. Jessie guessed they'd be considered the mean girls today, bullying anyone who didn't fit into their idea of proper high school society. Jessie, with her country girl persona, was the target of some of that bullying, so Patsy was the last person with whom she would want to spend time.

"We're sitting in the VIP seats," said Patsy, "with my parents and in-laws, our kids and some friends. Why don't you two join us? I'm sure you'll be able to see much better from there. We have plenty of room. You know, of course, that my father-in-law is running for governor, don't you? He's going to make a speech at half time. This will give you a chance to meet the future governor of Hawaii. We're all excited about it."

"I didn't know he was running for governor," Jessie lied. She'd seen the posters on just about every telephone pole and store window between Hilo and Kahana and along the highway on the way to South Point. Even Moon Toli had one of Ed Sherman's posters tacked up on the wall behind the bar of the Beachhead Inn. But she wasn't going to give Patsy the satisfaction. She hadn't liked her in high school and that hadn't changed. Jessie knew she shouldn't still be carrying a grudge, but Patsy, she thought, was as irritating as a heat rash.

"Thanks, Patsy. That's kind of you, but we're with the Bradford Ranch group and Mac McIntire. We're just fine where we are."

Patsy's face lit up. "You mean John McIntire?"

"Why, yes, he's an old Bradford family friend. We practically grew up together. Do you know him?" Jessie looked at the crowd gathered around the food kiosks, hoping she'd see Mac so he could rescue them, but he was nowhere in sight.

"Lucky you," said Patsy. "John McIntire is quite the eligible bachelor. There's hardly a single woman in Hilo, and even some who aren't single, who wouldn't want her shoes under his bed." She pretended to swoon and waved her hands as though she were fanning herself. "But I'll bet you already know that, don't you?" She grinned wickedly. "I wouldn't mind having a fling with him myself."

In your dreams, thought Jessie.

"He and his wife divorced years ago." Patsy lowered her voice. "She's married to the top exec of the Hilo branch of Island Bank. Did you know that?" Jessie nodded and kept watch for Mac over Patsy's shoulder. "Very upscale," continued Patsy, lowering her head and looking out through the top of her sun glasses. "Quite a catch for the ex wife of a policeman, wouldn't you say?"

Jessie was saved from answering when a voice from the kiosk window called, "Next!" Finally, she was at the head of the line. She'd finished giving her order when she heard Mac call her name and saw him weaving through the throng of people. She was relieved to see his face in the crowd as he moved toward them.

Patsy was still talking. Jessie tuned her out and reminded herself that she had sworn that if she ever returned to live in Hawaii, she would make an effort to stay away from snobs like Patsy Sherman. Whenever she was with Patsy, she felt like slapping her.

Mac reached them in time to pay for the lunch and help with the plastic bags laden with food and drink. He had taken off his dark glasses and his eyes looked as blue as the ocean they'd passed that morning along the coast road. Jessie was glad she was with him and glanced at Patsy, whose tongue was just about hanging out as Mac nodded at her. "Hey, Patsy, good to see you. Hope you're enjoying the rodeo," he said, as he ushered Jessie and Catherine away from her and led them back to the bleachers.

"Nice to see you, too, Mac," said Patsy, as she watched them move through the crowd and out of sight.

When they got back to their seats, Jessie's neighbor, Frank Gomes, was talking with Billy and the others. He took off his hat, smiled with his teeth clamped onto his cigar, gave Jessie a bear hug, and shook hands with Mac.

"Jessie, I was hoping I'd see you before you left. Rod would have loved being here today, wouldn't he? We used to get together with some of the old timers behind the bleachers, have a few beers, and talk war stories about our young days. It's sure not the same without him."

"Thanks, Frank. I miss him a lot, too," said Jessie, returning his hug. She introduced Catherine.

"I hear you're going back to California," he said.

"Yes, Cathy and I are leaving on Monday morning. You want to sit here with us? There's plenty of room and food."

"Thanks, but my wife and family are waiting for me. I just stopped by to say hello. Take care, Jessie. I hope you come back soon and if you change your mind about leasing some of your land, let me know." He tipped his hat. "Aloha to you and your beautiful daughter. See you guys later," he said to the others and made the shaka sign.

It was nearly dark when bull riding, the final competition, was over. The all-around cowboy who won the silver belt buckle and trophy cup was from Maui. Second place went to a paniolo from Mauna Loa ranch and third place went to an Australian.

As Mac, Jessie, and Catherine headed toward the parking lot, Catherine said, "Well, this is my last rodeo, you guys. I couldn't stand it another second. Talk about animal abuse. Oh, my God! Is it even legal?" She started to walk away from them. "Where are you going?" asked Jessie.

"Didn't I tell you? Mary and Harry offered me a ride home, so I'll leave you now, Mom. Sorry, I thought I mentioned it. See you back at the ranch." She giggled. "See ya later, Mac. It was nice meeting you. Hope we run into each other again."

"Uh, nice meeting you, too," said Mac, perplexed, as he watched her walk away. Catherine smiled as she joined Mary and Harry. She and Mary winked at each other and climbed into Harry's pickup truck.

Mac and Jessie didn't spend any time alone together the entire day. They now looked at each other, bewildered. "What just happened? I wasn't expecting this," Jessie said. "What brought it on, I wonder?" She stared after Harry's truck as Catherine and Mary waved.

"I suspect your daughter and your housekeeper planned a little surprise for us."

"Were you in on this?" asked Jessie.

"Nope," he said, "but I wish I had been. I've wanted to get you alone all day. Finally, here's my chance." He opened the door and helped her into his SUV. "Come on, you can pick up your ride at my place."

The drive back to Volcano wasn't as scenic as it was when they were heading toward the rodeo that morning. The zigzag road seemed precarious in the dark and Mac was concentrating on making those sharp, winding turns. They didn't talk much.

When they reached the cottage it was drizzling and foggy. Mac asked, "Want to come in for a brandy or hot chocolate?"

"Well, I don't know." She glanced at her watch. "It's late and I don't like driving at night." She looked into his eyes. "If I do come in, I'm spending the night," she teased, leaning over and kissing him on the lips. They made love on the living room floor in front of the fireplace, but didn't bother to light a fire.

Later, as they sipped brandy before a fire, Mac said, "I know you're going back to San Francisco on Monday, Jessie, but don't stay away too long or I'll have to go to San Francisco and bring you back. For now let me give you a tour of the rest of the house." He picked her up and carried her up the stairs in his arms. "The bedrooms are up here."

The next morning as they were walking to her truck, Jessie said, "Well, the secret's out, I guess. Now that Mary knows about us, it'll be front page news in the South Point Gazette."

"I hope so," said Mac, "because I want everyone to know I'm in love with you. Once word gets around, it'll be harder for you to stay away. I promise, I'll come and get you if I have to. I love you, Jessie."

She leaned into him as they stood with their arms around each other, "I love you, too, Mac."

"Then why are you leaving?"

"Because I have to, there are some things I need to sort out."

As she drove away heading to South Point for the last time, she wondered if she would ever come back. She looked in the rear view mirror. Mac was still standing there.

28

SIX MONTHS WENT BY WITHOUT ANY NEW LEADS IN ALLEN Bradford's murder. Mac had moved on to other cases. There were the usual ones – cock fighting, drugs, domestic abuse, and burglaries – and some not so usual. A homeless woman was raped and murdered in broad daylight in an alley downtown. They caught the guy with the help of a security video from a nearby shop and within a few days the story was off the front pages and television newscasts.

Mac promised Jessie he'd follow up on anything, even the smallest lead, but on the chief's orders, Bradford's mysterious death was officially designated a cold case. Mac and Brian still worked on it on their own time, but weren't any closer to solving it than they had been before.

Mac spoke with Sachi several months ago and she was just as nervous with him as she'd been with Brian. He picked up on the same vibes that Brian did, that she knew something, but wasn't talking. One day he said to Brian, "Kid, I think it's time we had another chat with Sachi Gonsalves, the two of us this time."

"I was thinking the same thing," said Brian. Before he could continue, another detective knocked on the open door. "Mac, Brian, there's a call about a disturbance at a house just outside of town. The uniforms are on the way and the captain wants you two to take it. The dispatcher said alcohol is involved and a possible shooting. Sounds like a cock fight gone bad."

"Great," said Mac. "All the usual crimes tied up in one big package. Let's go, but hold that thought about Sachi Gonsalves." They checked their Glock revolvers, Mac grabbed his hat, and they hurried out to the Expedition.

At the edge of town in a rundown neighborhood of ramshackle houses, they turned onto a dirt road and into a yard where a small crowd was gathered. Mac and Brian got out of the truck and waded through the mob. Two men, both of them with bloodied faces, were sitting on the ground. They were still struggling to get at each other as a couple of policemen held them apart and handcuffed their hands behind their backs. A handgun had been kicked away from the handcuffed men. Mac picked it up. The crowd was getting restless and starting to move closer. Mac yelled for them to move back and settle down. He recognized the two combatants. They were regulars.

"Ernest, Benny, how many times do we have to come down here to break up these fights? And this time you have a gun. You guys are goin' to jail again and not only for fighting and gambling, but on a weapons charge. Who got shot, Tommy?" Mac asked the officer who was handcuffing one of the men."

"Nobody," said the officer. "This guy shot into the air." He pulled the man to his feet.

"Make that weapons charges," said another officer as he pulled out a handgun that was stuffed into the waistband of the second man's pants.

Cock fighting is illegal in Hawaii, but that doesn't stop people from raising fighting roosters and organizing fights in the old plantation camps and the seedier neighborhoods of the cities and towns. Hilo was no exception. Fist fights are common during the events, usually caused by gambling that goes awry when the losers refuse to pay up or someone is accused of cheating. Alcohol and drugs are often involved as are weapons, mostly knives, but guns are showing up more often.

One rooster lay dead. The other one, though injured, was limping around, pecking at the grass. Mac figured somebody was going to have chicken for dinner that night. He told the crowd to break it up and go home before they all got arrested. God, he hated this part of his job. It was almost enough to make him quit and move to his ranch.

He'd bought Bradford Ranch. As an extra bonus, he bought the cattle and horses. Jessie was long gone when the deal was made and Billy handled everything. It was now Mac's place, but he still lived in the cottage at Volcano to be near work.

When Mac and Brian returned to the office after the cock fighting melee and were writing their reports, they resumed their discussion about Sachi Gonsalves.

"We should talk to her again before she goes to join Billy," said Mac, looking up from his computer. "He's over on Maui now and I hear Sachi stayed to finish out the semester at the university. Once she leaves it won't be easy to get to her. This time instead of asking questions, we'll tell her we're zeroing in on Nobu as the suspect in the Bradford case. We'll let her think he's our guy. What do you think?"

Brian had finished his report and was reading a file on another case. He shut down his computer and looked at Mac. "What do I think? I think it's a great idea. She'll probably want to protect Nobu. Maybe she'll tell us what she knows just to take suspicion off him. We should go together, though, like we're ganging up on her."

"We won't call first," said Mac. "We'll just drop in and catch her off guard. The chief knows I've been working the case on the sly. He doesn't want me to spend any more time on it, but let's try it one last time. If nothing new comes up, we'll put it away for good. It'll be a last ditch effort." Mac knew he would always be working on it, but he'd keep it to himself. He was curious and he knew Jessie would want to know what happened.

He stood up and picked up his hat and jacket. "I'm going to the ranch this weekend, by the way. I'm driving down tomorrow morning. You know how to reach me." He grabbed his cell phone and put it in his breast pocket.

"Got a hot date this weekend, Boss?" asked Brian.

"Nope, and if you're referring to my house guest, Melissa Albright, I never see her. I've already told you that I lent her the ranch house so she wouldn't have to stay at a hotel in Kona or Hilo while she's interviewing the cowboys in the South Point area. I haven't been down there the whole time she's been there. Don't get funny." He stopped at the doorway and turned to face Brian who was grinning from ear to ear.

"Wipe that silly grin off your face, kid. This was her last week at my place. She's supposed to be cleared out by now and on her way to Parker Ranch. At least that's what she said. In any case, I'm staying at the cottage tonight, alone, as usual, if you must know. What's the smirk about?"

"Nothing! Shootz! A guy can't even smile around here. I guess I've been listening to the scuttlebutt about you and the blonde from L.A. who's been staying at your ranch, that's all. It does sound pretty cozy."

"I don't even want to hear about it," said Mac, shaking his head. "Don't you guys have better things to talk about? You're on duty this weekend. Go fight crime. As I said, you know how to reach me. Talk to you on Monday." He put on his hat and flung his jacket over his shoulder, picked up his briefcase and walked out the door. "And don't call me boss. We're partners. When I make captain, you can call me boss."

"You still outrank me, Lieutenant," Brian called after him. "Don't be so sensitive."

As Mac drove out of town he thought of Jessie's warning about the rumor mill. He never figured he'd be a target because his personal life was boring and his love life was non-existent. He hoped Melissa would be gone when he got to the ranch tomorrow. About a month ago, she contacted Guy Matsumoto and asked if he could give her the names of ranchers she could interview for a magazine article she was writing. Guy had given her Mac's name among others. Mac wasn't pleased that Guy had referred her to him. He was a cop not a cowboy. Still, he agreed to an interview. Since he only stayed at the ranch a couple of days a month, he offered to let her stay at the house for the two weeks she planned to be at South Point.

She was good looking and nice enough, but he couldn't imagine her riding horseback with the wind blowing her carefully styled hair from underneath a straw hat. She'd never been on a horse, she told him, and declined his offer to take her horseback riding. They'd ridden Rod's old Land Rover instead. Why her editor would send someone who couldn't even ride a horse to write an article about cowboys and ranching was a mystery to him. Anyway, she was young enough to be his daughter.

He stopped off at a fast food drive-thru on his way out of town and got a cheeseburger, fries, and a coke. It was raining again. So, what's new? It always rains in Hilo, he groused. It would be foggy and cold at Volcano. When he got home, he'd get a fire going, pour himself some Scotch, and figure out a plan for a meeting with Sachi. She seemed such a fragile little thing. He didn't want to scare her off, but he wanted to see if she'd tell what she knew in order to protect her brother.

If they expected her to tell them the truth about her father and her brother, Tak, they'd have to handle her with kid gloves. This might be the break they were looking for. Damn, I wish I'd thought of using Nobu as bait sooner. What's the matter with me? Jessie, I guess, gotta get her off my mind. I can't let my personal life interfere with my work. He turned on the windshield wipers and, eating his burger and fries, drove home.

In the morning he'd head to the ranch. Things hadn't changed much down there since he bought it. He still hadn't decided on a name. There was already one McIntire Ranch on the island and he needed to come up with something that seemed right.

Since Billy left, he was managing the ranch himself, keeping the books and paying the bills. Tarzan did repairs, tended the cattle and horses and other chores, supervised a new ranch hand, and generally looked after the place. They spoke by phone several times a week. Tarzan was unofficially his foreman. He'd make it official one of these days when things were more settled. Tarzan, now married, had brought his bride to live with him in the cottage that Mac had remodeled for them.

Mary came once a week. He rarely saw her, but knew when she'd been there because he'd find baked goods in the pantry and home-cooked meals in the freezer. The house was always tidy, the sheets changed, the laundry folded neatly.

He kept the furniture Jessie left. Guy Matsumoto said he'd suggested that Jessie leave some of the old furnishings for the new owners until they got around to redoing the place. He hoped Mac didn't mind. "You can always get a crew to move the stuff out if you don't want it," he said. Mac hadn't changed a thing. One of these days he'd fix up the house, get some new furniture. He settled into a comfortable routine going to the ranch on weekends and his days off. That is, until Melissa Albright came along.

To avoid any sign of impropriety, he didn't go to the ranch while Melissa was there and asked Mary to come in more often for those two weeks. He wasn't aware that Mary kept in touch with Catherine and was telling her what she imagined was his every move, and that, in turn, the news was relayed to Jessie. The South Point Gazette had expanded and was now reaching the California coast.

He heard the rumors making the rounds at work after his colleagues learned that the attractive young blonde journalist was staying at his house. When Melissa told him her next stop would be Parker Ranch in Waimea and that she'd be staying at a guest house there, he was relieved.

Parker Ranch with its 450,000 acres of rolling hills and thousands of heads of cattle is considered the largest privately-owned cattle ranch in the United States and is 100 miles and two and a half hours away from

South Point. Far enough, Mac hoped, to dispel any notion that he and Melissa were romantically involved. The smirks and knowing looks of his colleagues were getting old. He expected her to be gone when he showed up in the morning.

He wished he had something new to tell Jessie about the case, so he'd have an excuse to call her. When she first left, they'd spoken on the phone or emailed and texted nearly every day.

That tapered off after a couple of months. He assumed that she was living it up in San Francisco because whenever he mentioned her coming home to Hawaii, she usually said she didn't have time and changed the subject. He was busy at work, so he didn't have time to brood about not having a love life.

Melissa was gone by the time he reached the ranch early the next day. Mary was there. He didn't expect to see her on a Saturday morning. "I wanted to clean up after Melissa," she said. "I'll only be a little while. I guess she's not coming back, yeh? Her hair dryer, toiletries, clothes, everything is gone. She left a nice tip for me and this note for you." She handed him an envelope with a card inside and watched him open it. "Thank you for lending me your charming home, Mr. McIntire. Sincerely, Melissa Albright." He put it on the kitchen table knowing Mary would read it. <u>Mr.</u> McIntire? Really?

It was great to have the house back. He dropped his shaving kit and briefcase on his desk and went out to look for Tarzan. He found him saddling Hoku and the bay mare, Big Red. They toured the ranch, checked on the herd, the water troughs, the fences, and then rode down to the cliffs. He couldn't believe he actually owned the place. "Tarzan," he said, "you're looking at a very lucky man." He was quiet for a moment. "One thing is missing, though."

"What, Mac? Jessie?" Tarzan asked. Mac nodded.

"Yeah, I miss her, too," Tarzan said. "I've known her since I was about 15 or 16. I used to come here with my dad when he worked for Rod. She was really nice to me and I always looked forward to seeing her. It'll take a while to get used to her not being here. I thought you two were an item."

"So did I, but I guess I was wrong," Mac said. For such a little person, she sure left a big, empty space in my life, he thought.

29

Monday morning he was back on the job. Brian had the day off after his duty watch on the weekend, but he called Mac. "I've been thinking all weekend about us going to see Mrs. Gonsalves," he said when Mac answered the phone. "I don't think we should put it off. How about we drop in on her tomorrow when I'm back at work? Like you said, surprise her."

"First thing in the morning," said Mac. "I've been thinking about it, too. We'll pay her a friendly little visit. If it doesn't work out, at least we tried. What do we have to lose?"

Maybe they'd finally be able to solve the Bradford murder case. If the tactic worked, Sachi could be the key. Whatever she knew would have to come out. Even if everyone involved was no longer around, which he figured was probably the case, it would be good to know what happened and he could give Jessie some answers. He hoped the ruse would work.

He reviewed the investigation that began nearly a year ago. According to the people he interviewed, the Miyamotos had lived in near seclusion after Allen Bradford disappeared. Most people believed it was because of the close friendship between Bradford and Miyamoto. Mac suspected the family closed ranks because they had something to hide. Maybe that was just a cop's suspicious mind. He was sure he was right. Sachi was just a kid at the time of the murder, but she lived in that house. If there was a secret to be kept, she'd have to know about it.

In the morning he sat in the passenger seat reading his old notes aloud while sipping coffee as Brian drove the Expedition to the Gonsalves home in an upscale subdivision in the lush hills above the city. Mac had looked at his notes the night before, but wanted to double check. He hadn't read them in a long time and needed to refresh Brian's memory as well as his own.

Sachi was surprised to see the two detectives on her doorstep. It was only eight o'clock in the morning. She was wearing workout clothes and a yoga DVD was playing on the big screen TV.

"May we come in, Mrs. Gonsalves?" asked Brian. "Detective McIntire and I have a few things we'd like to discuss with you."

She sighed as she stood in the doorway with her hands on her hips. What now? Nobu was doing his community service and sticking to the requirements of his probation. As far as she knew he was behaving himself.

"Oh. Okay, but I have a class in less than an hour, so make it quick." She closed the door and led them into the living room. Cardboard boxes were stacked everywhere. The room was in disarray, evidence of her imminent move. She turned off the TV and cleared some empty boxes off the sofa and chairs.

"I'd offer you something to drink, but the kitchen is a mess. You probably know I'll be leaving at the end of the semester to join Billy on Maui." She made a sweeping gesture. "That's why all the boxes. Please, sit down." She sat opposite them with her hands folded in her lap.

"What's this about? Is it Nobu? He hasn't done anything again, has he? I talk with him every day and he seems to be…"

Mac interrupted her. "Sachi, it is about Nobu, but it's not what you think. He's been a model citizen after the incident last year. He's sticking to his sentence – two years probation and 200 hours of community service. I see him from time to time mowing the grass and trimming the shrubs and flowers at the parks around town. We're here on another matter, the Allen Bradford case."

She blinked her eyes and did a double take. "What? What does Nobu have to do with the Bradford case?"

""Mrs. Gonsalves," said Brian, "we think your brother may have been involved in that murder along with other members of your family. That's where our investigation has taken us."

She stood up. "Are you crazy? Nobu wasn't even here when that happened. He was away at school. I don't understand. In what way do you think he was involved?"

Mac told her they knew Nobu was at school on Oahu during that time, but they'd checked the records and on the day Bradford disappeared, Nobu was marked absent from his classes. It was a lie, there were no records that went back that far, but he said it anyway. "He could easily have taken a flight to the Big Island and gone back to Oahu without anyone knowing."

"And committed a murder? It's not possible," Sachi said, angrily. "I'm not going to listen to this nonsense. You're accusing my brother because you have nothing else. After all this time, that's the best you can come up with? How pathetic. Why are you involving my family? Why can't you leave us alone?"

When they didn't respond, she continued.

"Look, I know Nobu is hot-tempered and he broke the law last year. It was the first time he'd ever been in trouble. He's straightened himself out and is doing well now. Please, don't do this. It isn't true. You're making a big mistake."

Mac and Brian shifted uneasily in their chairs. They didn't want to bully her. But if they could just get her to give them some clue about what happened, the whole thing would be over. "We need to close the case," Mac said.

"And from what we've learned through our investigation," said Brian, "your family was cooped up in that house for at least a week after Bradford went missing. You were there the whole time, didn't even go to school. We don't think it was only because a friend of your father's had disappeared. We think it was because your family knew that Allen Bradford was murdered."

"That's not true! Why do you suspect Nobu or anyone in my family, for that matter? I've told you before we don't know anything."

"We've been investigating this for almost a year, Mrs.Gonsalves," said Brian. "The leads always end up with your family. Nobu is the only one alive today who could have been involved, or maybe knows who was involved. We believe that he might have been an accomplice. We're going to talk to him again, but we wanted to give you a heads up, give you a chance to tell us what you know."

"Haven't we been through enough with my mother's death, Nobu's arrest, this big move Billy and I are making? I can't believe you're doing this now. I'm calling our lawyer. You'd better go. Please. I have to get to class. Or do you want to arrest me, too?" She was on the verge of tears.

Brian looked at Mac, who nodded. They stood up and walked to the front door. "We're under a lot of pressure to solve this, Sachi," said Mac. "We'll let ourselves out. You know where to reach us."

After they left, Sachi looked up the number of Nobu's attorney in Honolulu, but changed her mind about calling him. Instead she called her husband. "Bill," she said, "you have to come home. I need your help." He knew it was serious when she called him Bill. That's the name she used when she was troubled.

Billy had been offered several jobs – a couple on the Big Island and one on Maui. He wanted to accept one on the Big Island, but Sachi pleaded with him to accept the job on Maui. "Billy, let's get away from here, go someplace different and start over. I can always get a job at the community college there. Come on, it would be good for us. We've lived here all our lives. Don't you want to do something different? Please?"

The next afternoon Sachi picked up Billy at the airport. As he drove to their house, she told him about the detectives' visit. "They think Nobu had something to do with Allen Bradford's murder?" asked Billy. "I thought they figured out that he wasn't even here when it happened. He wasn't, was he?"

"Of course not, he was at school in Honolulu. I thought they had that figured out, too. Nobu and I both told them he was at the university," said Sachi, "and that's the truth, but they said they learned that he didn't attend classes that day. I don't even know how they could find out something like that when it happened so long ago. Billy, I have something to tell you. Something I should have told you before, but I hoped I'd never have to."

Billy turned and looked at his wife. Tears were streaming down her face. "What is it, Sachiko-san?" he asked, using his pet name for her. He pulled over, parked on a side street, and put his arms around her.

"Let's go home," she said. "I'll tell you when we get there." She sat quietly with her hands clenched, looking straight ahead, until they were parked in their driveway. "Tell me what's bothering you," said Billy.

"Not out here. Not until we're inside," she said.

"Okay, Sachi," he said after closing the front door behind them. "Tell me. What's going on?"

She started to cry again and led him to the sofa. "You know I would never knowingly hurt anyone, don't you, Billy? You're always teasing me that I can't even kill the ants in our house."

He took her in his arms. "I know, honey. You wouldn't hurt a fly. So?"

"So, I know who killed Allen Bradford and it wasn't Nobu."

"YOU know? How do you know? Who is it?"

"I was there, Billy, I was right there when it happened."

"You've known all this time and you never said a word, not even to me? Why didn't you tell me, the police, John McIntire? Who did it, Sachi? Was it someone I know? Who was it?"

30

When Jessie got back to San Francisco it was business and work as usual. Compared to the turmoil and chaos of her summer at South Point, life in the city was boring. She began to question the reason she sold the ranch and left Hawaii because San Francisco seemed to have lost its appeal.

She hadn't done any of the things she'd used as an excuse to return to the Bay Area. There were no nights at the opera or symphony, nor plays or concerts. Except for a few outings with friends and Catherine, she worked all the time.

And there was Mac. They called each other every day at first, but the calls had tapered off. She hadn't heard from him in several months. He'd promised to let her know if anything new turned up in the investigation. Was he still working on it or had he moved on? She still hadn't told him what she learned from Sumi Miyamoto and her guilty conscience was keeping her awake at night.

When Guy Matsumoto and Billy called to tell her Mac bought Bradford Ranch, she didn't know how to feel. She signed the papers they faxed to her, but it was awkward. Had he planned it all along? He never said that he was interested in buying the ranch. She didn't know whether to be happy or sad. Had he done it for her or did he just want it for himself? Tarzan was working the ranch for Mac and Billy was now managing a spread on Maui. The last time she spoke with Mac, he hadn't changed the name yet. He said he was trying to come up with something. What other changes would he make?

Her phone rang late one night when she was at home grading papers. It was Catherine. "How about doing a spa day with me, Mom? I've submitted my thesis and I'm waiting for the appointment for my orals. I need to relax. I thought we could go have a facial and a mani-pedi. I can't think of anyone I'd rather do it with."

Jessie put down her red pen and straightened the blue exam books on her desk. "Oh, I don't know, Cathy," she said. "I don't think so."

"Really, you don't think so?" chided Catherine. "You've been mooning around for that cowboy ever since we got home. If you're not going back to Hawaii to claim him, get over it."

"Mooning around? I have not been mooning."

"Yes, you have. And that city lifestyle you said you couldn't give up? When was the last time you went to a concert or a museum or the opera? Not once in the last six months. Okay, there was that Clint Black concert at the Civic Center, a cowboy concert. You aren't over Mac and you know it. You've got cowboy on the brain."

"Mac and I aren't keeping in touch these days," Jessie said. "Our little romance is over, as brief as it was. And I'm not even sure it was a romance."

"You two were calling each other all the time when you first got back. What happened? Oh, and by the way, maybe the reason you're not hearing from him these days is because he's got a girlfriend. Did you know that?"

"What?" Jessie stood up and began pacing around the room. "Of course I didn't know. How would I? Who is it, anyway?" She paused. "Not that I'm interested."

"You know who. I told you about her, that writer who's staying at his house. Aunty Mary tells me everything. The South Point Gazette isn't half bad. CNN could take a few lessons from Mary Chin. I've learned a lot from her about news gathering. I swear she missed her calling. She should have been a reporter for one of the tabloids."

Jessie knew that ever since they'd returned from Hawaii, Catherine and Mary had been calling, texting, and emailing each other. Catherine never told her much about their conversations and Jessie didn't ask. Mary worked at the ranch house once a week these days because Mac was rarely there except on weekends, but she had her eagle eyes open for any tidbit she could pass on to Catherine. They'd been plotting to get Mac and Jessie together ever since the rodeo.

A couple of weeks ago, Mary told Catherine that a journalist from Los Angeles was on the Big Island to interview Hawaiian cowboys for an article on Hawaii's ranches and paniolo. The woman had interviewed Mac and according to Mary, they were dating.

"Maile's South Point Gazette is alive and well," said Catherine, "and this is a hot item."

"Oh, my God, wasn't 2,300 miles far enough away to escape the gossip?" asked Jessie.

"Her name is Melissa," continued Catherine, ignoring her mother's remark. "Melissa Albright. She's young, about my age, tall with long blonde hair, and stays at the ranch."

Why are they always tall and blonde, Jessie wondered. She walked into her bedroom and looked in the full-length mirror at her five feet three-inch reflection. She straightened her shoulders and stretched her neck, holding her head high. That didn't help. It made her look like E.T. Nope, she was short and no amount of shoulder straightening and neck stretching would make her look taller, and her unruly, curly light brown hair could never be mistaken for long and blonde. Standing there barefoot, wearing a t-shirt and pajama bottoms with her hair pulled into a pony tail, she didn't think she could compete with a tall blonde, especially a young one.

"Aunty Mary doesn't like her, says she's kind of stuck up."

"Who?" asked Jessie as she stepped away from the mirror.

"Melissa Albright," Catherine said, exasperated, "Mac's new girl-friend. Aren't you listening to me?"

When Catherine asked if the journalist and Mac were sleeping together, Mary said, "Well, you can always tell a woman is in a man's life when you find her tooth brush and hair dryer in his bathroom and her clothes in his closet and dresser drawers, yeh? She wears French perfume, very expensive." Mary lowered her voice to almost a whisper. "I only have to change the sheets on one bed," she said. "Don't tell me they aren't sleeping together." Catherine decided to keep that information to herself.

"You're going to lose him, Mom, and you're not even putting up a fight."

"I don't intend to put up a fight and that's that. I hope he's happy with what's-her-name. Leave me out of it. Listen, I have exams to grade, so we'd better say goodnight."

"What about our spa day?"

"Oh, some other time, honey. I'm so busy with school right now. Maybe when the semester is over, okay? Thanks for asking, though. I love you. 'Night."

"Goodnight, Mommy." Catherine clicked off. She planted the seed. Now it was up to her mother. If knowing that Mac had another woman in his life didn't spur her into action, what would?

So, mused Jessie, she lost Mac, not that she'd ever had him, really. They had circled around each other for a couple of months and now he was with someone else. It's not as if they'd had a romance. It was more like a couple of one night stands, wasn't it? Did she give him up for the right reasons? If so, why was she so upset?

She went back to the full-length mirror, lifted her t-shirt exposing her midriff and bare breasts and examined her reflection again. She was 51 years old, past middle age. Does someone like me get a second chance, she wondered, turning sideways and patting her flat belly. Well, at least I don't have that middle age spread yet. Hmm, the yoga and pilates classes are paying off. I still look pretty good, but how do I compete with a girl in her 20s? She pulled down her shirt. I guess I don't. I've been tossed aside for another tall, young blonde yet again. I should be used to it by now.

Catherine was right. She hadn't done anything since returning to San Francisco that she couldn't do in Hawaii. She missed the ranch and Mac. He said he'd wait and he didn't. In just a couple of months he found someone else. No wonder he hadn't called in a while. Was that girl staying at the ranch with him? <u>Her</u> ranch?

She still hadn't told him what she'd learned about her father's death. If Mac ever found out she knew what happened, he might never speak to her again. There was nothing to lose now. She wanted to tell him, but how? Over the phone? Face to face? She'd have to figure out some way to do it. "If only I'd been honest with him from the beginning, I wouldn't be in this mess. I'd probably be with him, well, maybe," she said aloud.

31

It had been a while since Mac and Brian spoke with Sachi. The semester was almost over and she'd be leaving for Maui soon. Both men read the Bradford file again, reread the notes of the interviews, the details of the Miyamoto family's movements at the time. They couldn't have been more thorough if they'd used a magnifying glass.

For a time, even Sumi Miyamoto was a suspect. There was motive. She could have wanted Bradford out of her life. Perhaps he persisted in continuing their affair. Or he may have wanted to end the relationship because he was involved with someone else and she killed him in a fit of jealousy. But two blows to the back of the head hard enough to crush his skull? They discounted that theory about as quickly as they thought of it. Bradford was a big guy and Sumi was small, barely five feet tall and as thin as a stick of bamboo. It couldn't have been her, but how to prove it was Hideo and Tak? Even if they were able to prove their theory, would there be an arrest or a trial? It was almost certain that everyone involved was dead. Why continue?

"Maybe we should just leave it alone, like the chief says," said Brian one day. "It's taking a lot of our time. My brain can't take it anymore. I mean, how many times can we go over the details? Nothing clicks! What do you say? Let's put it away."

He glanced at the box marked COLD CASE with Allen Bradford's name and case number written across the sides in bold black letters. It sat on the floor in a corner of their office. Inside the box were the items that were collected at the scene – the gold watch, the wedding ring, and the belt with the silver buckle, the boots, his wallet containing $54.00, his driver's license, the coins they found under the skeletal remains, remnants of clothing. "It's all ready to go," said Brian. "What do you say?"

He stood at Mac's desk, looking down at him and at the files of new cases piled in front of him. "What's going on, Boss? It's Jessie, isn't it? You're doing this for her, aren't you?" He leaned over until his face was just inches away from Mac's and said slowly, softly, parsing each word, "She's probably gotten over it and gone on with her life in California." He straightened up. "I bet she doesn't even think about it anymore. People move on, you know. That's what we should do. Especially you," he said, jabbing his finger at Mac.

"You're right, kid. It is about Jessie. Maybe she doesn't think about it anymore like you said. I'd still like to work on it for a while longer. Tell you what, we have our hands full now with the airport murder. We'll give that case our full attention, not that we aren't. I'll keep investigating Bradford on my own, put it on the back burner and go over it whenever I have time, just me. How's that? It'll save your sanity and we'll be doing what Chief Lindsey wants, sort of."

"Okay, by me," said Brian. "I thought when we put a scare into Sachi Gonsalves we'd have some kind of reaction from her by now. I hoped our little plan would work. It looks like we were wrong. Maybe she really doesn't know what happened or she's tougher than she looks. It's always the innocent looking ones you have to watch out for."

They were investigating the rape and murder of a young woman whose body was found in a grassy field near the airport a couple of days ago. So far, they had no leads. It was a high profile case because the girl was the daughter of a U.S. Senator from Maine. She'd been on vacation visiting her sister who lived in a dorm off campus near the university and one day she disappeared.

Because grounds keepers found her battered, decomposing remains in a field near the airport, the media dubbed it the Airport Murder. Chief Lindsey ordered Mac and Brian to work the case 24 hours a day if they had to. "Put Bradford in cold storage where he belongs," he said, eyeing the box in the corner of their office, "and leave him there. I mean it," he barked, glaring at Mac. "I know you've been working on it on the sly. I want that stopped right now."

Unbeknownst to them, the Bradford case was soon to rear its ugly head again. This time, no matter how much they'd studied every detail, they were in for the surprise of their lives.

They planted the seed in Sachi's mind that Nobu was their number one suspect. She knew her brother wasn't guilty of the murder, but felt the detectives were determined to prove he was. She hadn't heard from the detectives since that day several weeks ago, but was certain they were still going after Nobu. She was tired of looking over her shoulder, the sleepless nights, jumping every time the phone rang.

When Billy came home after her last meeting with Mac and Brian, he wanted to call their attorney immediately. Sachi talked him out of it. She wasn't ready to tell anyone except Billy what she knew. Now with Billy working at his new job on Maui, she couldn't keep it a secret any longer. She called their attorney, Imori "Mo" Ishinaga. She didn't tell him every-thing over the phone, but just enough so that the attorney would know the situation was serious. Mo Ishinaga had successfully defended Nobu last year. Maybe he could do the same for her. He advised Sachi not to say anything more. "Don't contact the police. Do not say a word to anyone. I'll see you tomorrow morning." He booked the last flight from Honolulu to Hilo that evening.

Then, she called Billy. He said he'd take the first plane out. She assured him that once the lawyer was handling things, everything would be all right and he could go back to work. "But I need you here now, Bill."

"Just hang on," Billy said. "I don't want you to be alone, Sachi. I'll leave for Hilo tonight and I'll stay until Mo has things well in hand. I'll have to come back to work, but I can always go to be with you if things get tough. Don't worry, I'm coming, baby. I'll be there in a couple of hours."

Mo showed up at the Gonsalves home the next morning in a rented Lexus sedan and carrying a Gucci brief case. After spending a couple of hours with Billy and Sachi, he drove to the police department and sauntered into Mac's and Brian's office. The detectives were out, but Mo left a note with his phone number and a reference to the Bradford murder case. When Mac and Brian returned later that morning and found the note, they were intrigued. Had their ruse worked after all or were they being sued for harassment?

"I wonder what it's about. Isn't this the attorney who handled Nobu Miyamoto's case?" Mac asked, handing the note to Brian and picking up the phone.

The attorney said he'd been retained by the Gonsalves family regarding the Bradford murder case. Could they meet in a half hour, privately, away from the police department, at his office on Kilauea Street?

"We'll be there in 15 minutes, if that's all right," Mac said.

"Maybe we got lucky and our little trick worked after all," said Brian. Mac shrugged his shoulders. "We'll see," he said. "I'm not taking anything for granted."

When Mac and Brian were led into a conference room at the law office, they were surprised to see Sachi and Billy Gonsalves seated at the table. They reached across and shook hands with Billy and nodded at Sachi. "What's going on?" asked Mac, looking into Billy's eyes. Mo walked in before Billy could answer, shook hands with the detectives and sat next to Sachi. He motioned for the stenographer who accompanied him to sit at the end of the table.

"Mrs. Gonsalves has prepared a statement," said Mo. "Before we begin, I want you to know that she is making this statement against the advice of counsel." He looked at Sachi. She was pale and looked as though she'd been crying. "Are you sure you want to go through with this?"

"Yes, I'm sure."

"Do you want me to read it?" he asked as he handed each of the detectives a copy of a handwritten note.

She shook her head. "No, I'll read it," she said softly. She cleared her throat and straightened her shoulders. "I, Sachiko Ruth Miyamoto Gonsalves, am making this statement of my own free will. I am not under duress and I have not been coerced. My brother, Nobu Miyamoto, is innocent of any involvement in the death of Allen Bradford. I killed Allen Bradford 37 years ago when I was 14 years old. I did it to protect my mother who I thought was being attacked by Mr. Bradford. I found my mother, Sumiko Miyamoto, and Mr. Bradford in a compromising position in the garden of our home at Kahana Sugar Plantation. He had his arms around her and he was kissing her. My mother tried to pull away and was struggling to get free, but he wouldn't let her go. I thought she was in danger. I yelled at him to leave my mother alone. He started to turn toward me, but he was still holding her while she struggled to get away from him, so, I hit him on the back of his head with a piece of granite from the top of a stone lantern. I hit him twice, hard. I didn't mean to kill him. I just wanted him to let go of my mother. I thought I was protecting her."

She looked up. "That's all I have to say," she said. Surprisingly, she felt free for the first time since that day in the garden. She had carried the burden for so long that it was almost comforting to finally tell her story. She looked at the faces of the men sitting across from her. How will they judge me, she wondered. As a murderess or as a young girl trying to protect her mother? Whatever happens, my biggest regret is that Billy could be hurt by this.

It was only several seconds, but it seemed as though a thousand minutes passed before anyone said anything. It was Billy who broke the silence.

"Mac," he said, "I just found out about this after you last spoke with Sachi a few weeks ago. At that time you told her you suspected Nobu. I swear I didn't know until Sachi told me. She's carried this with her all these years wanting to protect her family, telling no one, not even me. Nobu was never a part of it. When she thought you might arrest him for something he didn't do, she had to come forward and tell the truth." He put his arm around her shoulders. Sachi didn't respond, but sat quietly, as if waiting to see what her fate would be. She kept her head down, not looking at anyone and felt that she was 14 years old again and it was still that terrible day.

Mo spoke up. "Detectives, let's leave Mr. and Mrs. Gonsalves for a few minutes." He led them to a vacant office down the hall, gestured toward some chairs, and sat at a desk across from them.

"Now, gentlemen," he said, "we have to discuss what charges, if any, will be brought against my client. I'm asking you to consider that Mrs. Gonsalves came forward of her own accord. Let's be clear, this is a very, very cold case, an act committed when she was just a child trying to defend her mother. I believe that those facts should merit leniency, extreme leniency, as in no arrest, no charges. I advised her against making the statement, but she was adamant about wanting to keep you from accusing her brother." He leaned back in his chair, clasped his hands together behind his head, and smiled sardonically.

"By the way, that was a clever ploy, detectives. You knew damned well that Nobu Miyamoto didn't have anything to do with the death of Allen Bradford, but your little ruse worked and you got your statement." Mac noticed that the lawyer was careful not to use the word confession. Mo leaned forward and tapped on the desk with his manicured fingernails. "So, now what, boys?"

"As you well know, Counselor," said Mac, "there's no statute of limitations for murder, especially first degree or capital murder. I'm not saying this fits into either of those categories, but let's consider the facts. A man was killed. We have only the word of the person who committed the crime that it was unintentional and that she did it to defend her mother. There are no witnesses, no one to back up her claim." He looked at Brian. "Anything you want to add?"

"It would help if there was a witness," said Brian. "Everyone who might have been involved is dead, as far as we know, and Mac is right, we only have her word."

Ishinaga wasn't going to let these two small town yokels get away with anything. He was going for the jugular. "Come on, you guys. She was just a kid. She acted on impulse. Surely, you don't think she planned to kill the man? You're not going to be hard asses about this, are you? You can pursue this if you want, but I'll offer a deal to the DA and it'll be a deal she'll definitely accept, I promise you. This is a no-brainer. Do you really want to make this public and possibly ruin the lives of Mr. and Mrs. Gonsalves? Between them they don't even have one traffic ticket."

"We don't want to be hard asses," said Mac. "I'm still in shock about the whole thing. Sachi Gonsalves is the last person I…we… suspected. Isn't that right, Brian?" Brian nodded, for the first time in his life at a loss for words.

"We don't have all the facts," said Mac. "Who put the body in the cave? There must have been accomplices. Who were they? Are they still around? Is Sachi trying to protect somebody? We didn't get the whole story. Don't try to tell me a 14-year-old girl drove Allen Bradford's body to the site and dragged it down that cliff." He glanced at Brian.

"Well, all I can say is I hope they haven't sold their house here in Hilo yet," said Brian, "because she can't go to Maui until this is settled and we have some answers. We've been working on this case for nearly a year. This is the break we've been hoping for and it's been a long time coming. You expect us to let her off? Just like that? It'll be between you and the DA to work out a deal."

"Are you going to arrest her?" asked Ishinaga.

"Can we have a moment, Mo?" said Mac. "My partner and I need to talk."

When they were alone, Mac said, "I don't want to arrest her. Not now, but we have to question her. I know Ishinaga will hover around like a grandmother as if she's still 14 years old. I hate to have it get out – the press, the media – they'll be all over this, and we don't have all the facts yet. She has to stay here in Hilo to finish the semester. It's only what, a week or so? Let's get her to tell us who else was involved. Then, we can talk to Chief Lindsey, either that or we arrest her now."

"We can't talk to the chief," said Brian. "Remember, he's in Honolulu at the chiefs' conference. He won't be back for a couple of days. We could call him, but, well, what other choices do we have?"

"I guess we keep quiet until the chief gets back," said Mac. "She confessed without any coercion on our part. She's probably glad it's over and will probably give us the details now that it's out. We should question her while we're here and she's still talking."

"We already know who the accomplices were, don't we?" said Brian. "Frankly, I don't think Nobu was involved. The Marine sergeant said he saw only Tak and Hideo driving through Waikea that morning. Nobu may have known after the fact. But I agree, let's keep it quiet until the chief returns."

Mac opened the door and motioned to Mo. He told the attorney what the plan was. "We want to question her now, in your conference room, alone, without you and her husband present. We need to know exactly what happened and who helped dispose of the body. We expect you to try to work some magic with the DA and offer a deal. Just let us talk to her and we promise nothing will be leaked to the press, but that could change in a heartbeat."

"It's not up to us, anyway," Brian added. "The chief is in Honolulu and won't be back for a few days. He'll make the final decision."

"Yeah," said Mac, "and remind her that she'll be monitored and that we can arrest her today if we want to. I want her to appreciate that we're giving her a pass for now."

"You think I'm going to let you talk to her without me being present? You're nuts! No way are you guys getting her alone," said Mo. "The husband can wait in another room if you want, but I'll be right there to make sure you don't infringe on her rights. She retained me as her attorney and that means she doesn't even have to talk to you at all, but if she does, I will be in that room. You hear me?"

"What's your problem?" asked Mac. "She's already confessed. All we want are a few details, but yeah, I suppose you'll have to be there."

With her lawyer at her side, they spoke with Sachi for several hours, got some answers that satisfied them for the time being, and turned her over to Mo and Billy. They left the law office and drove to the police station.

32

"WHAT THE HELL? I'M BLOWN AWAY," SAID MAC AS THEY DROVE to the station. "I can't believe it. That is the last thing I expected. You?"

"I'm speechless," said Brian, "plain, fucking speechless. Who would have thought that a little girl killed the guy? Do you think she's telling the truth? She could still be trying to shield somebody." He parked the Expedition and they didn't speak again until they closed the door to their office.

"I had my doubts at first," said Mac, "but I believe her now after speaking with her. She killed Bradford, it was unintentional. Tak and Hideo cleaned up the scene, drove to South Point, and put the body in the cave. I'm sure no one else was involved, just like she said."

"Well," said Brian, "so much for not working on our time off anymore. We'll stay on it until we clear up everything. So, we'll keep it quiet until we can figure out what to do, all the while working on the airport case. If we keep this up, we're going to be moonlighting for the rest of our lives."

Mac didn't think it would take long. "Ishinaga is sharp," he said. "He'll work out a deal with the DA so fast we won't know what hit us. What I'm worried about is when we tell the chief about this, he might want us to slap the cuffs on her, bring in the press, and make a circus out of it. He's running for reelection next year. This could be a feather in his cap. Ishinaga said he's going to see the DA today. We'll wait and see how that plays out. We should hear from him tomorrow. If he and the prosecutor work out a plea deal that we can live with, I think we should agree to it and put an end to the investigation."

"The chief is going to be pissed if he gets back and finds out that we made an agreement with the lawyers without his approval and you're gonna be glad you bought that ranch, Mac," said Brian. "We might not have jobs if the chief finds out we kept anything from him. You may just get to be that cowboy you've always wanted to be sooner than you planned. And, me, I'm gonna be your ranch hand, shoveling manure. If we don't go to jail, that is. Shootz! We better know what we're doing. This has to work out, Boss, or we'll be toast. We should call the chief now, tell him what's going on."

"Okay," said Mac, "we'll phone him, but not until tomorrow. I hope he exercises some restraint and doesn't call a press conference. I think we can keep him quiet until Mo and the DA work out a deal. It shouldn't take long. I just wish we had a witness to corroborate Sachi's story. That would solve all our problems. I should call Jessie tonight, though. She'll want to know this latest development."

"Good idea," said Brian. "Call and tell her what's up. Maybe this will help rekindle your love life." He didn't really know what was going on between Jessie and Mac, but knew that things had cooled off between them. He figured it was because absence didn't really make the heart grow fonder after all.

"Thanks, Dear Abby," said Mac. "Maybe that can be your new vocation if things don't work out here – advice to the lovelorn."

"We're gonna continue with the airport murder now, too, aren't we?" said Brian. "I think we're close on that one. There've been a lot of tips coming in."

"I know," said Mac, "looks like everything's coming together. It's about time we got a break. Tomorrow might turn out to be a big day for us."

As Mac drove home that night, he thought this is the kind of news that would warrant a phone call to Jessie. He promised to keep in touch and tell her if anything new turned up. Well, he had a lot of news for her now. What time was it in California, anyway? He looked at the dashboard clock. It was 7:35 and figuring in California time, there was a three hour difference. He'd call her at 11 o'clock her time. He'd be parking in front of the cottage by then. He called as soon as he got home. Jessie answered. "It's Mac," he said. "Are you sitting down?"

"Mac, it's great to hear from you. How are you? Should I be sitting down? What's going on?" She hadn't heard from him in months. They talked for a few minutes about the weather, Catherine, school, the ranch, but the small talk was killing him, so he got to the reason for his call.

"Listen," he said, "I have some news, big news. There's been a break in your father's case." When he finished telling her about Sachi, there was silence on the other end. "Jessie?"

"I'm here, Mac. I heard you. I...I just can't believe she confessed. What's going to happen now?" She spoke softly with no emotion.

She was so calm. Mac thought she'd be shocked it was Sachi who killed her father and relieved that the case was solved, that it was finally over and she might even shed a tear or two. Instead, there was just this... calm.

Again she asked, "What's going to happen now? Have you arrested her?"

"We haven't arrested her yet. If we had a witness who could verify her story, we might let her go," he said, "but since we don't have a witness, it might go to the grand jury, then to trial. She has a good lawyer. He got her brother Nobu off with probation and community service after he shot up his neighborhood last year, if you remember. The lawyer is slick. He'll

236

try to work something out for Sachi with the district attorney. No guarantees, though."

"A witness, you need a witness? Does it have to be someone who was actually there?"

"Jessie, a witness is someone who witnessed the event. What are you getting at?"

"Well, what if someone who was actually there told another person what happened? Would that person count as a witness? I mean, say, if the actual person who was there was...uh...dead, for instance?"

"Okay, maybe. It would be hearsay, though." Mac wasn't sure where she was going with this. "Are you trying to tell me that you know of someone who is a witness?" he asked. "Someone who knows what happened besides Sachi and her mother, but who wasn't there?"

"Yes."

"Who?"

"Me."

Now, it was his turn to be at a loss for words. He was standing in the middle of his living room when he called. He dropped down in a chair and rubbed his hand back and forth across his forehead as if he had a headache. He couldn't believe what he just heard. "You? You are the witness who wasn't there? How did that happen? What are you talking about?"

"I'm sorry I kept it from you, Mac, really. I tried to tell you so many times, but I just couldn't. I didn't want to get Sachi in trouble because it wasn't her fault and she was just a kid when it happened, and then there was Billy working for me. It was awkward. Please listen. Remember when I visited Sumi Miyamoto at the nursing home? She told me what happened. I walked out of there not knowing what to do. Then, she died. I almost told you when you called about her death, but I didn't know how and anyway, you were in such a bad mood. If you only knew how often I wanted to pick up the phone to tell you what I knew."

"I wish you had. I've been chasing my tail for a year. I can't believe you did this."

"Mac, I'm so sorry. I hated not telling you. It just got harder and harder as time went by. Now you know why I've been indecisive about everything, about us. If you never speak to me again, I'll understand. What happens now? Are you going to arrest her? I'm willing to go back and testify on her behalf. Could I do that? Would that help? I mean, it was my father and Sachi was trying to defend her mother. Isn't that sort of self defense? What if I don't want to press charges?"

There was a long silence at Mac's end. Jessie thought he had hung up. "Mac?"

"It doesn't work that way," he told her. "It's murder. It's not up to you to press charges as if she stole your purse or something. The state decides whether to bring charges in a capital case, even one that's 36 years old. That's what we're dealing with now. We just found out a few hours ago. Tomorrow we'll see what our chief says. He may want to arrest her, I don't know. In any event, her attorney will probably try to make a deal and the DA will have the final say. If we had a witness, it would make a decision much easier."

"Well, I'm a witness, aren't I? I can come any time. Just let me know when."

"You may not have to come here. A deposition should be enough. You can go to an attorney in San Francisco, give your account, they'll record it and send your statement to the court here and it will be used as testimony. I'll work on it."

"I can do that." She was disappointed that he didn't say she should go to Hilo to testify. It must mean that he doesn't want to see me, she thought.

"Okay. I'll get back to you." He clicked off. He felt like he'd been hit by a truck.

33

Jessie hadn't heard from Mac in a week. She'd expected him to call back sooner. She was deep in thought and talking to herself. *I knew this day would come. He's angry and I don't blame him. If only I had done things differently, but I really couldn't think of any other way to handle it.*

If Sumi hadn't died, maybe I could have persuaded her to tell Mac what she told me. It might have cleared Sachi, but how could I have been sure? It's too late to undo the damage. Mac's been trying for nearly a year to solve a crime that I could have solved for him months ago. She thought of his curt response on the phone.

He'll never forgive me. I'll wait to hear from him. If they needed a deposition, she'd give them one. Actually, she was glad the secret was finally out. No matter what happened with Mac and her, at least this wouldn't be on her conscience anymore, but she'd always regret that she hadn't been forthcoming.

She'd just finished preparing the final exam for the semester. Tomorrow her assistant would make copies of the test and lock them in her desk drawer. Final exams were in two weeks and summer hiatus would soon be here, but she had no plans except to teach a six-week summer class on Hawaiian history. Afterward, she thought maybe she'd go to Hawaii and try to work things out with Mac, but now that seemed unlikely. She planned to teach the summer class and not worry about what happened next. So far only four students had signed up for the class, so it might be canceled.

Who was interested in Hawaiian history, anyway? Most of her students thought about surf boards and sandy beaches. They didn't care that the United States military deposed Hawaii's queen in 1892 and kept her prisoner in her own palace until she died in 1917 so that wealthy sugar planters could take over the islands. She was disappointed that out of 20 students in an average class, only about half really paid attention to her lectures. Very few of them received an A in her classes, but she handed out quite a few Cs to students who took the class solely to satisfy their requirements, not because they were interested in history, American, Hawaiian or otherwise.

Jessie had written her doctoral thesis on the history of the Hawaiian Islands. She was surprised when she first arrived in California in the early 1980s that many people, even some professors at the University of California at Berkeley, knew very little about the 50th state 2,300 miles away in the middle of the Pacific Ocean. Upon learning that she was from Hawaii, some people expressed surprise that she spoke English and others wondered if she was an American citizen. It irritated her when someone asked how she liked being "in the States" as if she had come from a foreign country.

She declared her major in American history early on. Her plan was that when she became a teacher, she would include in her curriculum a lesson on the history of her birthplace. That's what she had done for her entire teaching career. Each semester she devoted several class sessions to Hawaiian history. This summer's 6-week session was a first time effort. If it was successful, she might do it every summer.

The past year had been a roller coaster ride starting with her uncle's death, selling a 500-acre ranch with a thousand head of cattle and a string of horses, and learning of her father's murder. She felt overwhelmed by it all, including her relationship with Mac, which she realized she'd handled badly, like a kid with a school girl crush. Mac hadn't called since she told him she'd known it was Sachi who killed her father. Would she ever hear from him again?

Her friends and Catherine tried to cheer her up. They went out to dinner, took spa days, and shopping trips. She even dated a couple of times. Those events were pleasant, but often uninspiring. Someone even suggested she try online dating. She refused. She didn't need a date that badly.

"What you need is a hobby," Catherine told her during one of their late night phone calls. "How about going line dancing with Greg and me?"

"Line dancing? Puh-leez," Jessie said.

"We're thinking of switching to salsa," said Catherine. "Maybe you'd like that better."

"Thanks, sweetie, but I don't think so. You don't have to babysit me. I know you mean well, but really, I'm fine."

"How about a cruise, then? Aunty Mabel told me she's planning to go on a European river cruise in September. Maybe you could ditch teaching next semester and go with her. You need a diversion."

"Cathy, remember when I went on that Alaskan cruise with your Aunt Mabel a few years ago? I couldn't wait to get back on dry land. I know she's your Dad's aunt and a favorite of yours, and I love her, I really do, but she's too much for me. I can't keep up with her. She's a spinning top and never stops talking. I'm exhausted after just having lunch with her."

"Well, you've either got to get over that guy you left behind in Hawaii or call him and tell him how you feel. I saw a bumper sticker the other day that sums up what you need to do. I think you could learn something from it."

"Hang on," said Jessie, "a bumper sticker? I hate bumper stickers, you know that."

Catherine ignored her mother's statement. "I know, but this one is so right for you. It said, 'Pull up your big girl panties and deal with it.' It's time for you to deal with it, Mom. Come on, call him."

"He doesn't want to have anything to do with me. If he did, I'd have heard from him by now. He's angry and I don't blame him. No, that's over. Life goes on. Is he still with the blonde, by the way? Just curious."

"Oh, Aunty Mary told me it's over," said Catherine. "I think the woman finished her interviews at South Point and moved on to Parker Ranch. She's probably back in LA by now. Mary was never sure what happened. She told me that a note the girl wrote to Mac thanking him for letting her stay at the ranch referred to him as Mr. McIntire. We figure that she wouldn't call someone mister if she'd had an affair with him."

"You've seen *Sex in the City*," said Jessie. "One of the characters calls her boyfriend Mr. Big."

"Don't be silly," said Catherine, "that was his nickname. Oh, I hear Mac's working on a new murder case. The media is calling it the Airport Murder. A very big deal since the victim is the daughter of a U.S. senator. She was there as a tourist visiting her sister and turned up dead near the Hilo airport. Mary says she wouldn't be surprised if this case gets Mac promoted to captain. If he solves it, that is."

"I've read about it online," said Jessie, admitting for the first time that she was following Mac on the Internet. "But he's also still working on your grandfather's case. I don't think the media has picked up on that again, though. It's old news. You know how it is. They only report what's happening right now, especially if it's sensational. I would like to know what's going on with Sachi Gonsalves, though. Has Mary said anything?"

"I don't think Mary knows anything about Sachi, especially since Billy is working on Maui now. At least she hasn't mentioned it to me. She'd be giving me all the details if she could. I certainly haven't said anything about it. When you told me Sachi confessed that she committed the murder, I couldn't believe it. What a shock! And you knew all the time. I don't know how you kept it to yourself for so long, not even telling me. Would you ever have told Mac about it if Sachi didn't confess?"

Jessie didn't answer. She liked to think she would have told Mac everything, but she wasn't sure.

"Oh, this should cheer you up," Catherine said. "Mary told me that Ed Sherman, your friend Patsy's father-in-law, lost the election last fall. I forgot to tell you. Anyway, if you ever see her again, you won't have to listen to her crow about her father-in-law being governor. Does that make your day?"

"That is good news, but she's not my friend." Jessie hoped she'd never see Patsy again, but if she did, she was certain that Patsy wouldn't bring up the unsuccessful grab for the governorship.

Several days later, Mo Ishinaga called. Detective McIntire had referred him to her. Would she be able to give a deposition in the Sachiko Gonsalves case? He understood that she had some information that might be crucial in proving Mrs. Gonsalves' innocence. He could recommend an attorney in San Francisco if need be.

Jessie said she had an attorney. What exactly would a deposition entail, she wanted to know.

"It's like giving testimony at trial," explained Mo, "except that an attorney will ask you questions out of court and your answers will be recorded on video and presented to a judge as if you actually testified at trial."

"Okay. I'll call my lawyer now and see when she can fit me in." She gave Mo her attorney's phone number so he could fax the details of the case to her office.

"Is tomorrow afternoon all right?" asked the assistant when Jessie called to make the appointment. "There's been a cancellation. She can schedule you in at two o'clock if you're available."

The next morning, after teaching a class on post civil war America, Jessie took a cab downtown. As she waited for the attorney in a conference room on the 10th floor of the Transamerica Pyramid Building on Montgomery Street, she thought of her visit with Sumi. It was as if Sumi Miyamoto had just spoken to her that morning, it was so fresh in her mind. Jessie could almost hear Sumi's voice as she spoke, huddled in her wheel chair under the patchwork quilt.

* * *

"One day, ichiban long time ago," Sumi began in a voice so soft that Jessie had to lean forward to hear her, "Allen-san, he came to my house. I was in the garden. We had not seen each other in many months, so I was surprised to see him. I told him he must go, that Sachi would be home from school soon. But he said he wanted to talk, so we sat on the bench in front of the koi pond. He told me that he still loved me and he took me in his arms and tried to kiss me. I struggled to push him away at first, but he was so big and I was not strong. He held me tight and we kissed. Then I heard the garden gate open. It was Sachi.

"I was facing her and I saw her shocked look. Allen had his back to her, so he didn't see her. He was still holding me in his arms and kissing me and I was struggling to get free. Sachi ran to us and she picked up the top of the stone lantern and said, 'Leave my mother alone!' He looked startled when he heard her voice and started to turn toward her. That's when she hit him on the back of his head with the top of the stone lantern. He made a noise like he was in pain and put his hands on his head. She hit him again very hard and he started to fall. I tried to hold on to him, but I couldn't and he fell to the ground. Blood was coming from his head. Oh, it was so bad, ichiban bad.

"Allen! Allen!" I screamed, but he didn't move. Blood was in the grass by the koi pond. "Sachi, what have you done?" She didn't answer. She just stood there holding the piece of granite from the lantern. It was covered with blood and blood was on her hands, on her dress. She was crying and I began to cry, too. I tried to wake Allen again, but he still didn't move. I didn't want to leave him alone, so I sent Sachi in the house and I stayed outside with him. I kept calling his name, trying to wake him, but he never woke up. I knew he was dead. I waited for Hideo and Tak to come home.

"Allen and I, we loved each other, but I was Hideo's wife. I knew Allen had other women, but he told me that I was the one he loved. Sachi didn't know about Allen and me. I don't think Hideo knew or the boys. They never said. I was afraid for Hideo to see what happened, but there was nothing I could do. He and Tak came home together and when they walked through the gate, they saw me sitting on the bench and Allen lying at my feet at the edge of the koi pond and all the blood."

Sumi stopped talking and took a deep breath. "I am ichiban sorry, so sorry," she kept repeating. Tears were streaming down her cheeks. The tears made little rivulets in the crevices of the wrinkles of her skin. She took off her glasses and laid them in her lap. She wept, making little sobbing sounds and dabbed at her eyes with a handkerchief, but the tears kept pouring out.

"Hideo made me go in the house with Sachi," she continued. "He didn't know she was the one who hit Allen until later. He locked the gate and he and Tak moved Allen's body to a corner of the garden behind the bamboo trees and covered him with some rice sacks so no one could see. They washed the blood from the ground. Sachi and I stayed in the house. She was so young, only 14 years old. She didn't mean to kill him. She thought he was hurting me and only wanted to help.

"Hideo and Tak came in the house and Hideo made me tell him what happened. He looked so sad. He and Tak talked together. In the middle of the night they went back outside. They didn't tell me what they were going to do. After a while, I heard the car drive away. I went outside in the garden. The top was back on the stone lantern, the blood was washed away, and the garden was quiet and beautiful. It was like nothing bad had happened. I went back inside and put Sachi to bed. I told her she must never speak of this, not to anyone, ever. That was the last time we talked about it. Hideo and Tak never mentioned it again." She dried her tears and reached for Jessie's hand. "It was ichiban hard time."

It took a few seconds for Jessie to speak. "Where were your other sons?" she wanted to know. "Did they help Hideo and Tak?"

"Oh, no. Nobu was at the university in Honolulu and Isaburo was in medical school in California. Albert died in the army. It was only Hideo and Tak. I don't know if they ever told Isaburo and Nobu what happened, I'm not sure."

* * *

Jessie didn't have to tell the story word for word for the deposition. She answered some personal questions at first, but most of the questions pertained specifically to Sachi's case and Allen Bradford's death and what Sumie Miyamoto told her. As Mo Ishinaga said, it was as if she were testifying at a trial.

It took several hours and then they were finished. The stenographer clicked off the video camera, picked up her laptop, and left the room. "How did I do?" Jessie asked as she wiped away tears with the back of her hand.

"You did fine," said the attorney, handing her a box of tissues. "We'll send it off to Honolulu this evening. If they need anything more from you, they'll let you know. You're welcome to sit here for a while if you need to." Jessie couldn't wait to get out of there. "Thanks," she said, "I'm okay."

She left the law office feeling wrung out, flagged a cab, and went home. It was emotionally draining to dredge up what happened at the nursing home with Sumi and to answer all those questions. She wanted to call Mac, but what would she say to him? She threw herself across her bed and had a good cry.

Two weeks later Mo Ishinaga called to thank her. "Because of you," he said, "the district attorney has decided not to bring charges against

Mrs. Gonsalves. Your testimony was responsible for that decision, Miss Bradford. I'm sure you will be hearing from Mr. and Mrs. Gonsalves very soon. They owe you a great debt of gratitude."

But it was a long time before Jessie heard from Billy. She never heard from Sachi again.

34

CATHERINE WASN'T GOING TO LET HER MOTHER PINE AWAY IN San Francisco while Mac was probably doing the same thing in Hawaii. She decided if anything was to be done to bring them together, she had to be the one to do it. At least she'd try. She called Mac.

"Remember me?" she asked when he answered the phone. She was nervous, but pressed on. "We need to talk."

"Of course I remember you," he said. He was at work, alone in the office. "How can I help you, Catherine? Is everything all right? Is your mother okay?"

"Yes and no," said Catherine. "Detective McIntire, do you love her?"

"Excuse me?" He got up and closed the door.

"Just answer yes or no. Do you love my mother? If you do, you'd better do something about it. I've never seen such stubborn, childish, stupid people in my life as you two, playing these games, not speaking to each other, no phone calls for months on end. She's been moping around like a lovesick teenager. Life is too short. If you love her, tell her. Or better yet, man up and come and get her."

Mac was speechless. Finally, he said, "I told her I loved her when she was here last year. That hasn't changed. I begged her to stay. She wasn't interested." He paused for a few seconds. "What else can I do? She's a stubborn woman."

"She's stubborn, all right. She thinks you're angry because she kept the information about Sachi Gonsalves from you. She knew it was wrong, but considering the circumstances, her relationship with Billy and all, what else was she supposed to do? You must understand what she was going through. You're not that dense, are you? She planned to tell you all along, but couldn't figure out how to do it without hurting the people involved. Are you still holding a grudge? C'mon, give her a break."

Mac felt as though he were being interrogated. "I've never held a grudge. Okay, I admit I was a little pis...ticked off at first, but I got over it."

"Then, let her know you're over it. Call her. You're an adult. Can't you figure it out? I'm not telling you to marry her, not right away. She's afraid of commitment and given her experiences with men, I can understand why. She always chooses the wrong ones, but I think you're the guy for her. She's cancelled her summer class, so now would be a good time to contact her. As far as she knows, I didn't make this call. It's up to you now. Goodbye." Before Mac could say anything, she hung up.

He sat for a few minutes staring at the dead phone in his hand. "Well, I guess I'll have to do something about it," he said as Brian walked in.

"Talking to yourself, Boss? Ever since we wrapped up the Bradford case and the airport murder, you've been acting a little goofy. I think you need a vacation."

They'd arrested two suspects in the murder of the young woman found in the field near the airport. It hadn't been a difficult case. It turned out that she was riding an expensive bike and caught the attention of two men who followed her, raped and killed her, dumped her body near the airport, and stole the bike. The bike was featured in all the media reports, yet people saw the men riding it all over town.

Hilo is a small place. It didn't take long for the calls to start coming in to the police department about a bike like the one that was on the television news shows. Some people even knew the men who were riding it. Mac and Brian found where they lived and walked up to the front door. They saw the Schwinn Super Deluxe Cruiser bike leaning against the wall outside their apartment. As the news reporters later stated, they were "…arrested without incident." DNA testing sealed their fate. It was the easiest case Mac and Brian had ever handled and they received accolades from the chief, their colleagues, and the senator from Maine.

Mac put his phone on the desk and looked up at Brian. "You're right, kid, I do need a vacation. Tell the chief I'll be back in a few weeks." He picked up his jacket and hat and strode out of the office.

"But Mac, that's what I'm trying to tell you," Brian called after him, waving some papers in the air. "The chief signed these vacation vouchers giving us two weeks off. Mac…?"

"I don't have time to talk," Mac called over his shoulder. "I have a plane to catch. I'm going to San Francisco. See you in two weeks."

It was the last day of classes and the final exam was over. Jessie and her student assistant, Julie, collected the blue exam books and put them in Jessie's briefcase so she could grade them at home. A student assistant from the office next door peeked in. "Psst! Julie!" he said, "you've got to see this. Come quick."

They stepped out in the hall for a few seconds, then, Julie went back to the office. "You won't believe it, Jessie," she said. "There's this cowboy out in the hall. Looks like the real deal, cowboy hat, boots, jeans, the whole thing, and he's headed this way."

Jessie was sitting at her desk facing the door. She looked past Julie. "Mac! What are you doing here?" She stood up.

Julie turned around. "It's him!" she said. She looked from Mac to Jessie. "You know him?"

"Julie, we're done for the day," said Jessie. "You can go home early. See you next semester, okay. Thanks for everything and have a great summer." She turned to Mac, hands on her hips.

"What do you mean walking into my office like John Wayne? Why are you here and how'd find me?"

"There's only one San Francisco State University in this city," he said, "and the cabbie knew just where to drop me off. I'm a pretty good detective. I just followed the leads right to the History Department." He closed the door, pulled her close, and kissed her.

"Jessie, I've come to take you home. I've been miserable. I can't live without you."

"You seem to have gotten along just fine without me so far. What about the blonde journalist?"

"What? Who told you about her? Okay, you have your spies. Mary and Catherine, right? Look, I was never involved with that girl. She's young enough to be my daughter, for Christ's sake! She's probably back in LA where she belongs. She didn't even know how to ride a horse."

"So I heard. Are you still angry that I didn't tell you what I knew about Sachi?" Her voice softened. "I'm so sorry, Mac. I...I just..."

He touched her lips with his finger tips. "Shhh. All right, I admit I was mad at first. But I've thought about it and I understand why you did it. Look, when we get back home I'll answer all your questions. We can talk about everything then. All that matters now is that I love you and you love me." He drew back and squinted, looking into her eyes. "You do love me, don't you?"

"Hmmm...I'll have to think about it. How long will you be here?"

"I've got two weeks. Don't take too long to think about it. I'm a patient man, Jessica Bradford, and I love you like crazy, but even I have my limits."

Ten days later they were married at a wedding chapel in Reno, Nevada with Catherine and Greg as witnesses. The next morning Jessie closed up her house and she and Mac were on a Hawaiian Airlines flight to Kona. Jessie looked out the window and watched as they flew farther and farther away from the California coastline. I'll always miss San Francisco, she thought, but Mac is right. My roots are in Hawaii. I belong there. She turned and looked at her new husband. He smiled, watching her.

"I love you, Babe," he said.

She laid her head against his shoulder and said, "I love you, too."

THE END